You can't kill the Song

GAIL STRICKLAND

NIGHT OF PAN

THE ORACLE OF DELPHI TRILOGY, BOOK ONE

Gail Strickland

TABLE OF CONTENTS

GREECE
THERMA
THRACIANS
ABYDOS
TROY
AEGEAN SEA
THERMOPYLAE
CAPE ARTEMISION
Persian Empire
PHOCAEA
DELPHI
EUBOEA
MARATHON
CORINTH
ARKADIA
ATHENS
SPARTA
CRETE
N

Night of Pan

—A state where one transcends all limitations and experiences oneness with
the universe.

"Know Thyself"

—Inscription on the Temple of Apollo
Delphi, Greece

Dawn hangs heavy with the storm sweeping up from the sea far below us. A smell of brine and salt-crusted cypress suffuses the faint morning light. They walk me in silence through my village. No one is awake, no one sees me as they force me through dark, rough-barked pines—skeleton trees lit by lightning—on down the old stone path leading to the sacred spring of Kastalia, named for the girl who fled Apollo's embraces.

My guards look up, when an owl swoops low above me, his talons clutching a squealing mouse.

Now! I wrench free. Run into the dark pines. A hot wind blows rain hard against my face. Branches whip my arms as I stumble forward. Push uphill. Grunts and shouts and sandals slap muddy ground behind me. Closer.

"Stop her!"

A hand grabs my hair and jerks me to the ground. I twist between hairy legs, roll into a tight ball and shove my head straight up into his groin. The priest's shocked scream echoes off mountain walls to my left.

Leaping to my feet, I hurl myself up the precipice, scramble over scree and around scrub pines. Another lightning flash illuminates brush, cypress trees and thickening pine forest. I know this mountain. Every goat path. Every crevice and stream. I hope the priests don't. Far below me, their shouts grow fainter. I climb higher up the rock face heading for my cave. Around the old cypress charred by lightning. I slow down as I cross flat boulders slick from the rain. Almost there. I peer up toward a thicket of laurel and push harder uphill. A cascade of rocks below forces me to stop and listen. I hear a priest call out and another answer, but they are far down the mountain. They're off track.

Not much farther. My best friend Sophia and I have a cave. Cramped and dripping of white lime and stinking of bat droppings, but our secret hide-away.

It's silent in the forest. Nothing but rain against stone and pine needles. I relax a little and slow my pace.

Looking around, I realize I need to head more to the east, toward the sun just flaring over the cliffs. It's not far now. I hurry my steps thinking how Sophia and I played there as children, pretended we were goddesses. She wanted to be Aphrodite. Not me. I was always Athena—a warrior. It's been a long time since we met there, slipped away from Mama to just be alone. To dream.

A flute, low and breathy, sings from the rocks high above me. One note followed by silence.

I stop.

I'm imagining things. *It's not the first time.*

I smile to myself and think of my wanderings on this mountain. Hard blue sky above rock-stubbled trails. But I never felt alone. I don't remember when it all began. A whisper in the wind, words I could not quite understand. An old cypress, gnarled and shredding its bark that seemed to watch me pass.

Probably just a bird. I push on.

There it is. Laurel branches obscure the opening, but I drop to all fours and crawl inside.

"Sophia, you're already here."

She's huddled before a twig fire, her back against the rough wall; arms wrapped around her knees.

"Thaleia. Thank the gods." Her eyes are wide. Frightened. Vulnerable.

How can I think of leaving her behind?

A small jug, several cloth-wrapped parcels and a woven basket filled with nuts and figs are spread across the uneven floor before her.

"Sophia, how did you get here so fast?"

Her smile is her only answer. She jumps to her feet, ducking to not hit her head on the low ceiling and hugs me. When she finally pushes back, tears flow down her cheeks. "How did you get away from Diokles?"

I laugh. "Some young priest won't be after any priestesses for awhile."

Sophia's smile quickly changes to a frown. "Thaleia, are you sure this is what you want? Today is your wedding day. Your parents will be furious. Not just your parents—the whole village. What about your father's promise to Brygos?"

"I won't do it, Sophia. I can't marry Brygos."

She looks at me and rests one hand on my shoulder. "Here's the food you asked me to bring from your wedding feast." Stepping back, she squats beside the bundles. "Where will you go?" She won't look at me. "What's your plan?"

"I haven't thought that far. All I know Sophia is that we've always been our fathers' property. I hate it! Today they would take me to Brygos. Can't you see? I am his possession as soon as I walk through his door. The moment his mother welcomes me with apples and figs, I belong to Brygos. No better than a pig or loom… an *amphora* of wine for him to consume."

She finally looks up at me. A bat scurries and resettles in a dark recess. "But, Thaleia, how will you live? Our fathers, our husbands take care of us. We have no rights, no property, no money."

Are we really that different? I've always known that she doesn't see things the way I do. Stunned speechless with the idea that my best friend will never really understand, I look at this girl I've known my whole life. We laugh and dance and work together, but will we never dream of the same future? I stare at her as if I've never really seen her before.

"I'm more than a man's property! You're only a year younger than me, Sophia. It will be your wedding day soon enough." My words unsettle me. They feel dark and false. That feeling I get sometimes, when Mama knows I've spent the day up the mountain, and I tell her I spent the day weaving or spinning yarn. And she knows I'm lying but doesn't say. That feeling in my stomach. But I ignore it and sit beside Sophia, take up her hands. "Will you let them claim you? Take you from your home and parade you like a sacrificial goat to Timon's home?"

Sophia blushes, pulls her hands from mine and studies them. Her betrothal ring, gold carved like asparagus, shines in the firelight. Sophia was engaged to Timon when she was five. I was at her ceremony. I felt much older than Sophia. I was six years old. I had been through it all before—Papa betrothed me to Brygos, when I was five and Brygos twenty. He was already a respected fisherman. Papa said he wanted to keep me safe, wanted a husband who could take care of me, but I only remember that I couldn't bear to stand next to him. He reeked of fish.

The idea of a wedding day meant nothing to Sophia or me. The pig pushing her snout in the dust looking for grubs. That's all we cared about! From my ceremony, I remember fish and from Sophia's, I most remember the old sow, whiskers poking straight down from her fleshy chin and the promise of a ram and three ewes on her wedding day.

Sophia's mouth twitches. She draws her lower lip up and bites the upper to stop the quivering. She is silent.

"I don't mean to upset you. I guess you don't mind being engaged to Timon. He's so handsome. That long black hair."

"I love the way it hangs down over his eyes." Sophia smiles. "You never really wanted to marry, did you?"

"Brygos?"

"If Papa knew how often you ran off. He thought we were both spinning and weaving—learning the skills of a dutiful wife. I worried, Thaleia. *You* never worried. Did you even know that I did your work as well as my own? Worked twice as hard so you wouldn't get in trouble? Did you even notice?"

"You should have come with me, Sophia. Up the mountain. Together." I drape my arm over her shoulder and pull her close.

"Now you're leaving me forever." Sucking in her breath, she tries to speak, tries again, but tears well in her eyes. "I wish I was brave like you. Is this the last time we'll be together, Thaleia?" She lifts my chin and looks closely at me. "You can tell me."

"No, Sophia, you're like my sister."

Three bright flute notes sing just outside. I hold my breath and pull Sophia deeper into our hiding place.

"Did they follow you?" Sophia hides behind me.

I shake my head and creep to the opening. Wind rustles through laurel. Somewhere close, water washes over stone. Nothing else. I tilt my head and strain to hear.

A breeze lifts the hair off the nape of my neck and caresses my back. "Sophia, we're being watched. I can feel it."

Several short notes pierce the thick air. Like a snake, one low note slithers up my back. As if the music is alive and waiting. I can't shake the feeling that someone's just beyond in the rain shadow. Waiting. A shiver courses my spine, but I step out into the open. I have to know.

"Thaleia, no." She grabs for my sleeve but misses.

Rain pummels me. Sophia comes up behind. I grab her hand and pull her beside me, strain to hear through the downpour. There's a strong odor of wild garlic.

I squeeze her hand and take one slow step closer toward the music. Low, earthy notes draw me another step. Colors swirl between the trees as if ambrosial storm clouds descend from Olympos. Blue and green mist sweeps between the rain-soaked pines. The music shifts. The colors swirl and ripple orange and yellow. "Sophia, it's so beautiful!"

I hook my arm through Sophia's and take another step.

Iridescent blue and wine-red settle around us.

An urge to follow the music overwhelms me. A command to follow. Like rage and hatred and passion and love. I have to know who's playing. "It must be a god, Sophia."

"Thaleia, Diokles is out here looking for you." She tugs me back into the cave.

The flute-notes patter through rainfall growing more and more distant, fading up the rock-face. "Come on, Sophia. You said you wanted to be brave. Come with me!" I pull her back out into the rain.

"No, I can't." She tries to jerk free, but I won't let go.

"Don't you want to know, Sophia? Come with me up the mountain this time. Together. Let's find this god together." I always could talk her into doing things she later regretted.

She sighs. Smiles. We scramble up the rock incline. At last we stop and bend over gasping for breath. I pull wet hair back from Sophia's face. She looks pale. "Just a little farther?"

I peer through pine needles—spiked thorns against the slate-gray clouds—try to locate the flute, but the music is everywhere. Is it a bird after all? The notes swoop and soar around us like a dove in flight but too wild to be a dove, more like a raptor, angry and wild. I whirl in circles trying to find the bird if there is one, but the wind scatters the melody.

We push uphill against a rising storm-wind. I can barely hold on to Sophia's hand as I swing around trees in our path.

Sophia stumbles, her foot caught on a tree root hidden under pine straw. She lunges forward managing to throw both arms out to break her fall. The wind howls as it sweeps across bare granite slabs. A warning. A threat. Suddenly, I don't want to know, but the music calls again. It is a flute. It has to be.

For one mad moment, I don't care about anything or anyone. I have to follow the music. I race after its call.

I abandon Sophia crumbled in the mud.

Running blindly with the wind blurring my vision, I scramble on my hands and knees over boulders in my path to crags unfamiliar to me. Heavy rains course down my back until I can run no farther. At a meadow's edge, I sink to my knees. My vision bends and eddies, swirls with sunrays and slanting rain dancing between ancient pines.

Sophia catches up to me.

"I'm sorry, Sophia." Part of me wants to reach out to her, to defy this feeling that's turning me into someone I don't recognize.

But five low, melting notes call. Soft and warm like candle wax. I glance at Sophia. Barely able to breathe, I squeeze her hand. We step together into a meadow bathed in sunshine. The storm is behind us as if the soggy pines form a barrier. We follow the music's sweetness into the heart of the glade that is suddenly silent.

No melody.

No wind.

What is this place? Fear spikes up my back.

The wind picks up again, blows hot and violent, tangles my hair across my eyes and mouth. The flute music fades, and still I strain to find it mingled with the storm-winds—amber and rust like a painter's brushstroke across barren clay that paints a memory at my mind's edge. Just out of reach.

I reach out as if I can caress the beautiful colors, but they sink back into the poppies and grasses. The storm comes and goes. Black, menacing clouds race overhead followed by brilliant blue skies. My scalp tingles. I wrap my arm around Sophia's shoulder and pull her close beside me. A god is playing with us. I know it. And there's another thing I know—my fate will unfold in this meadow.

Another low note sighs from the needles of a massive pine at the far end of the clearing. A sudden wind whips the grasses like the sea—shiny, leaden and shiny again. Treetops bend low, dancing a frantic circle around us.

Out of the corner of my eye, I catch movement, a stirring in the old pine's shadow. The tree trunk is thick, gnarled, its few high branches twisted.

"What's that? Did you see something? Thaleia, come on!" Sophia screams and grabs my elbow, pulling me back from the tree.

There's a smell of wet stone and something else—herbs and wild garlic, rain-soaked wool—the smell is overwhelming. Panic seizes me. Courses up my spine like a jolt of lightning.

Sophia takes two steps backwards away from me. Low, rumbling notes shiver the needles. I reach out to call her to me, but she backs another step away then bolts from the clearing.

"Sophia wait," I whisper. And though I desperately want to turn and run away with her, one low flute note filled with desire holds me.

The music changes to piercing, high shrills.

I turn back to face the pine. Take a slow step closer. Stare at the shadowed rocks beside the tree, until my eyes water with the strain.

One cautious step after another, I walk to within an arm's length of the old monarch. Its roots wrap around a smooth, limestone boulder like a squid clinging to the seafloor.

The shadow thickens to movement… slow, almost imperceptible.

Is that an arm? Sunlight plays across taut muscles. The arm lifts reed pipes then disappears behind the tree trunk.

I try to peer into the black shadows. My ears roar with the heightened sounds: weeds rub against one another; a lizard slips between dead leaves; two branches beat against the trunk of the pine, a drumbeat to the wandering melody of the flute.

The music compels me to take a step closer. And another.

CHAPTER TWO

PANIC

A sun-bronzed hand thrusts from the shadows, grabs my shoulder. Ebony fingernails dig into my forearm. Panic fills me. My feet feel like they grow tendrils snaking into the dirt, rooted with the poppies and wild grasses. I can't breathe or cry out.

A hairy leg steps from behind the pine. I don't move.

A satyr squats before me, his muscled thighs matted with bristling fur that curls over hooves. His broad chest—sturdy as an old oak—heaves.

The air between us is charged with light and a hum like a swarm of bees.

A quizzical smile crosses his face. He lets my arm go and steps back.

I should run, but I can only stumble one step away, afraid to turn my back to this creature, half man, half goat smelling of garlic and musky wine.

My heart, filled at first with mindless terror is stunned by the delicate lift of his fingers as they dance across his flute. The rippling notes tighten my chest; conjure images of deep forest dancing down to a wine-dark sea. Strong muscles shape his bronzed shoulders. With a tilt of his head, he seems to float from stone to fallen log, leaping and twirling with the music. Dark trees bend like an attending chorus, drawing the forest shadow away from the center of the glade until it fills with light and melody, motion and power. Needles cling to the satyr's curls.

He stops circling. His eyes are blue like the summer sky.

Pulling me close, he licks my neck. I stiffen in his embrace.

Once more he leaps around me.

I am drawn to his grace, the power of wild goats in the delicate lift of each leg, his hairless torso, gold with oil and sweat. Corded veins at his neck course with heated blood as he dances lightly before me then hides behind the old pine. Is he gone?

I whirl around as his hoof strikes an exposed rock behind me.

His knees prance as he plays quick trills on the flute.

The satyr kneels before me.

His silence, his breath envelops me. Like harsh ice crystals melting to warm spring waters, his gaze that once filled me with revulsion sweeps a rush of warmth up my legs. Longing tightens my heart and strangles my outcry.

With lithe fingers he lifts my hair, lets it fall strand-by-strand clinging against my breasts then leans his sun-bronzed forehead against my chest, snuggling into the crook of my neck. He peers at me, his face—wide like a bear's—inches away from mine.

I gasp.

I understand.

He is the god Pan, his eyes full of me. They know me. As no one understands me, this god, smelling of goat and thyme and garlic, his eyes laughing and full of scheming… this god sees into me. I smile back at his gap-toothed grin. His tongue works a hole where one of his front teeth is missing between full, smiling lips.

A tiny green hummingbird with a long, black beak and scarlet red throat flits around one of the satyr's stumpy horns then the other before deciding to land on his curls, golden bristles between the two.

When I laugh, his face smoothes. Gently, slowly, he lifts my fist, uncurls each finger, by blowing soft breaths as a potter does to keep the clay from cracking. He presses his panpipes into my hand and closes my fingers, one by one over the reeds. "Thaleia, I've waited for you." His voice is earthy, deep like black mud. Stroking the inside of my wrist with a light, quick caress, he trails claw-like nails slowly up the inside of my arm. The pipes are warm from his lips.

Though his touch is gentle on my skin, I pull back, when I see his hairy thighs and restless hooves. Waist up, he is a young man, but his legs!

"Do I scare you?"

I jump when his deep voice jerks me from my musing.

"Well, I'm not surprised. Just look at me. Even my mother thought I was ugly!" Pan prances a quick dance back, his hooves lifting high. Laughing, he throws his arms to the sky, "She abandoned me at birth! All the gods laughed the day I was born."

The satyr sweeps his fingers through a clump of poppies, plucks one and with a deep bow holds it up for me to take.

"Look at the flower, next to its petals… behind. There… do you see a light? Like a leaf shadow? Be the heart of the color. Feel with color. Find color in your body and hear its song. There you will find your power."

Pan strokes my cheek.

"Know thyself. It's really that simple, Thaleia. Trust who you are. You plan to run away and never return."

"How do you know?"

He wraps strong fingers around my arm and stares into my eyes. No, he seems to fall into my eyes, or I into his.

"You are needed in Delphi. Your destiny is here." He stands close before me, waiting, calm. His eyes hold the sky, his fingers the power of deep roots grasping rock and soil.

"Let me go," I say, suddenly afraid of his power over me, but my heart rebels against my own command.

A flash of lightning tears his attention. I twist free. There is another flash. The lightning bolt—Zeus' anger?—strikes the pine. We stand two stark shadows; the thunder's rage bursts around us, answered by a roar of fire. Flames consume twisted branches, making a torch of the old tree. Another flash and answering roar sweep over us.

Pan looks over his shoulder at the flaming tree, his back muscles ripple, tense; his nostrils flare… and then he is gone, disappeared into the woods.

I whirl around, stare into the pines. Strain to glimpse him. To hear his hoof sharp against the mountain's climbing boulders. Nothing. Did I imagine the satyr-god?

Drawing his flute to my lips, I blow one soft, tentative note, high and gentle. It is filled with unexpected sweetness. A sweetness so urgent, I sink to my knees in the limp grass; stroke the smooth pipes with trembling fingers, slowly over each rounded reed then again… again. My hand seems to move of its own accord.

My heart fills with yearning—a desire that seeps from the pipes, from me. From the solitude I feel as I sit and wait and listen for Pan. Remembering how he pried open my fingers and at the same time my heart and left behind hollow reeds. Simple dry grasses left long in the sun, until their parched skin contains the music's longing, the music's passion.

I look around the clearing. A poppy, limp at my side, touches my knee. Its stem is bent. The flowers trampled.

The wind feeds the flames. They lick the thick tree trunk. Dry needles drop like fireflies. The day darkens to twilight, while I wait. For Sophia? For Pan? I only know I don't want to leave.

At last, slow and cautious, I work my way down the mountain, sliding between wet rocks, until once again I find the goat's path. The well-beaten trail gives me confidence. I run its familiar track back to the opening of the small cave and peer in. There are the red cloth bundles of dried olives, nuts and cheeses Sophia stole for me. "Sophia?"

No answer. The cave is cold. Empty. "Where are you? I need you." My words echo off the stone. I sink to the hard floor. Pull a charred stick from the embers and draw Pan—horns, hooves, and his barrel-chest. My drawing smiles back at me as if to ask: *Well, what are you going to do?*

I stare at the panpipes in my left hand. They feel like a living thing against my skin, tingling with breath and heartbeat… magic?

But Pan? Papa told me stories about the satyr to be sure I behaved. *Never wander alone up the mountain.*

Of course I always did.

Pan will find you. It's not safe. Papa's voice, rough with warning, always thrilled me like a call to adventure.

I remember Pan's fingernail tracing up the inside of my arm. A shiver courses from my toes to my scalp.

Deep in the cave, water drips. Bats scuttle. Wind moans through a crevice like the Sirens. Time eddies as calm and smooth as a mountain pond that waits for a deer or wildcat or a shepherd's child to disturb the waters, to create ripples that flow to the other shore.

The panpipes rest quiet and alive in my palm as if waiting for me to decide. Do I run away like I planned?

Fire rushes through my body. I'm consumed with doubt and hope and determination. Like a fierce passion, demonic *Ate* sweeps over me, madness that steals my breath and fills me with power and desire. With all my heart, I want to leave behind Delphi, my parents' anger and their arranged marriage. Marriage to Brygos! I only want to turn my back on them all and never return… but in that instant, I know I won't. I won't run away. I will face Papa and the villagers and that horrible priest. With certainty I know that I can't turn back. Call it destiny if that's a name for it. I'd rather call it love. For Pan? Power? I'm not sure. I only know that the moment the god touched me, there was no turning back.

Pan's *syrinx*, the flute that summoned me, sings one low note. A sigh.

I stand up and walk to the cave entrance. It's night. There's a half moon. I wonder if Papa's looking for me? And Diokles? It doesn't matter. This is Pan's will—*dios d'eteleitou boule*—the god's will is accomplished. And what is my destiny? I can't imagine, but I know the mountain always called to me. The crags and ancient trees, meadow flowers and sparrows… was it Pan all along? Was it always the satyr who brought me from my home up the wild mountain paths?

I run to the edge of the village. Beneath the berry arch beside Apollinaria's clay oven, I sink to my knees, uncertain I want to walk the path to my front door, past the lanterns lit for the night, each doorway glowing a welcome, daring me to return home.

A branch cracks. I whirl around to face Pan.

But it's Brygos. He grabs my shoulders and pulls me against him, wrapping his arms tightly around me.

"Brygos! Let me go!" I shove him away. He looms before me blocking my way. A deep shame engulfs me, as a vision of us sharing our marriage bed flushes my face.

He rests his hands heavily on my shoulders then runs them up and down my arms.

"You ran away from our wedding. Afraid to be my bride?" His breath smells of onions and wine; his hairy arms still smell like fish. "You shamed me before everyone! You dare return now?" He grabs my chin and jerks my face close to his lips. "You will be my bride." His voice is low and commanding.

I don't answer, just step around him to his right. He stops me. I move away to his left. He pushes in front of me again. His leer grows wider with each of my attempts.

"There is a price to pass," he whispers, his lips close to my ear. I stand defiant before him, unable to move.

He doesn't wait for my answer. His lips are on my neck. My mouth. Jagged fingernails cut into my skin. His tongue forces its way between my lips. I push against his chest, but he wraps his arms around me and his body crushes me hard against the oven.

Pan holds my destiny… and it's not to be mauled by this disgusting, smelly fisherman. Power surges through me, and I jerk free. "How dare you!" I yank the pipes from my belt sash and blow one note, breathy like the wind. Another, sweet as honeycomb, calms me. I glare at Brygos and will him gone. The next note is piercing like an eagle's cry.

There is a charge of energy between us—a low rumble like the earth's bowels shifting.

Startled, I stop playing. My arm drops limp at my side.

Brygos jumps back. Shock washes across his face… and anger. "How did you do that?" His eyes narrow.

With slow deliberation, I lift Pan's flute, never taking my eyes from his.

"How dare you? You belong to me." His voice is a low growl.

"Never."

He towers over me.

With trembling hands, I blow Pan's melody, the notes cascading lower and lower like the Kastalian Spring falling from its source.

The slash of his mouth, tight and smirking, seems almost a smile. "You will die."

I stop playing and look at him one hard moment. "What?"

"If you don't marry me, Diokles will kill you and your parents."

I feel the truth of his words. There's a knowing he has about me… and I'm suddenly sure I don't want to hear it. Don't want to ask. But I do. "What do you mean?" I stand tall, hoping to appear brave. I feel light-headed. I can only whisper. "What do you know about me, Brygos?"

He steps close. His voice a low threat. "Ask your mother why your grandmother killed herself."

"What are you talking about?" I grab his sleeve. "She slipped and fell off a cliff. It was an accident." The moment I speak, I wonder if it's true. I remember my mother's face, the way it closes when I ask about her mother, the way she changes the subject. "Brygos, you're wrong."

His mouth smiles but not his eyes. They are hard and cold. Without another word, he stalks off.

I wipe my mouth over and over, until it feels raw.

Until I can stop shivering.

"What does Brygos know about me?" I'm talking to myself again. Suddenly aware I'm clutching the flute, I force my fingers to relax so I don't crush the reeds. "What did I just do?"

I draw a sharp breath. I want to close my eyes and think about Pan. Only remember his music, his smile, the power that rippled through his arms and shoulders.

Diokles will kill me if I don't marry Brygos? What does he know? Can he really force me to marry him? It is the will of my father, the priest, all of Delphi. Why?

I shudder.

Listen, the clouds admonish. *Listen*, whisper the boulders.

Listen. See. Know thyself, Thaleia.

A great calm fills me. A power to dream. To speak the god's will. I am the stone and trees, the wind itself. I am the mountain. I am the song.

For Pan, I would defy Brygos. I would defy them all.

CHAPTER THREE

WILL OF THE GODS

Diokles blocks the path before me as I try to sneak back into Delphi. He uncrosses his arms. Piercing dark eyes bore into me. He pounds his chest and coughs uncontrollably. After his fit eases, he steps closer—eye-to-eye. His breath smells sour like black olives rancid in oil. A vicious smile shadows his face, as he pushes lank, gray hair off his forehead. Slow and deliberate, he cracks his enlarged knuckles.

My throat is dry. We're alone. I can run away, but I don't.

"You will wish you never returned."

"I'm not afraid of you, priest."

"You should be."

Papa walks out our door a short distance up the stone path but doesn't look up.

A memory of the time we walked beneath the olive trees, and he told me he named me after the Muse of Comedy overwhelms me. We laughed that day and held hands twirling in circles.

And now? I want to run to him, to be safe in his arms. Why would he marry me to Brygos?

Flames sputter from dripping fat as he turns spitted chickens with iron tongs.

Diokles and I wait in silence.

Grabbing a greasy cloth tucked into his belt, Papa wipes his face and the back of his neck. Beneath the crease of a black, fringed scarf, unruly, thick curls cling to his neck and forehead.

Diokles sees me staring and turns, clasping his claw hand on my shoulder. "Icos!"

Papa looks around and sees us. His eyes widen.

"Icos, come control your…" The priest's voice catches, and he stares from Papa and back again at me before he finishes… "daughter."

With slow deliberation, I pry Diokles' fingers free, never taking my eyes from his.

"Wild like your mother!"

"Don't call Mama wild!"

Papa hurries over. There are deep creases worrying his brow. His eyes fill with tears. "You're home, Thaleia." He pulls me away from Diokles and hugs me tight against him. "I looked everywhere and couldn't find you." Running his broad fingers through my hair, he untangles a snarl. "I trusted that you'd come home to us." His eyes are dark with uncertainty, with his unspoken question.

"Papa, I won't marry Brygos."

I push back from his arms. "You have to understand."

"She violated her vows!" Diokles grabs my *chiton*; the red tunic sleeve falls off my shoulder, draping folds of cloth slip to just above my breast. I quickly tug it back into place.

"They were never my vows. I was five when you betrothed me to Brygos!" I glare at Papa. "You arranged this union!"

"Thaleia, where is your respect?" Papa gives me that look that always silenced me as a child.

Blood rushes to my face. I start to answer but remain silent.

Papa and Diokles lock eyes. The anger between them is palpable… and something more. It feels like there's a secret between them. A bargain? Pact? About me? What agreement would be made between a tavern keeper and Delphi's most powerful priest?

"Icos, take care how you cross me. All the city-states honor me. The Athenians, Corinthians… even the Spartans of the windy plain. They all built treasuries at my temple, filled them with gold and jewels to honor the gods."

Papa nods. "I do not question your authority, Diokles. But this is a family matter."

Though the priest is frail and withered next to Papa, he jabs his finger into my father's chest. There is a veiled threat in his words. "Even family issues are settled by the divine Oracle."

"Honorable Diokles." My father's voice is low, trembling with rage. "I will punish my daughter. You may be sure. You may leave her to me now."

"Thaleia!" Mama rushes out the door. She practically sweeps me off my feet as she hugs me and kisses my cheek and hair and hands. "You've come back. Are you all right? What happened? I didn't know where you were. I came to help you prepare for your wedding… you were gone."

I untangle from her arms. "How could you want me to marry Brygos? You married Papa, because you loved him. You chose your husband."

She stiffens and steps back but doesn't speak, just looks to Papa for an answer. His response is quiet but firm. "Your grandmother and grandfather were both dead. There was no one to arrange a marriage."

Mama gives the priest a strained smile. "Priest Diokles, you honor us." Her words are humble, but there is fire in her eyes.

"Hipparchia." The priest's eyes flash. He runs long fingers through his thinning hair. Papa draws himself taller and steps toward the old priest.

Maybe I was wrong. Would Papa have helped me this morning?

"We will deal with our daughter. You may leave her to us."

Diokles hesitates and then with a quick catch of breath, he turns his back and shuffles up the Sacred Way toward the temple.

Papa hugs me then holds me at arms length. His face is stern, worried but gentle, as if every emotion a father might have sweeps across his eyes. "Thaleia, you disobeyed me."

"I'm sorry. But Papa…"

"I love you, Thaleia. Never forget that." He looks away from me, stares at his feet and mumbles, "No matter what happens. No matter what anyone tells you."

"I love you too, Papa."

"You are definitely your mother's daughter… and that is not always a good thing. You will marry." He tries to laugh, when I jerk free, but there's fear behind his laughter. "Not today or tomorrow, I will allow you to wait. Perhaps until Sophia marries next spring."

"No. Don't marry me to Brygos."

"The gods and priests will honor the marriage. All this will be forgotten. You will give me a fine grandson."

I want to argue, but at least this gives me time to figure out what to do. I should have just left for good. *Why did Pan tell me to return?*

"What happened to Grandmother? You always told me her death was an accident, but Brygos said…" My words drift away.

"It doesn't matter now. All that matters is that you are safe."

Mama takes my hands, turns them to study my palms. "Thaleia, marry Brygos."

I take a deep breath. I have to know the truth. It feels good to ask. To let my question hang in the air, to shatter the idea that our family is simple and loving, not riddled by shadowy secrets.

"Brygos said the priest would kill me… and you… and Papa. If I don't marry him."

"Live a simple life here in the village. If you do, Diokles will leave you in peace. Please, Thaleia."

I pull my hands free. "Mama, look at me." Pain floods her face, when she looks up in silence. "The gods will protect me."

"Like they protected me?"

"What do yo ı mean?"

"You don't know who you are, Thaleia."

"Then tell me!"

Mama is silent. She shakes her head. "I can't. You must trust me."

I grab her arm and pull her back to face me.

"Mama, you must trust me."

She smiles and hugs me. "I only know that I am your mother. Nothing is more important to me. The gods may taunt and challenge, whisper sweet longing in my heart. Nothing is more sacred to me than being your mother."

She glances at Papa. "But Thaleia…" She sighs and gathers her question, looks at me a long time as if she can find her answer without asking.

"I don't want to marry anyone. I have my own power." I stroke the syrinx tucked into my waist-sash. "The gods have a plan for me. I just don't know what it is." I look at Papa. "I know it is my duty to marry Brygos. I am to bear his children without complaint and be grateful that he loves me. But Papa, you call that love? What Brygos wants has nothing to do with love!" I shudder at the thought of his hands on me.

"It is the will of the gods." Papa's face darkens. A crease deepens between his eyes, before he smiles a stiff grin. "Besides, you need a home of your own. And, like I said, lots of children—fat, laughing grandchildren for me to carry on my shoulders."

"Did Grandmother kill herself like Brygos said?"

Mama blushes. Something in her face closes. "All is the will of the gods, Thaleia." Mama rests her hand against my cheek. "Will you question the gods?"

"Mama, something happened. Up the mountain."

"It's not safe up there alone, Thaleia." Papa interrupts.

Mama studies my face and waits for me to say more, but suddenly I don't want to tell her about Pan. I don't want to tell her about the god's magic meadow or his gift, or what I did to Brygos with my music.

"What happened?" There is a new light in Mama's eyes replacing her worry. I look away, fearful she will know my thoughts. When I was a child, it seemed she only had to look at me to know everything I was thinking.

"Nothing important." I hug Papa. "I'm glad I'm home." Maybe I can convince him I'm sorry I ran away. "You've given me time to think."

But this time it's Mama who doesn't let the subject change. "What happened up the mountain, Thaleia?"

"It was nothing. I thought I heard strange music. I was running away from the priests and scared. I probably imagined it."

Mama looks like she doesn't believe me. There is still a question in her gaze, but she doesn't say anything.

The day ends. A star-studded sky is peopled with the gods.

CHAPTER FOUR

SPIDER'S WEB

The next morning, the storm is past and there is a smell of the salt sea on the breeze. I am alone, looking out the women's quarters' window. Still trying to figure out what Brygos meant, I stare at the threads of a spider web then pull Pan's flute from my sash. Worn reeds darkened by the satyr's lips. The pipes rest on my open palm as if they landed there like the small bird that flitted around the satyr's horns. Trying to remember every moment of my meeting with the god, I stroke the flute. I was so afraid. Not now. I only want to return to the meadow, just get away from here.

Apollinaria—Sophia's grandmother, the oldest woman in our village—shuffles past, wisps of hair escaping from under the black scarf she knotted tightly beneath her sagging chin. Curls soften her chiseled face, hiding a widow's anger. When I was a little girl, I used to imagine she was my grandmother and that she'd bake fresh rolls and steam sweet apple with honey for me. I'd run up to her and take her bony hand, but she always pulled it away. Looked the other way. Made up some excuse and hurried off. I don't know when exactly, but I quit dreaming.

She shades her faint eyes, forced closed by the morning glare like clam shells against a cold current, with a hand fluttering and palsied. Peering in the window, she scowls, lowers her gaze and walks on down the path. Her crone's black mourning robes trail behind her on the dusty path.

"There you are, Thaleia!" I jump when Sophia comes into my room and hide the panpipes in my sash. "What was behind that tree?" Her whisper is strident like seagull cries from the cliffs.

"It was… there was… you ran away and left me there, Sophia!"

"I'm sorry, Thaleia." Sophia takes my hand. "I didn't mean to… are you alright? I thought you'd follow me and you didn't. I was too afraid to go back." Sophia steps away and stares at me. "What was it, Thaleia?"

"Later. Not here. I'll tell you later. Quick Sophia! Let's hide from Mama." I laugh, hoping to distract Sophia. We crouch and cross the common room, our bare feet softly slapping the stone floor.

My mother kneels in front of the hearth, her back straight and proud, holding an iron poker. A soft, green chiton dyed with summer leaves, drapes down her sun-bronzed back. She tightens her waist-sash without taking her eyes off morning cakes sweet with honey and a flaky crust I could eat all day long and then shifts the logs, making certain they don't flare too high or die out to embers. When she blows on the coals, honey sputters and crackles.

She calls out to us, loudly as though we are outside, "Thaleia! Sophia! The cakes are ready!"

Shaking with silent laughter, we press our faces into the soft lambs' wool pillows. This was our game before words, before chores. We stuff the wool into our mouths to keep from laughing out loud and crouch down in our hiding place. When we can no longer tolerate the oily taste, we stand up, pulling fuzz off our tongues. Draping our arms around each other, we stagger over to Mama, laughing so hard we can barely keep our footing.

She presses her hand into her side and stands, her eyes alive with a barely contained laughter. Seizing the flat pan by the blackened wood handle, she cuts big pieces and puts them still sizzling on clay plates, then hands one to each of us. "I'll be back in a minute, and then I have chores for you both." She hurries out.

Sophia and I wander back over to the window to eat the cakes.

Kala, one of Sophia's aunts, walks past, a laundry basket under her arm. "Good morning, Sophia." Her eyes flick up to connect with mine, her mouth tight, before she looks away and walks down into the shadows.

"Sophia, why do the villagers look at me like that? What did I ever do to your aunt? To any of them to make them hate me?"

"Besides the fact that you ran away from your wedding?" Sophia laughs a short, mocking laugh, but when she sees the look on my face, she quickly says, "Are you kidding, Thaleia? They see you up the mountain day after day. We're not even supposed to leave the house alone, and you're always running around like a shepherd boy. How can you even ask why they give you the evil eye? They think you get away with everything." She laughs a kinder laugh and shoves me back. "And you do. Stop changing the subject. What did your papa say? He must have been furious."

"He told me I could marry next year when you marry Timon."

"Oh Thaleia, we can have a double wedding. Did he really say that?"

She sets both our plates on the sill and hugs me tight then grabs my hands and swings me in circles, just missing a low bench and the shelf holding cups and jars filled with dried herbs. Two drying mint branches break off as my shoulder strikes them. The room fills with its sweet smell and a sharp memory of tea Mama always brings me when I'm sick.

"I told you. I will never marry Brygos."

She stops circling, her eyes wide.

"Did you tell your parents that?"

"Yes, well, not exactly. At least this gives me time to figure out what to do. Brygos told me that Diokles…" I don't finish my sentence.

I can't bear to look at Sophia. I turn away and study the spider web stretched across the window. Drops of dew sparkle and disappear with a breeze, so the web looks like tiny pearls strung deep across the stone sill. The web trembles and leaps with the struggles of a fly trying to pull its legs from the sticky trap. A spider scuttles close. Thrashing frantically, the fly buzzes. The insect rasp turns to screams.

I put my hands over my ears. "Oh, make it stop," I say.

Sophia looks at me, her eyes wide. "Stop what?"

"Its screams. Can't you hear them?" The moment the spider injects its venom, the poison seems to course through my body like a wildfire burning from the top of my head to my toes, scorching my chest and neck and belly. The fly's agony grows louder and louder.

I stare at Sophia, speechless, wishing I hadn't said anything. She steps closer to the spider web, her face washed by the thin sun, pale as sun-bleached bones.

The spider settles its soft, fat body and covers the fly. Strands of the web shudder. The spider starts to feed.

I cannot look away as the spider's black eyes stare into my own, before it turns back to chew the fly's wing. Each bite crackles like wood consumed by fire. I clutch the windowsill. It isn't just what I hear that frightens me, but what is lost. The spider brings death to the fly and at the same time devours the air around me. Devours the wind in the street. My own breath. There is only the fly's death left.

"A terrible thing will happen," I say.

"How can you know that?" Sophia asks narrowing her eyes.

The room shifts and spins. A prickling traces my arms and breasts, up my neck, tightening my throat, so I can barely breathe. I grab Sophia's arm, choke back tears. It seems the spider's web wraps sticky strands around me, binding me to the rock and soul of Hellas, as it traps the fly.

My chest throbs with pounding drums. Dust stings my eyes.

I am thrown into a clamor of horse-hooves, the scream of ungreased chariot wheels, and louder than Zeus' roar of sky and sea and raging storm—the beat of massive kettledrums and pounding feet against the Thessalian Plain. As if I would be trampled, I whirl to the right and left between black-clad soldiers, their masked faces one monster metallic shining in an alien Greek sun. A dark-skinned king in gold armor shouts guttural commands to a million marching Persians.

The vision fades. My breath slows. When I focus my eyes, I see only the spider's black eyes huge before me—black and evil and powerful as if they could draw me into the web.

I shake my head. Sweat beads on my forehead.

The spider is just a spider, spread-legged on its sticky trap. I shiver violently and reach out my shaking hand to touch Sophia's cheek.

She brushes clinging hair away from my face. "Are you afraid? A dead fly? A spider? They say spiders are messengers of the gods, so we are blessed."

I shake my head again, unable to find words to explain my vision. I feel surrounded by the black soldiers, haunted by the dark-skinned king; his gold armor flaring like mid-day sun on the sea. Tears flow unchecked down my face.

"What's wrong, Thaleia? What is it?" Sophia's frown changes to a smile. "You can tell me. I'm your best friend. Remember when we told that stranger that we were twins?" Sophia tries to cheer me up. "He only laughed at us."

I try to smile, but my attempt feels half-hearted.

"Can't imagine why he didn't believe us." Sophia twirls away from me, spinning wide circles, her arms flung wide. "Just look at us! You with your skin like bark of an olive tree, raven-black hair." She stops close before me. "And those midnight eyes of yours… you're gorgeous, Thaleia. But look at me! Pottery-red hair, green eyes… I'm a shrimp next to you! I'm no beauty."

She wants me to laugh, to come back to her, to tell her what scared me, so I try once again to smile but sob instead. "The Persians. King Xerxes. They will destroy us."

She stops mid-swirl. "What are you talking about, Thaleia?"

"You know how I've always known things, like rushing out the door to get to the old farmer, his baskets laden with honeycomb, before you heard the bell strapped to the old donkey's harness. Or, you know, I always knew Mama was calling us for supper before we heard her?"

Sophia walks over to the spider web and watches for a moment then turns back to look at me. She stares, her face white and unbelieving. She touches my fingertips.

I rest my hand on the panpipes. It's frustrating that Sophia doesn't understand me. I don't know how to tell her what I saw or about the satyr-god. She'd absolutely think I'm losing my mind. But I'm certain I saw King Xerxes in the chariot, son of Darius who the Greeks routed at Marathon ten years ago.

My vision leaves me with a vague feeling of dread, a feeling I mistrust. I want to believe it was just the fly's death. Nothing more. I squeeze Sophia's hand. I wish my life could be as simple as hers. But the kettledrums won't leave me. They echo in my chest, pound in tandem with my own heartbeat.

"I heard it. I saw it."

I turn back to look out the window. A soft rose light tips the tops of the houses—rough-cut stonewalls anchored to the side of the Phaedriades, our Shining Cliffs. I shake my head trying to clear it and peer past the neighboring houses to the cypress trees and pines lining the path down to the spring. They are gray and somber, but everything is as it should be. The morning. The smell of Mama's honeycakes bubbling on the hearth.

What happened to me? I am here in my home in Delphi—a scattering of red, blue and yellow huts that twist around the rocky contours of Mt. Parnassos, nothing more. I only imagined the soldiers. Everything here in my village is the same as always: thatched roofs lean down toward neighbors in earnest conversation. Old stone paths connect each doorway, slippery as river rock in winter storms. The gods honor my home… sacred and blessed. The barren stone of Mt. Parnassos towering over Delphi—most holy Sanctuary of all Hellas—is worn smooth with Apollo's footsteps. We *expect* the gods to make our mountain their playground.

But what do the gods plan for me? What is my destiny?

I stare at the spider devouring the fly and straighten my shoulders.

I dare the gods to manipulate me! But I can only think this blasphemy—can't even whisper my outrage to my best friend.

I whirl to face Sophia, pull her close, pressing red marks into her arm.

"Sophia, you didn't see anything?"

I want to believe Sophia sees and hears things the same way I do—the soft flute as I dance through a pine forest along the Sacred Way—the path that leads from our village to the high Sanctuary of Apollo—while lyre music seeps from the sap.

Her blank stare tells me everything. She will never see. None of the villagers will see.

CHAPTER FIVE

THE CHILD OF THE CLOUDS

A horn blare startles me. I rush to the front courtyard gate. Mama joins Sophia, and they crowd behind me. In slow cadence, four priests with drum and cymbals and clay flutes—purple headbands tying back their black curls—pace behind Diokles. He leans heavily on his cane, his steps unsteady but his head high. His eyes find me then look away as the procession passes.

The air is washed clean from yesterday's storm. A goatskin *daouli*-drum paces the priests' sandaled-feet. Their sonorous chant echoes off the stone walk.

"Twin serpents
Pythons brown of earth, blue of Apollo's sky,
join in sacred dance."

There's the priest I head-butted. I recognize him by his hooked nose. Two steps. He'll be right in front of me. I duck behind the twining grape arbor hoping its broad leaves will hide me.

"There she is. The new Pythia, Thaleia." Mama shouts over the procession. The young priest stops and looks at Mama, throwing the ritual in confusion, but with a frown from Diokles, he hurries on.

"Did Diokles really throw the last Pythia off the sacred tripod and declare Apollo's prophecies himself?" Sophia asks Mama.

"It's been almost sixteen years, since we've had a Pythia," she says.

A song swirls around Mama. Dark as the Underworld. The melody snarls like Kerberos, Hades' three-headed hellhound. For a black moment, I don't hear the priests' ritual, only the music rushing around Mama. Can she hear it? Angry. Strident. Her jaw is tight. She glares as four helot-slaves shuffle past, shouldering a litter draped with curtains. A young girl pulls aside the yellow silk as she's carried before us.

I cough from the dust and incense.

"Look, Sophia, it's her! Just like the other day up by our dream stone. When she saw me, she dropped something and ran away."

"What did she drop?"

"A wilted poppy petal." We share a smile, both remembering the day last week when Sophia and I visited our dream stone, and she spelled Timon's name on the white boulder—each blood-red petal moistened with a kiss.

But I turn away from Sophia as warmth rushes to my face with my dark memory of that day. At the time I thought I was jealous of Sophia. Ashamed at the anger I felt, because she was betrothed to marry Timon… someone she loves! Someone rich and handsome of high standing. And who did Papa choose for me? Brygos, an ugly, old fisherman.

But somehow, as the hooked-nose priest walks past, I understand that my dark mood wasn't only jealousy. There is some other connection between the priest and the dream stone. Something evil.

I shake my head to clear it. *Crazy. It's just wild imaginings.*

I push past Mama to get a better look at the new Pythia. Pale and fragile as the wing of a dragonfly, at most ten years old. The girl sweeps back her long, white hair with thin fingers.

She's beautiful!

Her skin is so translucent that it makes me think of scattered clouds and moonlight. She smiles directly at me then lifts her chin, purses her lips and sings the cry of a dove.

Why is she whistling like a bird? Her eyes, as blue as the summer sky, lock with mine as she purses pale lips and calls again. A thrill courses through me. As if time stalls, I smell pine-tart incense, feel the vibration of the lamb-skinned drumstick against the hide drum. And the dove song. At first my mind refuses to believe what it hears. I can hear words in her birdcall.

I am Pythia. Honor me for the great god Apollo chose me to speak his words.

Her words dance and slip like a catbird's mockery. She sings her birdcall once more.

I am Pythia. Honor me...

I look back at Mama and Sophia standing close together. A wistful look overflows in Mama's eyes. Does she hear the words also? She sees me looking at her and frowns.

The Pythia sings out again as the litter passes.

I am Pythia.

I whirl back to stare after her. There's something false about her. As she looks from villager to villager, her smile is more a challenge than a greeting.

I gasp with understanding and reach my hand toward the girl. "No. You're not, you're not the Pythia." I breathe out, my words spilling from me.

"What, Thaleia?" Sophia wraps her arm around my waist. "What did you say?"

"She's not, Sophia. She's not the true Pythia." The drums pound like Zeus' thunder, as the priests roar their chant.

"What?"

The child leans out from the curtains. Her eyes lock with mine. Jerking my gaze away in sudden dread, I see the daimona Kere. *The flaming Death-hag wraps itself around the pale girl. The death-daemon's fire-arms engulf the girl's white hair. Fire licks red and orange from the coach window, but doesn't touch the girl's face. Behind the flames, I see the Pythia's forced smile.*

I shake my head to clear it. The fire and daimona are not real. A vision. A premonition. In that instant, I know The Pythia's death will be my doing. I blink my eyes and the vision is gone. The girl draws back behind the curtains.

The procession is far up the Sacred Way, before the buzzing in my head clears, but I cannot shake away the dread. What does the girl have to do with me? I have to know. I turn back to face my mother and Sophia.

"Mama, why does the Pythia whistle birdsongs? Do you know how Priest Diokles found her? Why he claims she is the true Pythia?"

"Her father left her to die at birth." Mama's words are muffled by shouts and laughter as villagers fall in behind the procession. "He took her from her mother's arms and laid her among other forgotten bones on the wall of the unborn. Men choose which baby lives and who will die, left on the cliffs for black vultures." There is fury in her eyes, when Mama raises her voice to shout above the chanting and scatter of sandaled feet.

"Why did they want to kill her?" I touch my mother's sleeve to turn her to look at me. Maybe Mama knows that girl isn't the true Pythia. Maybe she can explain why I understand words in the girl's birdcalls.

"She didn't cry when she was born. They say she is mute." Mama lowers her voice to whisper in my ear. "That white hair, surely a curse from the gods. Her mother didn't even name her." Mama leans her forehead to touch my own. "They call her The Child of the Clouds."

"How did she… ?" I want to ask so many questions. I don't know where to begin.

"How did she survive?" Sophia says.

Mama strokes Sophia's curls.

"Her mother refused to abandon her. Instead, she hid her in a cave to be suckled by a goat, so the father never knew."

Mama is silent for a long while. "She was exactly the one the priests hoped to find. Easy to control because her father rejected her. And no one can understand her, because she doesn't speak, only sings the songs of the birds, so the old priest Diokles can claim to interpret her words."

"Claim to?" *Does Mama know I understand the girl's thoughts? I don't think so.*

In a lower, sadder voice as we turn to go back inside, she tells us how they found The Child of the Clouds. After many years spent searching for the new Pythia, Diokles finally dreamed of the wild girl. When he found her, she was almost blind from the perpetual twilight of her confinement. Her skin, translucent as a jellyfish, smelled of damp stone and goat. She slept cuddled among the other kids.

My mind wanders. I see Mama as if with new eyes. There is softness about her, but strength as well, easily seen in her arms as she raises them to pull back her raven hair. I always thought I was just like her. *But I'm not. I see it now… and she's hiding something from me.*

In silence, she pulls pans of sizzling cakes away from the flames and off to the side of the hearth, places uncooked cakes onto the already hot metal so the honey crackles, filling the room with its sweetness.

"Mama, why is The Child of the Clouds our Oracle? How can she be the Pythia? How does a cursed child become the high priestess of Apollo?"

"Through the will of the gods… if the priest allows it," Mama says to the fire without looking at me.

After an awkward silence, she presses her hand wearily into her side and stands, languid like a crow just catching the wind above the mountain. She shakes the flat pan, the honey sputtering and crackling, before she turns back to look at us.

"She defecated in the same corner, covering her excrement with a cracked wine jug."

Sophia and I giggle. "Mama!"

"I know. I know." Mama laughs. "But it gets stranger. When Diokles' shadow darkened the opening to the child's hiding place, the girl was whistling and warbling bird melodies. Faint birdsong filtered through tomblike walls—all she'd heard for years. The priest decided to bring her back to the temple. How can anyone argue? For almost sixteen years, Diokles controlled the oracle, while he told the elders he was still looking for the new Pythia. So, now when he claims he's found her…"

"Why didn't we have a Pythia for so many years? Was it because the temple burned and they had to rebuild it?" I have to know.

Mama sits beside the hearth. Staring at the back of her hand, she turns her gold wedding band.

"The last Pythia offended the priests," she finally says. She stares into the fire before turning back to look at me. "She was banished from the sacred tripod. Diokles forced her to reveal her shame. Forced her to choose."

"What was her shame?" I whisper, unable to speak louder. My eyes are locked with Mama's. A shadow darkens her eyes, but I am silent, unwilling to break the bond between us.

"She fell in love." Mama strokes her belly and smiles a distant smile. She blinks, comes back to us. She toys with a loose strand of hair.

"She got pregnant. The priests, well mostly Diokles, declared that a pregnant Pythia must be banished. He claimed she dishonored Apollo." Mama jabs the coals. They spark and flare. "He insisted that the Pythia could not care for a child and serve the god. If she wanted to continue to be the Pythia, to serve Apollo and speak his prophecies to the pilgrims, she had to…"

"Is that about the same time that Grandmother died?"

Mama is silent so long, her eyes unfocused staring into the fire that at last I say, "Mama?"

She stirs the fire with her stick. I smell honey burning. Her words are fiery. "Diokles told her she had to choose—leave the sacred tripod and raise her child or destroy the child." Mama whirls back to me, her face bright red. "What does a man know? Destroy her child? How can a priest demand such a thing?"

I stare into the fire. "That's horrible," I mutter, but don't dare look up to see Mama's reaction.

She grabs a thick wool cloth and lifts the blackened-pan from the flames. Without turning to face us, she whispers, "The gods are selfish… and nothing happens without the priest's blessing. Diokles wants to keep the oracular power for himself." Only in Delphi do women declare prophecies. Corinth, Bassae, Lenea—those Oracles are all men!" Mama whirls around to face us, her hands on her wide hips, her brow creased. "Only here in Delphi, the most sacred of all sanctuaries, do we have a woman. So Diokles threw the Pythia off the tripod seat and claimed her power."

"What's a tripod?" I whisper, afraid to interrupt her.

"The three-legged stool balanced over the steaming fissure that the Pythia sits on to commune with her god."

"Mama, when he banished the Pythia, did Diokles speak to the god Apollo?"

"That's what he claims," Mama says and sits down between us.

"He lied. I think it's a hoax. Only the Pythia communes with the god. Think of the pilgrims who came so far only to find a priest declaring the oracle. They came from the Greek colonies, Persia... far-off Egypt."

"Many in our village whispered that Diokles didn't want to find a new Oracle, that he turned a deaf ear to the god's commands," Mama says. "That way the priest controlled the sacred precinct, accepting bribes and treasures from supplicants. Apollo will judge. The gods destroy those who defy them."

"But Hipparchia, there is a Pythia now—The Child of the Clouds. So we have a girl again to commune with Apollo." Sophia's voice is strident, as if she would convince my mother.

"Like I said, she doesn't speak. It's easy for the priest to control her, when she sits the tripod and slips into trance. When even the stones speak to her and the smoke-filled chamber shimmers with a strange light and the music of the lyre."

Sophia and I look at each other. How does Mama know what it's like in the sacred chamber?

Sophia's eyes widen. "You ask her, Thaleia," she says while Mama tends the fire.

"No, you!"

A sparrow sings from the grapevine just outside the door. Mama walks over and peers up into the brilliant sunlight.

"They say, Thaleia..." she turns back to smile broadly at Sophia "and Sophia… that the god's possession is pure love. They say you don't hear the god's words, but feel them infused with your breath as hope and dreams as if anything imaginable is possible. Nothing needs to be explained or spoken. The Pythia feels the god's words in her bone marrow. She knows."

"Thaleia, remember the spider?" Sophia whispers, but I shake my head a quick no, hoping Mama doesn't see and question what Sophia means. I don't want to tell Mama about my vision. And I don't know how to tell her The Child of the Clouds is not the Pythia.

"I have a story to tell you. The Oracle is very old. Thousands of years ago, before Apollo claimed this Sanctuary, they say the great serpent Python declared the prophecies."

"Apollo killed the Python with his sword!" I interrupt, remembering a story the old priest told me. "That's why Apollo is the god of Delphi. He slew the monster serpent that was murdering villagers!"

Mama scowls down at us. "And who tells us that story? The priests. I don't believe the Python was killing villagers! And I don't believe the Python is dead."

"The Python *is* dead! Apollo killed it! The pilgrims smell its rotting carcass!" Sophia objects.

"No, Sophia, they smell a sweet smoke that seeps from the earth. I tell you the priests lie. The Python is not dead. The gods vie for power. Apollo is the most powerful god of Delphi, but in the cold winter, another god is worshipped—Dionysos."

Do I imagine it? As she speaks the god's name, fire flashes around her head and shoulders and her eyes char to black coals. I shake my head and it's gone before I can be sure.

Mama paces back and forth before us. "Apollo and Dionysos are like two brothers, two sides of a coin. The earth and the sky. Apollo is the god of light and reason, but Dionysos is wild and untamed. Imagine the Pythia communing with that bold god of pine trees and the sacred vine." Mama stops and looks out the window then speaks without turning around to look at us. "Both gods are honored in our sacred temple. There can be no divine light without dark earth." She shakes her head.

"Mama?" My voice is a whisper, my question caught in my throat. But I have to ask. I have to know. Mama stares and waits for me to finish my question. "Pan. The ancient nature god." I clear my throat and try to sound more casual. "You know, the satyr."

Mama nods. Her brow draws together, but she is silent.

"Pan is a companion of Dionysos?"

"Yes, where one goes, you'll always find the other. Why?"

"It's not important. I just wondered."

She waits for me to explain, but when I don't, she shakes her head. "Enough of this girls. I need to get back to my work." Mama walks out to the courtyard, turns at our gate to look back at me then jerks the heavy boarded gate closed behind her.

CHAPTER SIX

SACRIFICE

"Let's follow the pilgrims. Maybe we'll see The Child of the Clouds." I am gone and three houses up before Sophia catches up with me.

"Hey, you can't get rid of me that easily!" Sophia grabs my hand, and we run hand in hand past a scattering of clay and stone houses, clinging to the precipices of our mountain, uphill to the rocks and sky and gods.

Beyond the smallest village houses orange and rust, thatch roofs sun-bleached and tattered, we catch our first glimpse of meadows—beds of gold grass, glistening with morning dew, red poppies startling in the morning light. A metallic clanging of pots, sturdy swords, the huffing of tired horses carry down to us, just as we reach the wide stones of the Sacred Way—the path the Pythia and her entourage will follow on the ninth day of each month at sunrise.

I kick a pinecone sideways on up the path. First my right foot then left. I laugh, when I realize I am kicking it in time to Pan's melody. Forget The Child of the Clouds. I don't want to think about her. Or the spider. Or the Persian king and his army. Can there be a more beautiful morning than this? Cumulus clouds form in the heat, race across a vivid, blue sky, hinting of weather shifts and shorter days. But my heart sinks when I remember that early spring will bring my marriage to Brygos if Papa has his way. This time he won't back down. I kick the cone so hard it skids off the path and downhill, irretrievable.

"Sophia. What do you think? Has Priest Diokles communed with the god, translated the sacred hexagrams for the pilgrims just like the Pythia used to?"

"That's what Mama said." Sophia turns around while she continues to walk, glancing back down the path.

"I don't believe it."

"You've heard what they say—the priest sacrificed lambs to Apollo all these years asking for the new Pythia to be revealed." She looks around and lowers her voice. "You heard Mama say Diokles didn't want to find a new Pythia. He wanted all the gold and power for himself."

"And turned a deaf ear to Apollo? Defied the god?"

With my question, the Phaedriades sparkle in the morning light above us. Have the gods heard us? Feeling suddenly light-headed, I force my eyes to focus on the jutting stone cliffs. A shaft of sunlight flares off the rock face. Flute music whispers from a clump of poppies by the path edge. Everywhere I look, light throbs. I lose my sense of self, of time, of walking this well-worn path with my best friend. What's happening to me? It feels like I've fallen through a crack between… between what? Sleep and awake? The immortals and mortals? These visions coming and going are disorienting. I wish they'd just stop!

I smell goat. Suddenly strong, like wet wool left to dry in the sun. The smell is pungent and overwhelming, a bitter smell as if rancid olives and honey are mixed together. The odor sweetens as I look around thinking I'd see old Hestos' ram. The scent on the breeze changes to wild garlic and thyme.

Pan? I glance back at Sophia. Does she notice anything?

Something rustles in a scrub bush uphill from the path. I glimpse a bearded face crouched behind a scraggly cypress.

My heart skips.

It must be Pan.

Backing into the shadow of a pine, I hold my arm out to stop Sophia and pull her close beside me.

A hoof dislodges pebbles that fall just in front of me, dusting a small cloud. Behind the tree, Pan's haunch and leg lifts, drops, lifts again. I peer beneath the draping cypress branch. *Why didn't I hear him? When did I stop listening?* There is a distinct crack, a breaking branch and without any doubt, some feral corner of my mind—always alert, always waiting—knows it is the satyr.

I spin to look behind me just in time to see a goat leg disappear into dense laurel.

Maybe it isn't Pan.

Is it only Hestos' old ram standing on its hind feet half hidden there?

My eyes dart back to the face.

Two blue eyes wink shut and disappear.

Every needle on the cypress is outlined with a green glow. The shadow behind the tree, where I had seen the eyes, fills with pulsing light.

Sophia touches my shoulder. "Thaleia, what's wrong? Did you see something? Hestos? We'd better go back. The Sacred Way is forbidden for women to walk on. Only the Pythia and her servants can walk this path. Let's get out of here."

I catch my breath. Hestos is standing just above us beside the path, looking straight at us. A memory, just a hint of something like the smell of honeysuckle down by the sacred spring, flushes my face—Mama and Hestos stood close just outside the stone goat pen. She rested her hand lightly on his shoulder, and he turned to look at her. He smiled. Even though I was so young, too small to understand, I was flooded with a feeling of great sadness, of overwhelming loss trapped in his smile. His sorrow disappeared when his eyes flicked over to me, and he laughed. I never understood that moment, but I never forgot it either. It left me feeling like a thread connects Mama to the shepherd to me, and at all costs I must never break or tangle that thread. I don't know why. I just know.

"Come on, you fool goats. Milking time. Get up here."

The lead ram, the bell around his neck—clanging with each leap—and at least a dozen nannies and kids jump up the hill following the shepherd as he turns his back and heads to his hut.

"Sophi… I don't think he's seen us," I say, laughing behind my hand. "He's half-blind."

Hestos' eyes turned milky as she-goats nectar as he aged. About a year ago, he planted a red-barked madrone, a tree as smooth as Parian marble, between his door and the goat-pen. It made it easier for him to feel his way. His eyes were so dim that even his goats, who used every wile to escape him to higher grazing in younger times, sensed their old shepherd's world had shifted to vague winter grays with nothing left but solid stone and rough planks. They milled tightly around him, protected him from cliff edge and guided him to the last grazing he taught them to find.

So he tried to smell the wind, scrambling over creviced boulders to watch us splash in spring waters, turning his clearer eye, chin raised, tilted, peering at us like some old gander. It gave me the creeps. Even as he lost his sight, he seemed to always be watching us.

Sophia shuffles her feet in the dust of the path.

"Let's go back," she urges. "He might tell Diokles."

"Oh, come on, Sophia. Just for once, have some fun."

"Remember what happened the last time I followed you?"

"Yes, we found a beautiful meadow high up the mountain filled with magic music." I grab both her hands and swing her in a circle faster and faster, until we fall to the ground laughing. "We had an adventure together!"

She hesitates, smiles and pulls me to my feet. "Let's go." Her smile catches a moment as she peers up the wide, stone way, before I tug her behind me. We sneak past Hestos as he nudges the last of his goats into their pen, a small plot of trampled dirt fenced round with rough-barked limbs. Dead blossoms scatter in the warm wind;

chewed vines are shorn as far as the goats can reach, pushing their heads through the rails. A goat skull is lodged in a notch of the smooth madrone, decorated with withered laurel. The shepherd locks the gate behind them and disappears into his stone hut.

I look behind us to be sure no one else is coming. The light no longer shimmers. My head is clear. We turn a last uphill bend in the path. Massive Cyclopean blocks of the Sanctuary wall loom before us. I hold my breath and spider-crawl past the stone wall. Past a treasury, its bronze door bolted. Gulping deep breaths, I slip inside the high gate and into the Sanctuary. Music from flutes and finger cymbals, drums and a rattle of knucklebones drifts from the great temple.

Diokles is standing beside the sacred fire his back to me. The Child of the Clouds sits beneath the porch, in the stone's perpetual twilight, her pale face protected from the harsh sun. Sitting cross-legged on a pile of skins beside massive marble columns of the Temple of Apollo, her long hair loose, almost hiding her face, she waits, studies her hands resting cupped in her lap. With grace and purpose, she stands and tilts her head to the side at the sound of approaching drums, one deep bass shaping a driving rhythm, lifted with a high staccato of hand cymbals. In the bright morning light, I'm amazed by how young she looks.

Jumping up, hoping no one is looking, I race across the open space and crouch behind the rough Rock of the Sybil, a boulder lodged so close before the temple that it is shadowed by the fluted columns. Sophia skitters up beside me.

"What are you doing? They'll see us! Let's go back." Her voice is tight and high.

I grab her belt and pull her close to peer around the other edge of the rough hewn stone. If only I could melt into it, but I can't resist looking.

The temple courtyard stretches before us: marble stones, smooth, shining in the early sunlight, cluttered with wooden coffers filled with silver and gold coins, ransom for the gods, inscribed in many tongues. Carved on the lintel of the massive marble Temple of Apollo are the words *Know Thyself* and a giant, solitary letter—**E**.

What does that mean?

I'm distracted from my thoughts as slaves, many only children, hurry past, their bare feet scuffing tracks in the dirt blowing across the temple stone. They talk in whispered, chuffing sounds. A thin boy slips and falls just on the other side of our rock, but instead of crying, peers cautiously up at the rock's crest towering over him and scurries away. Bracelets of bondage on his wrists and ankles flash as he crawls across a strip of brilliant sunlight.

The adult *helots* are broad-faced, so black from working in the sun, that their dark eyes and thick eyebrows are lost, shadows without features. I guess from their black hair and almond-shaped eyes, that they are Persian prisoners from the battle of Marathon.

I've heard that when the last Pythia spoke the oracle in lofty hexameters to the priests, there were many more pilgrims. Then Delphi had power. But why travel to our barren mountain only to talk with priests? There are priests all over Hellas. So, over the years there were fewer and fewer pilgrims. But today the Sanctuary is filled with weary pilgrims—patricians in finely woven tunics, aged soldiers—all chosen by lot, looking exhausted by weeks and months of travel. They appear hopeful and doubtful at the same time. I look from face to face, wondering what question they have for the Pythia. Did they mistrust Diokles' long search for a new Pythia like I did?

The thick columns of the temple cast long shadows across the *temenos*. Black and stark.

Standing close before the altar fire, Diokles calls for silence then leans on his cane and glares from pilgrim to pilgrim, his face stern and proud. I wonder where The Child of the Clouds disappeared? Oh, there she is. She slips down to the altar to stand half hidden behind the flames. Two torches of tightly woven corn stalks burn steadily, slightly behind her on either side. The flames dance and flare, silhouetting her thin body through her tunic's soft weave. It hangs large on her, slips off one shoulder and drags the Sanctuary tiles.

I can't take my eyes off the girl. Her arms gesture a strange leaping dance, imitating the flames that roar high above her head.

Have these pilgrims come this far to find only a fake Pythia? And what will happen to this girl if the priests force her to commune with the god? For a moment, I feel sorry for her. A Pythia died once long ago, when the sacrificial goat did not shake off the holy water. The priests sprinkled the frightened animal with water, but it did not shiver. Would not shake off the cold libation no matter how many times they tried. The sign from the god Apollo was clear: He would not visit the Pythia when she sat upon the sacred tripod. He would not fill her with his divine knowledge.

When the priests—wanting their gold payment—forced her to take her place in the hidden chamber, the *adyton* deep beneath the temple and demanded she sit above the fissure steaming with the earth's fumes, she screamed. Convulsed on the leather sling-seat as if the god's possession were agony.

They carried her unconscious to her hut. She died the next day.

Will The Child of the Clouds die because she is not the true Oracle?

Do I care?

The goats, fat and restless, distract my thoughts, their hooves clattering in the muggy air. They look like attendants to the priests, each with a hind leg stretched toward the broad temple steps as if performing a strange sacrificial dance. Their cries echo between the columns.

Unable to pull my eyes away, I hear a low humming, like a wind between pines as the priests chant their way up the temple steps.

I smell blood, see it pulse over the goats. Red washes my vision, throbbing in rhythm with the ritual chanting that swells and echoes, resonating in my chest and throat, pulsing behind my eyes. The smell is bitter and raw.

For one horrible moment, I am the goats' terror. I am white fur and silver hooves. Caught in their horror, I shiver with the knowledge that I will be slaughtered. The knife. The blood spurting from our necks, when we are sacrificed, our throats slit. I am overwhelmed with fear and death and confusion.

I gag.

Shake my head until the vision clears. The goats, unharmed, tug against leather straps tied to rings pounded into the paving stones.

"Those poor goats!" I whisper to Sophia. "Hog-tied, led to slaughter. That's exactly how it felt when Diokles came to get me for my marriage."

Sophia doesn't answer me. With worried eyes, she nods toward the temple steps.

The Child of the Clouds turns and looks toward our hiding place. Her gaze is long and steady.

Does she see us?

Her pale lips silently move, but the chanting priests that flank her drown out any sound she makes. Their bodies sway side to side as they sing.

One priest turns to stare toward our hiding place. I pull back behind the boulder and hold my breath.

My ears throb with the priests' chanting cadence, pacing sandals against stone, bleating goats and the smell—once more I am overwhelmed with a smell of blood. All the other sounds fade, replaced by one word: *Sacrifice. Sacrifice. Sacrifice.*

CHAPTER SEVEN

WICKER MAN

A memory stabs me. One I'd forced from my mind—I was a virgin-maid in last year's fertility festival—the Agrionia. We pretended it was fun. But we knew. All the girls, dressed in black, running free up the mountain calling for Dionysos. One of us would be chosen as sacrifice for the god.

Every year one girl died.

There'd been riddles and roasted corn, cheeses and delicious harvest bread still warm from the oven. I remember hiding quietly behind a pine to watch the older women down by the spring.

"Carry the god Dionysos to the mouth of the Underworld." Mama's deep voice, hoarse in the night wind, urged the other women. "The god will find his mother there." Their torches flared across the god's wicker form shaped to resemble a man, dressed in purple robes. Twined grape leaves crowned his head; moonlight shone through his stick-skull.

The women shifted the wicker god shoulder to shoulder and heaved it into the dark water. "Rebirth. Salvation. Dionysos will find his mother and return to the wide-plowed earth with her." Mama helped toss the wicker man into the Kastalia Spring as if it was the body of the god descending to the Underworld to find his mother. The mother ravished by Zeus… murdered by Hera's jealousy.

At first it floated on top of the water, until dark currents from the Underworld, cold drafts from the earth's deep seeped between the god's twig chest and arms and two holes for the god's eyes to see his way into Hades.

Sacrifice. Sacrifice.

There was no sacrificial goat that night.

With a rush, I remember the rest of the night. Two priests in yellow robes burst upon us as we sat on a dead log pretending to cast knucklebones for our fortune. Animal snarls escaped their clenched teeth. We ran screaming up the mountain, into that cloudless night. There was one girl, small and dark. I didn't see what happened. But I remember her gasping breath. Her anguished shout. A death rattle of metal against flesh.

Silence.

I ran and didn't stop, until dawn crept over the Shining Cliffs, and I could run no farther. We all knew, when we went to the fertility festival that one of us would be chosen. For fertility. The crops. For sweet babes suckling at a mother's breast. We knew, and we went anyway, because next year we would be married and possibly big with child. So we did what the priests and villagers said must be done.

Why? Why did we obey the priests? Why didn't we question? Why did we just let that girl be slaughtered for the god Dionysos? And the one the year before? And before that? Why did we go along? We justified it all—in the name of tradition. It was needed for the crops and the babies, we told ourselves.

Blood rushes to my face. It burns like a fire blazes from my heart to my throat, as if my eyes would murder the wretched old priest.

Why didn't we rise up and stop it all?!

Sacrifice.

I'm dizzy, lost between that Agrionia-night and this sunlit day. Swirling smoke taints the deep blue sky; its musky perfume fills me. I am weightless and drifting. There is too much of the divine in this Sanctuary.

A girl dressed all in black forms in the smoke before me. She runs away, scrambles up steep rocks, grabbing the cliff stone, panting and pulling herself up. She turns back to peer behind her as if someone chases her.

The girl is Sophia!

No. Not again. Not this time.

I smell dust, feel the night wind against my face. Sophia's frightened eyes stare through me. A priest in yellow robes with black hair chases her. I hear his ragged breath, feel his thirst for sacrifice. "Sophia run!" Do I scream? She doesn't seem to hear me, only scrambles uphill with all her strength, clawing stone and gnarled trees. A cry tears from her, when the priest grabs her hair and jerks her head back. His sword flashes in moonlight. Blood fills my vision. Blood and terror and death.

Sophia!

An eagle's cry shatters my vision.

I shudder and grab Sophia's hand. "Sophia," I say. "Sophia, the festival for Dionysos, the Agrionia! You can't go!"

"What?" Sophia hisses. "Shhh, they'll find us." She pinches my arm to silence me.

"The priest will murder you," I whisper close to her ear and draw a deep breath to try to explain, to warn. But she doesn't hear. The Child of the Clouds tilts her head back and shatters the brilliant sky with eagle screams. Another cry escapes the girl's thin lips. She's seen me!

Diokles lifts his withered arms, raising a libation bowl above his head. The priests' chant grows louder and deeper. He motions for two priests to bring the sacrificial goat.

The Pythia's eagle call pierces the cadence. Mixed with the raptor's call, I understand one word, as if her birdcall cries only to me, as sharp as a blade: **Intruder!**

No!

The Child of the Clouds lowers her gaze and glares directly at me. I tuck back behind my rock and hold my breath.

There are more eagle shrieks—**I am Pythia. Oracle to the great god Apollo. Leave now or forfeit your life!**

We're discovered! The Pythia knows we're here!

I squeeze Sophia's hand and raise a finger to my lips for her to stay completely still. I pull back, flattened against the boulder. We don't dare move.

Sandals shuffle against stone. I hear a struggle as they pull the sacrificial goat through the side gate. His bleats sound a desperate scream past the Polygonal Wall. The sound of hooves scraping the temenos stone on beyond the sphinx atop its massive column and rough cries cut the silence. Tear the air as the priests and attendants wait for the acrid smell of blood, of life given to honor the god Apollo. The smell of sacrifice.

Will The Child of the Clouds show them where we are?

There is a plaintive bleat from the goat, closer, already on the Halos threshing floor. The priests gather for the sacrifice. I smell incense and sweet myrrh, imagine Diokles lifting a gold *kylix* in supplication. Will the Pythia stop the ceremony? Tell the priest I am here?

The ceremony continues, and I relax a little.

"Divine Apollo, give us a sign!" He calls the ritual. Now he will sprinkle the goat with water. I hold my breath. Will the goat shiver?

The chanting stops. I can't resist. I peer cautiously from my hiding place. The priests, initiates and slaves all stare at the Pythia, her pale hair billows in the morning breeze, sparkling like sacred waters in the sun.

The goat did not shiver. Apollo does not honor the sacrifice.

As one, the pilgrims catch their breaths. The Sanctuary is consumed by silence, a waiting hush as if the hand of Apollo swept aside wind and the sun's parching heat, the altar fire's crackle of wood consumed. As if the god stole all hope for his divine guidance.

Proud and defiant, The Child of the Clouds shatters the empty calm, purses her lips and sings the hunting call of a raptor.

Once again, in my heart, the eagle shriek becomes words.

Are you still hiding there, girl? What do you think the priest will say this time? How will he convince the pilgrims to cross his palm with gold? He'll find a way even if the goat did not shiver. They are such fools!

Her words resonate in my bones. But when I try to focus on them, they only sound like an eagle's call, but if I listen carefully to the birdsong, her words become clear.

Will the war cry of an eagle convince him? A pleading dove? The priest will say what serves his own purpose. He does not listen to the god. What will you do, if you discover I am not the true Pythia?

You're not the Pythia. You're an imposter.

The Child of the Clouds slips her fingers in and out of the high flames then steps beside the fire. She throws back her shoulders.

A sharp jolt courses my spine. "Sophia," I hiss through clenched teeth. "She knows we're hiding here. She'll tell Diokles. We're trapped."

"Would the Pythia betray us?" Sophia says so low I can barely hear her words, but I feel her cold fear.

"She's not the Pythia, Sophia."

Sophia stares at me, leans to look around the boulder, just far enough out to see the girl and quickly tucks back in. "What are you saying? Just look at her. She's wearing the leopard skin and the crown of laurel leaves." Sophia's eyes narrow. Her jaw is tight. "She must be the Pythia."

I jerk Sophia close, afraid her stare will draw the eyes of the old priest. He will feel us watching.

Death will be his answer.

It feels as though the blood stops running through my body. I smell the stone dust beneath me, incense and horse dung. Sophia tenses. There's nothing I can do but wait.

Leaning against the jutting boulder, hardly daring to breathe, I look back over my shoulder. Through the gate, the valley drops away from us, blue-green brush stubbles the limestone. The bay is an emerald green far below.

Is any of this real? Why do I hear voices? Should I believe them? Did I really meet Pan, or am I losing my mind?

The view stuns me. Dizzy, I clutch the stone.

Sophia nudges me with her elbow and nods toward the Sanctuary. "Thaleia, look!"

CHAPTER EIGHT

THE ORACLE OF ELEA

We peer cautiously around, still safely hidden on the other side of the boulder. A sun-dark stranger looms, his back to us. Thank the gods. He hasn't seen us. Maybe we can escape, while they're distracted by the barbarian.

He stands with crossed muscular arms, shiny as if rubbed with olive oil, and watches Diokles lift a libation to Apollo. He's tall, massive in height, dressed like a foreigner. Diokles seems frail and wizened in comparison. The stranger turns to the side to watch a young priest lead another sacrificial goat over, and I get a better look at him. In his middle years, there's something young and old about him at the same time. He has dark, curly hair and a black beard. Thick, red robes of an Oracle drape from strong shoulders and gold braids rope around his taut neck and across his chest.

All speak of power.

But his eyes are old, lost and unfocused. They deny his strength and shroud his face as if with a harsh memory. Slaves and pilgrims whirl a storm of activity past us. The Oracle backs out of the way, closer to our boulder, so I can't see him.

I jerk Sophia close. She kneels in the dust beside me. Another eagle cry cuts through the confusion.

Intruder!

It feels as though the blood stops running through my body. I smell the stone dust beneath me, incense and horse dung. Sophia tenses beside me.

I edge a little closer around the rock. Maybe this is our chance to escape. Crouching low on the temple stone, I peer around just in time to see The Child of the Clouds slip back into the temple shadows.

Diokles touches the Oracle's shoulder with hesitant reverence. They speak to one another in soft tones, but in the silence their voices carry.

"The signs are propitious, Parmenides. I'm sure Apollo will honor your sacrifice. As I approached the temple this morning, not one but two eagles crossed over the Sanctuary. If you will follow me… I will lead you to the pilgrims' chamber."

The Oracle stands pensive. He holds his strong hands out before him, as if presenting an offering to Diokles and studies the lines creasing his palms.

"No, Diokles. I will wait to receive my oracle from the true Pythia."

I catch my breath at his words. Does he know? Who is this seer? From his voice and cadence, his soft, even response, I think he must be from Phocaea, the eastern lands besieged by Darius and his Persian hordes.

"What do you mean, Parmenides, wise Oracle of Elea? The Pythia waits below in the adyton. The signs allow you to question her. If you will pay the tithe, I will lead you to Apollo's Oracle."

"The Pythia is here, Diokles."

"Yes. She awaits you below on the tripod."

"No. Not below. The Pythia is here." The Oracle's voice gets louder, more insistent. He looks around the Sanctuary.

I hold my breath behind the Sybil's Rock and pray to the earth goddess Gaia that the rock shadows hide us.

I jump when the Phocaean shouts, "*Menin Theou*, wrath of Zeus!

What do you take me for? A fool? I can feel her. She is here, I tell you!"

Crouching deeper in the shadow, I cringe at each shuffle and scrape of clay amphoras, startle at a donkey's bray. Its hooves clatter on the stone, dancing a staccato rhythm, as it tries to pull free.

Sophia tugs on my sleeve.

"Stop, Sophia!" My voice is louder than I want it to be.

"What was that?!" Diokles shouts and rushes toward our hiding place.

Sophia bolts. Her legs fly as she throws herself past Diokles. She dodges his grab and makes it to the *Bouleuterion*, the large meeting hall.

Run Sophia!

Every muscle in my body wants to run after her, to help her. I hold back. She's fast. If she doesn't get away, I'll be more help later if they don't know I'm here.

Forcing myself to wait, I pull farther back in the rock's shadow and listen with every fiber of my being.

I hear her run down the stairs between the Council House and the Treasury of the Athenians. Will she make it out the gate?

"Seize her!" Diokles' shout startles the doves. In wild confusion, they flap their wings, battering the slaves and priests. They scatter as if Apollo flies with the birds urging them to attack. Children yell at each other. Men curse at their horses.

Sophia cries out, but I wait, hold my breath until it feels caged in my chest. Unable to stand it any longer, I peer around the rock. Two men—slaves in dirty tunics, muscled arms gleaming with sweat—grab Sophia. She struggles to free herself. Her breath is short and shallow as she digs her heels into the paving stones. Her face is grim. She doesn't cry or scream again.

Come on, Sophia. Come on. My muscles clench, willing her to break free.

Abruptly, she collapses in their grasp.

No, Sophia. Don't give up. Can I get to her? There's a tunnel that opens up to the theater. It's so far. Too far.

The younger slave, barely older than Sophia, lifts her limp body and carries her to the temple steps, dumping her at the priest's feet.

"Sophia!" Diokles hisses his anger. "Why do you desecrate this sacred Sanctuary?" He motions for two priests to jerk Sophia to her feet. "Speak up!" Her face is pale, her eyes unfocused as she looks around the Sanctuary as if unable to understand where she is or why. Diokles shakes her.

Tears fill her eyes, but she is still silent.

When she looks over to my rock, pleads with her eyes for my help, I cringe behind the rock. I hear a dove call from inside the temple. The Child of the Clouds' words sting me with shame.

Good! They caught her.

I swallow hard.

I've got to help her.

I brought Sophia here. This is my fault.

Taking a deep breath, I step from behind the boulder. "Let her go, Diokles!" I'm surprised, when my words echo loud and strong off the Sanctuary walls.

My senses expand. There's a loud hissing like steam forced through a stone opening, or a Titan's hot breath or a thousand vipers set loose. The Phocaean's horse whinnies and dances. Animal cries and hissing mix with a roar from deep inside the temple. Like fire and thunder and the anger of all the Olympian gods combined. *The Python! The ancient god.* My gut wrenches with fear. Wails assault my throbbing temples.

I take a step closer to Sophia. It all stops. The fire-roar and hiss. With that one step, that one decision to stand up to the priest and help Sophia, a calm descends on the sacred grounds.

Slaves, priests and *therapon*-attendants stare at me.

Sophia looks terrified and relieved. "Thaleia!"

The Oracle Parmenides walks toward me, his arms wide, as if to welcome me.

A deep rhythmic clang of the priests' bells fills the silence.

I can't look at Diokles. My only hope is the other—the foreign Oracle. It's as if he calls me. Something tells me to beg his help. *Should I trust him?*

My ears hum as I strain to listen for the Python and take another step closer. I stare into Parmenides' dark eyes, eyes that bore into my soul. My mouth is dry. I force the words from my lips.

"I brought her here. She didn't want to come. I'm the one."

I try to keep my voice steady and firm. When the Oracle moves toward me, I stare at the ground and clasp my hands together so tightly they burn. I can feel Diokles' glare from beyond Parmenides.

The Child of the Clouds is silent and watching, high above on the broad temple step.

Say something. Do something. I try to give myself a courage I don't feel.

Taking a gulp of air, I look back up at Parmenides, the wise *Hierophant* from Elea. To my surprise, he smiles at me in encouragement. What can I tell him that will make him want to help me? If I tell him the priest is a fraud? If I tell him the Pythia isn't the true Pythia? How can I prove any of it? I look over at Sophia with a priest on either side clutching her arms. I have to try. I straighten my back and stride close before Parmenides. My words are loud in the silent Sanctuary.

"Diokles spent sixteen years looking for the Pythia and all that time insisted that the pilgrims believe his oracles!"

Diokles stiffens and shuffles down the temple steps to stand beside Parmenides.

I whirl to face him. "You banished the last Pythia and claimed you couldn't find a new one!"

He gasps and lunges at me, clutches my neck with withered hands and tries to force me to my knees.

"By the gods!" Parmenides seizes Diokles' arm and pulls him off me.

Power surges through me, emboldens me. I shout at the old priest. "How dare you accuse Sophia of desecrating this Sanctuary? You dishonor Apollo! For years you claimed the power of the Pythia, claimed to commune with Apollo? You say you hear the god's oracles? Lies, all lies."

Diokles grabs my hair and claps his hand over my mouth.

Parmenides clutches his shoulders, but before he pulls the priest off me, I bite Diokles' palm. He screams and jerks away.

"You only want power and gold. You don't understand the girl's birdsong. I do!"

Several priests seize me.

"Release her." Parmenides' voice is threatening. His low growl commands respect, demands they obey.

"Who are you, girl?" The *Hierophant* asks but looks as if he already knows. He glares at the priests still clutching my arms. They let me go and back away.

Diokles is not about to give in so easily.

"You are in my Sanctuary, Parmenides. In sea-shouldered Elea you may hold sway, but in this temple I hold power. He steps close to the dark priest, throws back his shoulders like a puffed hen and tries to stare him down.

Parmenides towers over the old man's stooped form, dark to Diokles' white age. He plants his feet side by side and silently looks down at Diokles. His crossed arms ripple with youth and vigor.

He speaks again, without looking at me, this time his words are low and kind. "Girl, I ask you again. Who are you?"

I take a deep breath and move so close to Parmenides that I smell the jasmine oil rubbed into his shoulder and a breath of mint. "I am Thaleia, daughter of Icos and Hipparchia."

He smiles and reaches long fingers, studded with gold bands and jewels to touch my cheek. His slight caress sends a surge through me. I draw a tight breath and feel a rush of blood redden my face. Glancing at Sophia, I twist my hair around my fist.

Parmenides turns back to Diokles. His face and voice fill with stern disdain. "Priest, I will leave now. Thaleia and her friend will come with me. I have found the answers I sought, no thanks to you."

"What!?" Diokles objects, but his words are cut short by a coughing fit. While he bends double trying to stop choking and find his words, Parmenides steps close to Diokles and rests his hand on the old priest's back.

"Do not harm this girl. The gods will honor her words of truth. If I hear you hurt her…"

Diokles straightens and shifts from foot to foot, struck dumb. He clutches his hands behind his back. For the first time I can remember, the priest is at a loss for words.

With a gesture from Parmenides, all his slaves jump to their feet.

I walk over to stand beside Sophia and take her hand. *Are we really free?*

"Sophia, are you alright?"

She nods, but her eyes are wide; her face pale.

"I'm so sorry." I squeeze her hand.

Children run to pick up bundles of bright, woven shawls, soft and limp, emptied of their treasures. Others hurry to gather bundles of food offerings and amphoras they had hidden in the column shadow to keep the water jugs cool.

Will we be allowed to leave with the Oracle? Did he save us from Diokles?

The stones shimmer as we pass beneath the portal—Sophia and I on either side of Parmenides, the silent Hierophant. Pacing two steps to his long stride, I smell smoke, the familiar scent of burning laurel, and a god's breath upon me. As subtle as a breeze. Warm. Moist. Spice-laden.

This temple is Apollo's home. Is it his breath I feel as a wind? Are we free because of Apollo's grace?

My back listens, tingles as if it has ears to hear.

There is a distinct crack, a breaking branch. I spin to look behind me. A large goat leg disappears into dense laurel just outside the Cyclopean gate to the Sanctuary.

Holding my breath, sharp pinpricks spike behind my eyes.

A flute melody weaves the morning sunlight.

Pan? Did you save us?

I stop rooted on the path, but Parmenides smiles a question at me and pulls me to the side, as six priests carry Diokles in a litter bright with yellow curtains and purple flags hanging limp in the still air. The old priest's withered hand draws aside the curtain as he passes. His eyes are molten hatred.

Catching up to Sophia and Parmenides, I crush her fingers in mine and stumble down the Sacred Way.

CHAPTER NINE

BETRAYAL

Parmenides brings us to Papa's taverna and disappears inside. I stiffen, when the litter stops directly in front of us; the priests lower it to the ground. One foot with perfectly trimmed nails then the other emerges from the drapes and Diokles steps out. I wrap my arm around Sophia's shoulder and raise my chin. "Don't touch us. Parmenides told you to leave us alone." I want my words to sound bold, but they still quiver.

Diokles crosses his arms. His gaze bores into me. Sophia nudges my foot with her sandal, urging me to be quiet.

"How dare you? You will answer to the council of priests," the priest wheezes and presses a wrinkled fist into his chest.

My throat is dry. I stare back at him and refuse to look away.

"The Sanctuary is sacred to Apollo." He pounds his chest and coughs uncontrollably. After his coughing fit eases, he steps closer.

Doubt rises in my throat like bitter milkweed. Diokles is the most powerful man in Delphi… maybe all of Hellas. He can destroy me if he wants.

"Never to be desecrated by woman," he hisses in my ear—looks around as if Parmenides might appear—before grabbing my shoulder. He drops his arm and steps back. "Have you heard me?"

I nod and swallow.

Diokles gestures to the priests who have been standing back waiting.

I don't let go of Sophia's hand. They surround us. Two in front. Two behind. Sophia's hand is shaking, but I can't look at her. *It's my fault. She didn't want to come to the temple. She warned me. Told me not to trespass the sacred Sanctuary.*

I squeeze her hand harder. Head high, I try not to look as miserable as I feel. He's right. They have every right to kill us. In the name of Apollo, with the god's blessing, they can lock us away with no food or water. Leave us to die in dishonor. Or worse. I shudder. They can stone us to death. No one, not my parents or Sophia's mother, no one can help us.

Maybe Parmenides could help. He may be the only one.

Pilgrims straggle past us like a river divided as if we are rocks mid-stream.

Parmenides appears at the door way and stares at Diokles. They do not exchange a single word, but the old priest straightens his hunched shoulders. He pushes Sophia and me toward Parmenides and shoves past him into the taverna.

The Hierophant rests his large hands on Sophia and my heads as if in blessing. We stand in silence. There's no need for words. After the pilgrims have all passed and the dust settled, Sophia follows Parmenides as he pushes the heavy door open. They both turn back to look at me.

"Thaleia?" Sophia says.

"I'll be right there. Just give me a moment."

The door closes behind them. Alone on the quiet pathway, I listen for music. For the clipped sound of hoof against stone. Nothing. Wind rustles the grape leaves trellised over the door. Fat sizzles on the hot coals of Papa's grill. A sparrow chirps from a nearby olive tree. Nothing more.

Pushing the door open, I ease from blinding sunlight into the dark room. Dripping honeycomb candles burn on long, wooden tables.

They cast a warm light on the clay walls and paint the travelers' faces amber. Egyptians, Achaeans, Aeolians. Quiet faces. Faces with dark eyes unfocused or staring at their hands grasping painted goblets.

I glance at Mama standing by the hearth and Papa serving wine to two old men laughing together, happy, drunk. They stop laughing and look up when we walk in. Their eyes alert. Do they know what happened in the temple? Has the priest already told them? "Mama, can I help?" Hurrying over, I pull a heavy pot filled with steaming barley off the iron hook.

Papa sends me a dark look and opens his mouth to say something, but he's interrupted.

"Icos, we need more wine over here… and eggs… and your patient ear." A traveler summons Papa with the broad accent of the Argive plain. The man is tall and lanky with a smile that lingers at the corners of his wide mouth. I saw him here twice last year. He must be losing a fortune buying audiences from the priests.

"Have you visited the Pythia, Icos? No, you wouldn't have. Lucky. You have your own world here." Papa refills the traveler's goblet. The man gestures around the room with it, spilling wine over his white tunic.

I look around for Diokles. There he is in a dark corner. His plate is already piled high with roasted lamb and figs, but he's not eating. His stern gaze is focused on Sophia, who stands close beside him. Her head is bowed as the priest talks and talks. Pointing one long finger in her face, he grabs her arm. She glances up and sees me watching her.

I rush to her side. "Don't touch her. The Oracle Parmenides told you to leave us alone." I look over at Mama, but look away, before she can question me. If she doesn't already know, I'll have to tell her, but later. Not here. Right now I have to help Sophia.

Diokles crosses his arms. His gaze bores into me. Sophia studies the cup she's holding, avoids my questioning look.

My throat is dry. I stare back at the priest and refuse to look away. The room around us is stunned to silence and the priest's words break loud and harsh over us like a maverick wave. "You *will* answer to the council of priests. The Sanctuary is sacred to Apollo. He glares across the room at Parmenides before grabbing my shoulder, but drops his hand when Parmenides jumps to his feet. Tension strands between them as strong as a fishing net. But Diokles is unwilling to completely let it go. He turns to me, his face a breath from mine. "Did you hear me?" With slow determination, he pushes back his chair and shuffles over to the hearth to get a cake from Mama.

Mama casts me a questioning look. She lowers her eyes, as she hands him a board stacked with the honey cakes, but not before I see a flare of defiance light her gaze as intense as a fire that follows the priest's slow path back to his table. The room is silent, filled only with the shuffle of Diokles' feet across the floor.

"So, Icos… you heard the Pythia?" Parmenides says, his accented voice soft. "Not this girl the priests call the Pythia now. The real Pythia, who came before her?"

Papa wipes his bloody knife on the cloth wrapped around his waist and looks around the room.

The priest glares at Parmenides and sits in his corner seat without a word. He stuffs his mouth with the cake. Licks honey from each gnarled finger.

At last. Here's someone to control the old priest. Someone to help me.

"No, Parmenides. No, I never had an audience," Papa says.

Parmenides wraps ringed fingers around his goblet. Presses it tightly against his closed lips. "She sounded like a raven crying out… no, more like a gull. I remember everything about her, though it was many years ago now. The Pythia was a young girl the first time I heard her, maybe fifteen at the most. She would be at least thirty years old now. Tell us what happened to her, Icos. Where did she go after the *priest* banished her?" He glares at Diokles.

Mama and Papa look at each other and quickly around the room at the men staring and waiting to hear what they will tell the Hierophant.

I throw a plate I'd filled with lamb to the dirt-packed floor, so everyone will turn to look at me instead. When Sophia rushes over to help, we stare a long moment into each other's eyes. I don't understand the guilty look I catch before she looks away.

"It's true about Mama, Sophia," I say while I sweep the shards onto a goatskin cloth that Sophia presses against the floor to keep it flat.

"She would have told you, Thaleia." Her voice is urgent and uncertain.

"Thaleia, bring me some lamb." Diokles raps his knife handle on the table. "Don't just stand there!"

Sophia jerks away and heads out the back door.

I grab a rag to wrap around the hot knife and cut some lamb from the bone and slide it onto a clay plate. The meat is so tender it falls away from the bone in shreds. I pile the plate high. I've crossed the priest enough for one day. For Papa's sake, I'd better appear to be the obedient daughter. But at last I know. I am certain. Mama was the last Pythia, the Forbidden One the villagers always talked about. The whispers I overheard throughout my childhood make sense now… why didn't anyone tell me?

Mama bends over the hearth stirring the coals. Her face is flushed, her mouth tight. I want to comfort her, draw her to me and stroke her hair, bring a smile to her eyes. Instead, I draw back my shoulders and walk over to Diokles.

"Here is your meal, Priest Diokles. Do you want cheese and barley?"

He nods a silent yes, stuffing his mouth with meat.

Humid heat slaps me as I leave the dark taverna. I squint, peering toward the back wall and see Sophia sitting on our bench—a slab of limestone balanced on two rocks with the wall as a backrest, where we spent hours playing house. Sophia was always the mother. I'd pretend to be her son and wander the yard hiding from the Persians, slashing a pine branch for a sword and always returning home victorious.

"Hey, Sophia."

She glances up at me, but quickly looks away pursing her lips.

The air smells of lamb, onions and rain.

"Do you hate me?"

A guilty look crosses her face, but she looks away and brushes some wet leaves off the bench and nods for me to sit beside her.

"Of course not. Why should I hate you?"

"Because I talked you into going up to the Sanctuary. Because you were caught by Diokles. It was all my fault." I want her to forgive me, to say it's alright like she always has, but her silence stretches awkward between us. I don't know what else to say. It was all my doing… and if she's not ready to forgive me…

The afternoon seems as gray as my thoughts, but I decide to try to apologize again later; to give her some time to get over her anger. "I'm sure now, Sophia. Diokles banished Mama from the sacred tripod because she was pregnant with me." I crush my fingers together and sit down beside her.

Sophia's words spill out in a breathless rush. "Thaleia, there's something I have to tell you."

The sky seems to crack open as a heavy rain spatters mud on our legs and feet.

"Zeus!" Sophia tenses, when I wrap my arm tight around her shoulder. We tuck back under the pine bough. "Do you want to go back in, Sophia?"

A quick up of her chin nods no, but she averts her eyes and won't look at me. Her words are choked, forced between tight lips.

"I tried to get you to run away with me up the mountain. I told you not to walk the Sacred Way into the Sanctuary." She turns full to face me. "You never listen to me!"

"You're right, Sophia. I'm sorry." I clutch her shoulders, wishing we could go back to what we were before. Before Diokles caught us in the temple and the Oracle rescued us. Before I met a satyr-god, who told me to trust my destiny. "Please believe me, I'm so sorry."

She sits stiff and silent, just letting me press my fingers into her forearms. Her face is hard and unforgiving.

Helpless to change her mind, I let go and fold my hands in my lap.

A brilliant flash of lightning scars the afternoon sky followed by a thunderclap. Raindrops as big as seedpods bounce off the hard-packed ground. I smell manure and wet hay as the rain soaks through the rough slats of our goats' lean-to across the yard.

"You're always getting me in trouble," she says finally. "Always telling me what to do. You really think you're special, don't you? This time you've gone too far."

Sophia grabs a handful of mud. Rolling it around between her palms, she shapes a ball, the sticky mud traced with lines of her palms. "It's all your fault. I had to tell him."

"What?" I jump up.

She ignores me.

"Sophia, look at me."

Breaking off a twig, she gives the clay ball features: a nose, wide-spaced eyes, long, straight lines drawn for hair. I stand speechless, while she carves the head.

"Sophia," I say. "Are you talking about Diokles? What did you have to tell him?"

"It's you, Thaleia." She holds the clay head up to show me, her mouth drawn into a tight smile. The face lays on its side in Sophia's open hand, a tiny head resting lightly against the curve of her fingers. She stands up and peers into the stormy sky. The sudden downpour stops, but dark clouds hang heavy over us.

"Sophia!" I grab her shoulders and lightly shake her, trying to make her look at me. "What did you do?"

At last Sophia looks me straight in the eye and answers. "I told Diokles that you have visions. That you have powers. You do, don't you?"

All around, water drips from over-laden branches.

In my gut, I know it's dangerous for the priest to know about my Sight.

"What did he say?" I feel suddenly weak in the knees and sit down.

"He said you're unnatural." Sophia sits beside me. "He said you will be judged by Apollo, Thaleia."

"How soon? When do I face the god?"

"I don't know. He didn't say." She watches a sparrow shake rainwater from her feathers and fluff them to dry. Our silence lasts a long time.

I take a deep breath and look over at Sophia. She looks miserable.

"Maybe Diokles can help you, Thaleia. Delphi is the center of the world, the exact place two eagles met—beak-to-beak, claw-to-claw—each sent by Zeus to fly in opposite directions around the Earth. Our village is the *omphalos*, the bellybutton of the world. He's the highest priest in the entire world. He's the one who can understand your visions."

"No, he's not." I shake my head as I fully understand. "That's the reason Diokles wants me married. That's why he threatens to kill me, if I don't obey the village rules. He already knows I have visions. He's afraid of me. Of my power to see things. A power he can't control like he does The Child of the Clouds."

I've put Sophia through so much. I want to keep her safe, but all I do is drag her into trouble. "Don't worry, Sophia. I don't blame you for telling him."

Her face is drawn. She places the mud head on the bench and wraps one braid around her finger, twists it to her head. Releases and twists it tight again. She bends over and traces a finger through the mud, doesn't look at me when she says, "I was trying to help, Thaleia. I thought maybe if I told, it would get you out of trouble."

As if suddenly aware of the danger she's put me in, she wraps her arms around me and sobs while I brush strands of hair from her face; pat her back; try to console her. "What's done is done. Don't worry about it, but Sophia, I tried to tell you in the Sanctuary. When I was watching the sacrificial goats, something happened. I saw something."

"What, Thaleia?" Sophia's eyes widen as she leans back.

"Sophia, don't go with the celebrants to the Agrionia."

She looks hard at me. "I have to. Diokles ordered all the *parthenai*-unmarried maids—to go the year before they marry."

"They…" How can I explain what I saw? Maybe now Sophia will believe me. "Just trust me."

But her anger flares. "You're always trying to order me around. Stop telling me what I can and cannot do. I won't stay home. It's tradition… and maybe it'll be fun." As if realizing that she's scolding me again, she smiles sheepishly.

"Sophia, please." I take a deep breath. I need her to understand. "In a vision, I saw the sacrifice at the festival for Dionysos. You Sophia. The sacrificed virgin was you."

"What are you talking about, Thaleia? That's just crazy. They choose a girl from descendents of the Minyan family. You and I can't be chosen."

Fear and doubt darken her eyes.

"He'll kill you!" I don't know how to explain, what to say.

Sophia picks up the head and carves lines for hair with her fingernail.

"Please, you must listen to me."

As I stare at my clay effigy in Sophia's hand, red waves envelop it. The tiny head moves side to side as if my fear brought it alive. Its jaws open and close, open and close twisting in a silent scream. This time Sophia sees it move.

She stares at me wide-mouthed then screams and hurls the head across the yard. It smashes against the stone wall. She runs out the back gate. It slams behind her.

CHAPTER TEN

THE LAST ORACLE-PYTHIA

Two ravens call across rain-laden clouds. The downpour has cleared the humid air, like the shattering of the clay head cleared my mind. I know what I have to do. And it starts with me no longer doubting. I saw the head come alive. I met the god Pan. I saw the priest murder Sophia in my vision. Now it's up to me to save her. That is my destiny. That is why the satyr told me not to run away.

I breathe in the clean smell like fresh-washed linens or fig-steeped water. Papa and Mama come out into the yard holding dripping bags.

Papa hangs the bags of cheese whey from our fig tree. He smiles at me but doesn't say anything.

"Mama?" I stroke her back. She heaves a deep sigh. "Mama, you were the last Pythia?"

Her hands shake as she takes both my hands and holds them. There are tears in her eyes.

"Mama?"

She looks up and draws my fingers to her lips, kisses each finger. Her first words are quiet. So soft, I am uncertain if I hear them or imagine them. "Yes, Thaleia. I was the last Pythia."

"You never told me."

She drops my hands, her face contorted. Her voice quivers with rage. "You saw, Thaleia! Diokles will do anything to keep his power, his gold!"

When she calms down, she looks a long, sad moment at Papa. "Maybe it's time to tell her?"

Papa's face slumps with uncertainty.

I squeeze Mama's hands once more, nod and pull her to sit beside me on the stone bench. "Tell me, Mama. Tell me about being the Pythia."

Mama's soft voice seems to walk me alongside her into the shadows of the great columns. I follow the shuffle of her bare feet as if they draw me deep into the temple. With her quiet words, we pass through a dark passageway, narrow with rough stone on either side of us, pungent with a sharp sweet smell. It all makes sense to me, like lines in a drawing at last making a face familiar to me, a picture that I've known for a long time and that is at last becoming clear.

But what she says next confuses me. I grew up understanding that the Pythia communed with Apollo in his temple. I learned that Apollo is the god of prophecy, the god who is both healer and destroyer. He may bring the plague and destroy or heal with his divine breath. Apollo is the heart of Delphi's power, the god that gathers pilgrims from the entire world. Why is she telling me about Dionysos?

"The priests thought I only communed with Apollo. They didn't know. In the winter months, Apollo left, but I was not alone. In frozen winter, another god claimed the Sanctuary. I would sneak off to the oracle chamber—the adyton—and Dionysos would come to me." She is silent, remembering.

"The new god from the East?" I say, wanting her to tell me more.

She looks at me with smiling eyes. "Dionysos, son of Zeus and Semele, god of sun-drenched vines and black earth and life unending."

Mama's face is on fire with the memory. Her eyes flash like the sun cresting the jutting cliffs above the temple. Completely still and silent, I wait to understand what she is telling me. I know there is more to her words than she has said.

"We worship Apollo, child of Zeus—the supreme god, the thunder god—and Leto. In our temple, we worship Apollo above all others, but I remember those winter days more than the summer days." She smiles and touches her lips lightly, before glancing up quickly at Papa. Her face flushes red. When she looks back at me, her mouth sets with determination.

"With summer's heat, I heard the prophecies of Apollo," Mama says, her voice low and monotone, her eyes distant as if once again she's under his trance. "In the winter, Dionysos' passion consumed me." Abruptly, she focuses her eyes on me. "I lived to be with my god. I yearned to walk alone into the sacred chamber, to breathe the earth's sweet fumes and climb the tripod. Each breath felt as if I would never draw another, but I could not leave my god. Each time I promised myself that I would wait until Apollo returned, until control and reason and the honored religion returned. But I couldn't stay away. Dionysos' raw power filled me. Every full moon, I went back, crept away from the priest's watchful eye and walked the path from my room. To him. To Dionysos. To my god. My god filled me, but I was desperate and lonely. Until I met your father." She smiles at Papa, and he moves to her side. He smiles back at Mama, but his eyes are sad.

"How did you and Papa meet?"

"The mountain gods brought us together."

I look sharply at Mama. Did she meet Pan?

Mama and Papa share another smile and this time their eyes are bright with a memory I can only guess. I wonder what really brought them together.

"When you were in my belly, I was scared. I knew there wasn't much time, until Diokles found out I was pregnant. I wanted you and Papa and a home. I wanted to serve the gods and you! There was enough love. But Diokles threw me off the tripod." Mama snorts a bitter laugh. "I know I broke the rules."

"If Diokles only knew!" Papa laughs.

Mama frowns, her eyes angry and sad. "He used my disgrace as an excuse to gain political advantage—anything to keep his power! I do not regret my choice, Thaleia. The gods devise their own plans. Yes, I was the last Pythia, the Forbidden One—the Oracle thrown off the sacred tripod, because I was pregnant. I still hear Apollo in my dreams. And Dionysos… I bake and wash and walk beneath a god-filled sky. The gods did not abandon me."

"Diokles wanted you to kill me. Before I was born!"

Mama looks at me and says nothing.

"You should be Pythia, Mama. Not that fake!"

"That time is past, my daughter. I want nothing more than our home here in the village. If we follow the traditions designed to keep us safe, it's like staying warm beneath a soft, wool blanket. Children are bred beneath that blanket. But tradition is not a living thing. It cannot grow. Yet, the children do. It cannot breathe or feel or wonder at the great mysteries of the earth. As the children always do." Mama smiles at me. "So it is the children who dare escape."

Pulling my hands gently from Mama's, I cross the yard and unhook cheese bags from the branch then squeeze the milk still oozing from the loosely woven cloth into a jug and hang the sack back onto the cut tree branch. I need to think. To understand what Mama is telling me.

Papa appears beside me. Rests his large hand on my shoulder. "Thaleia, come with me to the grill. We need to get that lamb off before it's charred."

I wipe tears from my eyes and set aside the cheese.

Diokles ordered Mama to kill me, but she refused. Mama forfeited her position as the most powerful priestess in all Hellas to save me.

I follow Papa around to the front.

Mama is the true Pythia.

Papa cuts slabs of meat off and places them on a wooden platter. "Here, Thaleia, carry this lamb inside."

There's so much I don't understand. How did Papa meet a Pythia? Weren't they always kept in chaste seclusion? How did he become her lover?

But there's no time to ask. A young hoplite, a Spartan soldier by his dress, rushes around the bend in the path. He glances up, grimaces with an attempt to smile at Papa. His leather tunic covers a loosely woven shirt soaked through with sweat. In one muddy hand, he clutches a long spear, a rolled scroll in the other. His face is without beard, unlined, at most two years older than I am. His eyes dart side to side; his brow furrows. Deep lines of worry, caked with mud, etch his face.

CHAPTER ELEVEN

King Xerxes of Persia

Papa nudges me away from the door as five or six more *hoplite* foot soldiers—their hair pulled back off hot necks—hurry inside. Their tunics are filthy. They smell of blood and fear.

I shove aside the door after them. The room is charged with men's voices. Everyone stares at the Spartans. The soldiers look exhausted. Sweat drips from their foreheads and hair plastered to skulls that recently wore crested helmets. One young hoplite already clutches a goblet of wine. His hands shake.

"Xerxes!" He gulps his wine. "He's already at Abydos!"

As soon as I can work my way across the room and get close to Papa, I stand on tiptoe and whisper in his ear. "Papa, King Xerxes, that's the Persian general, Darius' son?"

He nods.

"How can he be in Hellas again? Miltiades defeated Darius at Marathon ten years ago. They say 30,000 Persians ran with their tails between their legs."

I question Papa, but my mind is seared with the memory of my vision: black-clad soldiers marching across Greek soil, leading a King in a gold chariot. I look across the room at Sophia. I can tell by her wide eyes that she remembers what I said, when we watched the spider web—the first time I slipped into a trance.

"I can't explain now, Thaleia. Serve these soldiers. Help your mother."

I pour red wine mixed with cool spring water from a clay pitcher, but my mind spins. If my vision of the invading Persians is true, then my vision of Sophia's death…

Pacing from table to table filled with freemen and their slaves, tall warriors and brazen priests, holy men of Delos… heavy-limbed, dark or fair, I wait in silence, while the soldiers catch their breath.

My mind is chaos: Persian invasion. King Xerxes. Sophia. Persians. Sophia. I struggle to make sense of it all.

When a tall, swarthy hoplite—his face pockmarked as if he survived a plague—finally speaks, his voice is unsteady.

"The largest invasion the world has seen! Over a million Persians: warriors on horseback, chariots… and the king's own elite guard. Dressed completely in black, they compare themselves to our gods. They claim they can never be defeated, can never die. And their *hubris*! They call themselves The Immortals. They would claim the name of our own Greek gods!"

"What are you saying? You say the army is a million strong?" An older man, his face hardened like a beetle, a white scar at his throat, touches the soldier's shoulder. "There is no army that large."

"What beast is upon us?" Parmenides moves from his seat to join the men gathering around the soldier.

Papa slips quietly from soldier to pilgrim and back to Diokles to pour more wine. I notice he adds less water as the soldier continues his story, pours the *mavrodaphne* sweet and strong. He plants thick platters of lamb and sausage on the table. Mama crouches by the hearth pretending to be busy.

We wait to hear more.

The young hoplite looks up, stares around the room as if he can't believe it himself. "Half a million foot soldiers. Nomads from the east on camels. An entire navy… twelve hundred warships… maybe more!"

"Twelve hundred!" At last Papa stops his serving and stands directly before the storyteller. "You say they have twelve hundred warships?"

Standing close to the Oracle, I feel him tense, the air around him is charged like the sky before a storm. "Now, Spartan, you must exaggerate." Parmenides rests a hand on the soldier's forearm.

I wipe the table with my rag, glad for an excuse to stand amongst the men.

"They're building a bridge to cross into Greece at the Hellespont," says one young soldier with dark eyes that skitter from man to man. "Between the Black Sea and the Aegean. From Abydos across the strait to Sestos in Thessaly."

Far north of here, I think to myself.

"Is the bridge completed? Can this be true? The Persians plan to invade Greek soil again?" Parmenides' questions pepper the room.

"Yes, wise Hierophant, it is true," the first soldier says. "Phoenicians wove one line across the narrow waters with a cable of white flax, and Egyptians used ropes made of papyrus for the other to lash together ships: *triremes* and *penteconters*—double bridges covered with brushwood and dirt so the chariots and horses can have solid earth to travel across the water channel."

"Where are the Persians now?" I say, before I stop to think I shouldn't.

Papa squeezes my shoulder. The Spartan draws a sharp breath. The old man frowns. But after an awkward silence, the Spartan answers me, his words quiet and even, charged with conviction. "They built the bridge across the Hellespont onto the Greek mainland, it's true, but Zeus intervened for us. The gods did not betray us." Out of the corner of my eye, I see the young soldier kneel and touch his forehead to the packed-dirt floor.

"All-thundering Zeus brought a storm and destroyed the barbarian's bridge." The Spartan touches Parmenides' sleeve. "King Xerxes was furious! He ordered the sea lashed with chains and branded with hot irons. Then he beheaded his engineers."

"Beheaded his engineers? He's mad!" Angry words ricochet from wall to wall.

"New overseers rebuilt the bridge, and while the Persian king watched from his marble throne high on a hill, they crossed into our sacred Hellas!" The soldier's angry words rise above the outcries. "Xerxes plans to destroy Athens. All of Hellas! He will cloak our land of democracy with the mantle of his tyranny!"

Timon steps to the center of the charged room, walks over to stand beside the soldier. He rests a strong arm on his shoulder and looks around the room.

Surely Timon will have an answer. He will know what we should do.

But his words do little to comfort me. "Xerxes' empire is vast—Asia Minor, Egypt, Judah, Lydia, Mesopotamia!"

The soldier's eyes dart around the room now steeped in silent fear and anticipation.

"He would claim the greatest prize of all." Timon whispers his words as if Xerxes could hear and be drawn to us. He sits down heavily and stares off into the shadowed-corners as if he can see the hoards approaching.

No, Timon. Don't give up. There has to be something we can do.

"Don't be a fool!" A merchant in pristine white robes with ribbons of purple falling from his shoulders pushes his way between the soldiers. "We beat the Persians ten years ago at Marathon. Defeated them on the beach! Slaughtered them, as they tried to climb back onto their ships! They wouldn't dare attack again."

"Exactly. Xerxes wants revenge for his dead father," the first soldier interrupts in a loud voice.

Parmenides raises his hand for quiet. "He'll pass through Delphi on the way to Athens. He will want Apollo's treasures."

And her women. I ease away from the men to join Mama by the hearth. Her jaw is tight. Everything about her feels charged like a fire set but not yet lit with a coal. Sophia grabs my hand.

"He will never conquer us! Representatives of each city-state—from Athens, Milos, even mighty Sparta came together last autumn in

Corinth to form the Hellenic League." A merchant scowls and refutes the doubters.

"Impossible!" Timon leaps to his feet and pounds his goblet hard on the table, red wine overflowing like blood. "The poleis never united! Athens and Sparta are mortal enemies! What do you claim, merchant?"

"I tell you only what I heard! Are you calling me a liar? Xerxes sent his ambassadors throughout Greece to demand earth and water—to acknowledge their surrender. There are rumors the Thebans will follow Xerxes."

Diokles pulls himself to his feet. "Parmenides, we should not assume the Persians would ravage Delphi. They are known to allow those they conquer to worship their own gods. Govern their own."

The soldier whirls to face the old priest. "Are you defending these barbarians, priest?"

We hold our breaths to see what Diokles will do. He has the power to kill the soldier for his impudence.

Blood rushes to my head. I am dizzy. Fire flame and candlelight flare across an open mouth, a hand clutching a goblet, a sandaled foot propped on a chair… all frozen as if time stops. I sit and bend to touch my forehead to my lap.

I hear screams. Women. Children. Men snarling inhuman sounds in their death throes. Spider-web strands connect each man, woman and child. And I hear words—compelling and demanding that I speak.

A prophecy burns inside my chest and head, filling me with passion. It is impossible for me to pretend any longer that I am a dutiful village girl. A god's power seizes me and commands that I declare his words.

I lift my head. My vision leaves behind a sea-smell, brine and kelp, a warm salt-wind that draws me to my feet. "Pray to the winds," I whisper.

"What does the girl say?" The soldier steps around Parmenides to stand before me.

Mama drops her pan with a clatter and rushes over. As if from a great distance, I feel her lightly touch my shoulder. "Thaleia?" She shakes me. "Thaleia?!"

I'm intensely aware of my breath, Mama's touch on my back, the warm sea air filling my lungs.

"Pray to the winds," I roar, filled with truth—a truth so powerful that I cannot stop from proclaiming it. "Pray to the winds. They will prove to be mighty allies of Hellas!"

As abruptly as the sea-wind vision fills me, consumes me, the feeling is gone. I look around the room. Fire shadows dance across the floor. Papa, Mama, Timon and Brygos stare, their faces blank with disbelief. A slight smile crosses Parmenides' face.

Diokles is the first to break the silence. "Ignore the girl! She is a stupid, ignorant, willful child.

"It would not be wise to ignore this girl." Parmenides steps beside me and holds out his hand to draw me once more to my feet.

I am shaky but relieved. Parmenides will help me. He will protect me from the old priest if I need help. I move over so close that my chiton brushes Parmenides' sleeve. I take a deep breath. "Parmenides, why did I say to pray to the wind? Where did those words come from? Not from me."

"Do you feel like time stopped, like a chasm opened beneath you?" Mama lifts my chin and peers at me, before she says, "Like silk strands stretched between you and eternity?"

Tears of gratitude fill my eyes. Mama understands. I nod but cannot form words at first. At last I say, "Is this because I am your daughter?"

"Yes. All is the will of the gods."

I want to tell her about Pan, but everyone is staring at me.

Diokles snorts and then frowns at the Hierophant, then shuffles to the door without another word. The priest looks old, frail as the skeleton of a dried leaf with parchment thin skin, but still there is a whiff of power as he walks past. The look he gives the soldier silences his next words. Strong men in their prime move aside, even bow slightly. He passes between them, scattering them in his wake. I avert my gaze. Try to stifle my anger.

CHAPTER TWELVE

APELLAIOS-EARLY AUTUMN

JUDGEMENT

Throughout the sweltering summer, I wait for the Persians, wait to hear my fate at the hands of old Diokles. Only when I'm with Sophia do I feel rooted in the village. There's an odd peace when we wash clothes at the cistern or struggle back up the path with heavy amphora sloshing water down our backs cooling us in the brazen sun.

With the worry about the Persians, did the priest forget about me? The summer passes, filled with suspicious stares from the village men as I watch the northern path for another messenger, for news of the Persians. I hear they've traveled as far as the Vale of Tempe by Therma. Our soldiers, only 10,000 strong are no match for them, so they sidestep the unwieldy hoards and travel through the Sarantaporo strait, avoiding battle.

All the time, Xerxes sends ambassadors throughout Hellas—not to Athens or Sparta where messengers had previously been be-headed and thrown down a well—but wide-ranging. Our poleis city-states are divided. Stand and fight? Or give in to the inevitable. At Therma, many deliver up earth and water in surrender to the barbarian king on his marble throne.

Even Thessaly! Just north of Delphi. Great gods, who will stop them?

I try to help Papa at the taverna. Even smile at Brygos once or twice, when I think someone might notice, but it doesn't work.

Brygos arrives stern and formal at my gate after several interminable weeks. Long days leaning toward winter snow, but still swelteringly hot. Endless nights in which to wonder if Diokles forgot or forgave me for desecrating the Sanctuary.

The evening light is thin and brittle, when I am summoned with a silent gesture by Papa to serve spoon jams—the traditional offering to a guest—and boil thick barley tea to bring to the men's chamber to honor Brygos at Papa's request.

Papa and Brygos share no bonds of friendship. Their relationship frayed the last few years. I should already have married Brygos, managed his home and served him in bed, but the villagers whisper about my strange fits.

Brygos blames Papa. Gentle Papa who does not control his daughter, who instead turns a forgiving eye as I run wild, escape to the mountain to search for Pan and wonder who I am.

Brygos still wants to claim me, I'm sure of that—to wed me and tame me—but my shame in the villagers' eyes makes him wait, hoping Papa can shape me, bring me down from the mountain and back to the village ways. As summer swings to autumn, his love for me—was it ever love?—turns rancid. His gaze, when I catch him staring is often more hate than love.

"I heard Xerxes is building a road through Macedonia toward Pieria." Brygos' deep voice jolts me from my thoughts. "His army is raping and pillaging its way toward us. Soon nothing will stand between us and that madman."

Papa leans forward, his elbows on the table. "They say General Themistocles, the Athenian leader, disagrees with the Spartan king and wants to withdraw our Greek hoplites and only try to defend the Isthmus of Corinth! Would he abandon us up here on the mainland and only save the Peloponnese and Sparta?"

"There was talk of that, but now the defense is to be at The Hot Gates, Thermopylae. Have you seen it? That narrow pass of land on the edge of Mt. Kolyodromos? It's only a day's march north of here." Papa dismisses me with a wave of his hand but doesn't watch to see if I've left. I only go as far as the door. I have to know what Papa will promise Brygos, what he'll arrange about my wedding.

"Curse those barbarians!" Papa jumps to his feet and paces before Brygos. "There will be no place for the Persians to stand and fight, even if they are a million strong! Cliff above and below, with nothing but the sea to claim their bodies, shoved to their deaths by our brave soldiers!"

"But Icos, King Leonidas, though he rules all of Sparta, has only three hundred Spartans with him. The council would only allow him to take his personal guard, since he left Sparta in the sacred festival of Carneia. They would not let him form an army. He chose his bravest and strongest men, those with sons. No unmarried soldier, no father with only a girl-child, merely those with healthy sons could accompany the great king. He gathered more soldiers between Sparta and Thermopylae, but they're only ten thousand strong at the most. How can they possibly hope to defeat a million Persians? They are fools! We should deliver earth and water to the Persians, bow to their king and superior power and ask their mercy."

"No! The Greeks will never surrender! The Spartans are the bravest warriors of all!" Icos pounds the table and leaps to his feet. He paces past me without seeing me before striding over to the shelf and grabbing a jug of un-mixed wine and two cups. He doesn't bother to mix the thick drink with water but slams them down on the table and throws himself back into his seat.

I lean against the doorframe hoping to be invisible.

"Icos don't be stupid. How can we possibly hold back the entire Persian empire?"

"Stupid! How dare you call me stupid." Papa glowers at Brygos and stares him down.

Brygos clears his throat and throws back his shoulders. "We met last night by the village hearth to decide what we should do about Thaleia."

"What? Who met?" Papa pushes his palms flat against the table and jumps up to his feet. His fingers turn white as he clutches the goblet. "Without me?" He throws back his head and downs the wine. "You think you can meet without me to decide what happens to my child?" He slops more wine into his cup and pushes his face into Brygos'.

I back out the door and hold my breath.

"The village elders. You know, all of us." I hear Brygos shuffle his sandals back and forth beneath his chair. "They appointed me spokesman." Self-importance crackles in his voice. But I know that Brygos is only a puppet for the elders.

Papa pushes his chair aside, screeching the carved legs against the floor stones.

"Do what about Thaleia? How could you meet without me? She's my daughter."

"You forget, Icos. She was to be my wife." He looks down at his hands clutching the table as if contrite, as if sad that I am not yet his wife. But his hatred is thinly veiled. "She can't be allowed to get away with this! She thinks she's better than all of us. She violated the temple. She dishonored Apollo. Even if she was my betrothed, she can't be allowed to disgrace us." His voice is low and threatening.

"She is better than all of you! You don't deserve to look at her. You're vile and stupid... you aren't worth her smallest finger. Now get out! Get out of my home. I deny your betrothal. I deny *you*! Get out!"

It's all I can do to stay quiet. Will I get out of this marriage? Will I be free of Brygos? I pull two deep breaths and duck out of sight as Brygos strides past the open doorway, pacing from one side of the room to the other.

"Icos, listen to me. This is beyond your family." His voice grows suddenly louder, imbued with the authority granted him by the assembly. "She must go before the priests. She dishonored Apollo. The god will decide her fate!"

"The gods be damned! When did they ever help me? When did they help my wife or my child? Get out!"

"Never question the will of the god, Icos."

Papa paces back and forth between the hearth and the table. His eyes are wild.

"I always knew they would want her back. I knew the gods would claim her." He slams his hands on the table. His face contorts with rage. "They can't have her! I will keep her here in the village."

"Unless Apollo forgives her, she must die. There must be a sign." Brygos' voice sounds stiff as if he memorized the assignment given him.

They're going to kill me. I challenged Diokles. He'll take my life.

"Get out!" Papa yells, hurling his chair against the wall. A lamp shatters, white shards scattering like bones on the stone floor. They crunch beneath Papa's sandals as he backs Brygos out the door.

"Thaleia!" Papa shouts. "Thaleia," he sobs. As I come back in the room, he is standing in front of the hearth, his arms stiff at his sides. When he sees me, he speaks in a quiet monotone as if afraid he won't get the words out if he waits. "The festival of Dionysos is tomorrow, the day of the new moon. Tomorrow the priests will proclaim your fate." He looks a long moment into my eyes. "Thaleia, why?" Rubbing tears from his eyes, he turns abruptly away. At the door, he looks back. His sorrowful gaze is dark with grief as black and helpless as I've ever seen. "Run away, Thaleia. Get away from here."

"But Papa."

"It's your only hope."

"Where would I go? I can't leave Delphi. I can't leave you and Mama… And the god…"

"Save yourself. Run wherever you planned to go your wedding morning."

I look down at my clutched hands unable to look Papa in the eyes. "I didn't have a plan. I had no idea where I was running."

"Thaleia, that old priest will kill you. He always wanted you dead! Power. He lusts for gold and his own twisted honor. He has no honor! You challenge his power." Papa hugs me close.

"I won't leave you Papa."

"He's found the perfect excuse to destroy you at last and blame it on the gods." He holds me away from his embrace and looks deeply at me as if seeing me for the first time. "Go… and know I love you."

I rest both my hands on Papa's shoulders. "No, Papa. I won't run away. This time I will stand up to Diokles. It is my destiny."

Papa shoves me back. "Thaleia, for once in your life, listen to me!"

"My destiny is to save you, the village… Hellas."

Papa gazes at me in complete disbelief, but I hold his gaze and wait for him to understand. Each minute is so long. Time to notice his sun-rough skin. The way he yanks the cloth from his sash stretched tight beneath his heavy belly and wipes his neck. Time to see love shine from his eyes.

He shakes his head. His shoulders slump, and he backs away. "You've gone too far this time, Thaleia. I can't help you. May the gods take pity on you. Perhaps Dionysos…" He doesn't finish his sentence. He spins away from me.

And he is gone.

Early the next morning, I stand in Sophia's home waiting to be dressed and anointed. Iona Sophia's mother, squats in front of the hearth, her shoulders and hips like a great amphora, black in her mourning robes. I smell fear in the room, where I never expected to find it.

"*Yia sas*, good day to you, Thaleia," Iona greets me. Why *Yia sas* now? The formal greeting is for priests and elders, villagers who you can't approach, probably shouldn't trust, a lifetime away from pebble games in the dust of our stoop and chasing the crows from cornfields. I grew up lingering around this warm bake-oven sharing hugs and fingers sticky from honey on fresh baked bread and mugs full of steaming *rizogalo*—rice pudding with wrinkled raisins and cinnamon.

Sophia stands behind her mother's dark form, the firelight dancing across her smooth features.

"*Yia sou*, Sophia." I want my words to touch her, to bring her close.

"*Yia sas*, Thaleia," is Sophia's distant reply, as she glances at her mother.

Her formal words, constrained by ritual, chill me. This is real. This ceremony, arranged by Diokles, will lead me to my death.

With a gesture, Sophia walks to my side and unties my waist sash. The panpipes fall to the floor. I snatch them up and place them on a pillow by the hearth.

Where are you, Pan? You told me to help my village. And now? What do you expect me to do? He's going to kill me!

Sophia picks up the panpipes. "Where did you get these shepherd's pipes?"

Sophia's mother frowns, her face folds and wraps around stern eyes like bread just starting to rise. "Sophia, bathe her feet. I'll be right back. I need thyme and wine."

"Sophia." I reach out to reclaim the flute. "You asked me what happened in the meadow. You asked who was behind the tree… when you ran away." I try to smile at her to show her that I don't blame her, but my smile is stiff and I imagine not very convincing. She hands me the panpipes, and we both sink to the floor facing each other.

"Tell me, Thaleia. Who, what was behind that tree?"

I don't want to hide anything from Sophia any longer. Pan abandoned me. And Papa.

Sophia will understand. She will know. She has to.

"Sophia, it was a satyr."

With a sharp gasp, she peers at me to understand what I'm saying.

"It was the god Pan."

With rushed words, trying to explain it all before Iona returns, I tell her everything—how it felt to look into Pan's blue eyes and his hairy legs and hoofed feet… and tail and horns! My words spill out faster. "He told me I shouldn't run away. That my destiny is here in Hellas. But now Diokles…"

Iona steps through the back door, her outstretched arms holding Mama's wedding gown. Embroidered blue jasmine drips in the soft folds of cloth. She lifts my chiton off me and slips Mama's dress over my head.

"Your mother wants you to wear this," Iona says and glances sideways at Sophia by the hearth. "In the spring, Thaleia, you will wear this chiton and stand beneath the nuptial arch with Brygos, your husband. But she wants you to wear it today…" Iona pulls my hair back from my face. Tears fill her eyes. "In case the judgment is…" She turns away, crosses over to the hearth and returns with a clay mug of hot wine, raisins bursting as she drops them cold into the steaming drink.

In case the priest kills me and blames it on Apollo. Say it, Iona. That's what you mean, isn't it?

Sophia rubs olive oil scented with fresh mint into my shoulders. She works the oil on my hands, between each of my fingers, finally massaging my palms over and over, until they burn with their own fire.

I straighten my shoulders and let them tend to me. *Diokles is a power-hungry liar! I'll show him. The gods speak to me… not him.*

They color my lips with purple beet juice, darken my lashes with kohl and rub sweet berries to redden my cheeks. All the while, Sophia hums a wandering melody, as she wraps a soft girdle round and round my waist, until it lifts my breasts. She stands back as though to survey her work, and while Iona's back is turned, smiles at me as if to reassure me that we're in this together. That somehow everything will work out.

"Child of Demeter, daughter of Gaia's womb," Iona recites, her deep voice a monotone whisper. She circles me three times, twining honeysuckle and columbine around my waist. "Virgin of night and dawn… blessed by immortal fir… and the gods everlasting."

Her touch is gentle, yet not tender. She keeps the ritual between us, never meets my eyes. She plaits my hair into three braids, wrapping the ends with strands of pale ivy. At last satisfied, she nods to Sophia.

I take three slow breaths and will myself to stay calm. *Remember Pan. Remember Apollo spoke through you. Be brave, Thaleia. Be strong.*

Sophia flings open the door.

We stand like three silent statues facing somber faces. All the villagers wait outside. I am surprised to see it is already late morning. We have spent hours in seclusion and ceremony. As I walk over the threshold, an omen-filled wind blows, whipping my hair free from the braids, beating the grapevine against Sophia's wall, sweeping clouds across the sun casting us in black shadow.

I look around at my neighbors' anxious stares. Hestos leans on his crook, both hands folded across a worn ram's horn handle, smooth as marble, his white eyes almost hidden beneath his bushy eyebrows. Behind him are Sophia's aunts, but they look down at their hands when I meet their eyes. A crow cries from a nearby plane tree. What little confidence I found in Sophia's familiar home is gone the moment I see all the villagers waiting outside her door, eager to hear my judgment. Will Apollo condemn me? Will he speak at all or will the priests simply claim he condemns me?

Mama and Papa walk quickly down the path and without speaking a word, stand close on either side of me. Papa smells of oak fire and buttered chicken. The familiar smell comforts me.

"Keep your eyes open, Thaleia. Don't be afraid." Mama brushes hair away from my eyes, leaves her hand a moment on the top of my head. "Just do what they tell you to do, Thaleia. Don't argue with them."

"Mama, don't worry. The gods will not abandon me." I squeeze her hand and give her my best smile. I hope it is reassuring.

"I chose your name wisely, Thaleia—to burst with life."

The priests' chant is upon us, sweeping me up in a procession of flaming laurel branches, the flames whipping and straining, almost blowing out and then lifting in a sudden lull.

"Twin serpents
Pythons brown of earth…"

Two young girls, at most four years old, dressed in red and orange and blue tunics, brush the path stones with pine boughs, rhythmically swinging them from side to side in time to the chant. Someone places a burning branch in my hand and steps into the procession. Hands, some gentle, some rough urge me to the front of the gathering. The villagers' chant roars as we wave rough pine torches. Their pitch-dipped heads flare against a brilliant blue sky.

CHAPTER THIRTEEN

DESTINY

I walk in solemn time up the mountain. Mama and Papa pace at my side, their faces like bronze masks, stern with worry. I don't know what else to do. I'll go along and wait for a chance to escape. I don't care what Pan said.

Two priests lead us in cadence. They throw their call to the high stone. Their deep baritone voices swell around us as we walk on to the rhythm of their alternating cries.

Someone stumbles behind me. A woman coughs. The priests' dirge continues, as they swing censors with smoking laurel to purify our way.

"Thaleia! Thaleia!" My name ricochets from villager to friend to priest, tossed with each shout returning to me, before they resume their chant in chorus.

Diokles' voice cracks a command, sounding like thin ice crushed underfoot. "Sing praise to Apollo! We bring Thaleia to be judged."

My nervousness transforms my neighbors' faces to grotesque strangers squinting in the bright sun. Restless robes of yellow, red and deep purple dance around me and sway to the rhythm of plucked lyre and flutes, trilling and swooping to low moans.

"Apollo, speak to me now if you will judge me. Let me hear your command," I say, my words drowned out by the drums.

There is no answer.

We are past the village. Timon plays a tympani drum that leads us uphill past Hestos' sheep pen. The goat skull stares back at me as the sun spills over the top of the Shining Cliffs.

Pinnacles of gray limestone tower above me. The massive Temple of Apollo looms with each step, its fluted columns seemingly carved from the sharp rock outcroppings. There are few trees growing this high on the mountain, and those surviving the winds are stunted, twisted in their climb to the clouds.

Why are you here? The stones and trees ask.

Because it is my destiny! I want to shout back, but my answer is unspoken. *Because Pan gave me his syrinx. Because I understand the Pythia's birdcalls. Because Pan chose me.* My thoughts race and fill me with defiance.

I see everything with new eyes.

A flute calls from the rock face off the Sacred Way.

"Pan, where are you? Will I die, because they think I'm mad? You told me to return… for this? To be murdered by the priest for a false Pythia?!"

Suddenly, everything comes alive around me. I hear whispers mingle with the flute music as if the notes are weaving a riddle.

What is your destiny?

A halo of light circles the boulders and gnarled trees, even the red poppies lining my path. Their question echoes in my mind and demands an answer.

Is this Pan's magic?

The voice urges me to see, to remember the song of the universe Pan urged me to hear… to know I am not alone.

Pan, you honored me. Know thyself, you commanded. And I do now. I am the girl who knows the Persians will attack and a spider can scream… and a friend will die. But why? Why Pan? If that's who I am, I don't want to know my destiny. My destiny brought me here? Diokles intends to murder me in the name of the gods. Is that my destiny? What good does it do if I die? Answer me that! Have you led me here to abandon me? Why?

A cloud roils above our procession and rumbles words. Words I can't quite understand. The dust lifting from the path sparkles and sings. Pan's music swells in my chest—sharp staccato notes that sting like hornets. It sings the gods. Stars. Sunlight searing off hot and slanting limestone. The music is all the kosmos… and the music is a girl walking up the temenos to a priest's wrath. It sings my dreams, my fears. I cannot listen carefully enough to hear the story, the notes that declare my destiny.

"Great god Pan, what would you have me do?" I shout.

The morning sky swells with the villagers' chants. Bones from sacrificial goats rattle in time to the priests' demand: "Judge her. Apollo the Far-Darter, we bring Thaleia to be judged by you. Judge her with your power and your wisdom."

I force myself to keep walking up the Sacred Way, but every muscle strains to hear Pan's reply. Struggles to be worthy. Mama smiles a question at me. Is this how she felt every time she approached her god? What game are the gods playing with me?

At last, I hear Pan's words mingle with a swallow's cry.

"Know thyself."

His music grows louder. We're almost to the Cyclopean Gate.

Once again the flute echoes from the rock cliffs above our procession threading through a warm sea wind rising from the bay far below. Out of the corner of my eye, I see the villagers' eyes turn like schooling fish and my heart lifts as Pan's music sweeps clouds from the sky.

Do you hear the god? No, they only see Timon perched above us swinging his drum side to side. They only hear the priests' call for my judgment by the Far-Darter god.

Mama takes my hand.

"Do you hear the flute, Mama?"

"No."

I'm not sure I believe you. There is fire in her god-touched gaze. How did I not see it before?

The flute melody disappears in a confusion of screeching children. They scramble to surround us, pushing one another, laughing, holding hands and running ahead to hide behind stone sanctuaries beginning to line the path as we near the temple. They peer back at us, giggling as if we don't know they are there. Young boys break off sticks from low branches of pine and beat on the wall, a stony cadence to propel us into the Sanctuary, to lead our steps to the ritual of the priests.

We walk between two worlds—the Forbidden One and her daughter—between Divine and mortal. What joy did it bring her to speak with her god? Did he ever fill her life with grace and ease?

Will Apollo spare me?

I want to break free and run with the scattered children, gather them like chattering magpies trying to catch flying wheat at winnowing time, but the old priest waits above to declare my fate.

Our procession approaches the Cyclopean Gate. Swallows glide from the high wall.

Hoping to call Pan to help me, I snatch the panpipes from my belt and play a fragment of the song that brought me to the god.

Mama whirls to face me. Stops me in my tracks. I stop playing and stand frozen. A young boy stumbles against me and the procession flows around me. Squinting my eyes against the searing sun, I search the sheer cliffs hoping to see the satyr.

Mama grabs my shoulders and turns me to face her. "Where did you find those panpipes?"

"Mama, I met Pan."

She catches her breath.

"Pan? When? How?" Mama clutches both my hands.

"In a magic meadow. The day I ran away. I wanted to tell you, but didn't think you'd believe me."

"The god talked to you?"

"Yes." I look around to the high gate and clouds. "He's here now."

"Where?" Mama follows my gaze.

I shake my head. "He's here. Pan's spirit lives in every tree, every summer cloud. When he plays his flute, the wind whispers his words." I hold out the flute to show her. "He gave me his syrinx."

Mama caresses the reeds. Her eyes wide.

Pan? Where are you?

I play again, my notes more desperate and piercing, but the god doesn't appear. The crowd pushes Mama and I closer to the towering gate—stones hurled in place by giants.

Children circle around me, their bare feet shuffling on the stone path. Laughing. Shouting.

The drum waits, suspended and then turns its course to follow my melody. Its deep bass gives me courage. I find the rest of the memory; play the high trills and swoops of Pan's song.

Sophia pulls small hand cymbals from the broad belt binding her waist and starts a new rhythm, thin at first like the sound of hail. The others circle us with soft, shuffling feet on the worn marble. They sway side to side chanting in a low monotone.

The chant leaps above us to the Phaedriades before slipping back to swirl around me. Soon I will enter the Sanctuary. The Child of the Clouds will supposedly consult Apollo.

The priest will judge me.

I clutch the panpipes so tightly I fear I will crush the reeds. These pipes aren't a mad vision. Pan gave them to me. They are real.

Diokles breaks their circle. He holds out a thick, wooden bowl to me, only me. His faded brown eyes stare over the steaming bowl. The pale skin of his arm sags, so thin that I can see blue veins. I lower the panpipes. As my music fades, the villagers stop their chant.

"Drink." The cup brims with a bubbling liquid, brown and murky as river mud, but sweet smelling with honey and nutmeg.

Poison? I don't care! The gods will protect me.

Strips of mushroom, speckled purple and sandstone float on top. Sophia backs away. I seize the cup with both hands; empty it with one gulp. The mushroom drink burns my stomach. It is vile-tasting and bitter and gags me.

Papa silently passes a large *kylix* of wine round the circle from each grasp to the next. The circle completed, he offers the last draught to me. He does not meet my eyes. Distant and solemn, he speaks,

"Dancing beat of sacred drums
Twining, twining
Weaving a living web
Of flute, bird
Of a child
Child of god"

We dance a whirling, pounding dance. The men break free from the circle to leap, howling, slapping the soles of their feet and thighs.

I join the women, as the men circle us. The drink spins my mind and my vision. We link elbows, our hands clasped behind our backs and turn side to side, chanting the old song.

The mushroom drink burns my stomach. I'm going to retch. Sick and disoriented, I want to vomit it up. Run down the mountain. Hide in my room.

Pan, where are you?

My vision spins. Bright-colored women's skirts flow around me, dancing with the music. Each low beat pulses brilliant patterns in the blue sky, where a poppy appears, shifting and dancing with the drums.

"Know thyself. It's really that simple, Thaleia. Trust who you are." I hear Pan's voice clearly. I whirl in every direction to see if he is here, but his voice is nowhere. His voice is everywhere.

"Look at the flower, next to its petals… behind. There… do you see a light? Like a leaf shadow? Be the heart of the color. Feel with color. Find color in your body and hear its song. There you will find your power."

My body sways slowly side to side; my shoulders touch Papa's as only the men and I walk through the gate-arch into the Sanctuary. I will my feet to run away, but the music and the drink force me into the Sanctuary. We pass the Treasury of the Sikyonians and *Kouroi*—stiff statues of young men. It feels like their marble eyes follow me.

At the bend in the stone path, we step beneath long shadows of the Treasuries of the Boetians and the Athenians constructed like small temples—Mama told me they are filled with sapphires and silver, gold kylix and jewels of the Orient—the treasures that Diokles claims.

I look around to find Mama, but all the village men—their faces red with a passion to see me judged by the god—surround me. The girl who ran free. The girl who defied them at last put in her place. I smell their thirst for revenge. For justice. For my death.

Past Kassotis Spring. And the Rock of the Sybil, where Sophia and I hid. It seems so long ago! And beyond, the wide steps of Apollo's Temple. And beyond Diokles.

Once again, slow, steady drumbeats throb, their rhythm wraps around me, chilling me like a winter stream. I hug myself and hold my breath. Each low note pulses through the last, urgent and demanding. My body sways slowly side to side.

I feel disoriented but step away from Papa, slip out of my sandals and walk barefoot across the white marble stone farther into the temple courtyard. Halos of light surround the doves that line the lintel above the shadowed terrace of Apollo's home. They sit completely silent, feathers ruffled against the wind.

Diokles glares and squints into the sun, before he slowly makes his way across the courtyard toward me. His back is stooped, and he leans heavily on a cane tipped with a gold goat's head.

A wind swirls around me, honey-thick and alive with girls' voices. They sing droning hexameters from Apollo, as they caress my hair and laugh in my ear.

They are the spirits of all the Pythias, a chain threading back to the ancient prophet who first communed with the Python deep in the earth's womb.

The girls' voices grow louder and more insistent.

Save us, Thaleia, child of the gods. The old priest denies us. We who are linked mother to daughter like moonrise to sunrise and again to moonrise. Don't let the priest destroy the ancient wisdom.

A thrill courses my spine. My head clears. With a jolt, I know what I must do.

I will stop the priest's lies.

I slow my breath, harnessing its rhythm to the old man's careful steps. Now he will judge me. The villagers will do whatever he tells them. He moves his right leg forward, drags his left one then paces his right foot forward once more. With each step across the worn marble, I breathe a shallow breath and wait, until at last he reaches me. Stretching his withered hand to lightly touch my shoulder, he peers at the men.

He scowls and pounds his cane against the stone two times. "Thaleia desecrated the Sanctuary." Diokles' voice is deep, commanding in a way I have never heard. "No women are allowed in the god Apollo's sanctum! Only the Pythia." Flush with righteous power, he points his withered finger at me.

A pregnant silence thickens, while I wait. I force my eyes to focus and read the inscription carved into the stone portal above me: Know Thyself. *Now.* It needs to be now. With long strides, I mount the temple steps and stand between the young priests. They thrust their torches before them; bow their heads to Diokles.

I straighten my back. "You see one woman before you, but Mama and I stand here together. We are stronger than you know."

"How dare you!" The town's potter pushes his way through to stand just beneath the priests. "You violated these holy grounds." The crowd pushes closer.

The Child of the Clouds walks from behind a stone treasury and heads straight toward me. I whirl and point at her. "*She's* the imposter! Diokles claims to understand her birdsong and calls it Apollo's prophecies. It's a lie!"

"You dishonor the god." Diokles climbs the stairs. The initiates move aside to let him pass. He clutches my arm. I'm surprised at his strength as his long nails cut into me.

But I won't stop. I don't care what they do to me, kill me, banish me. I no longer care.

"All of you knew my mother was the last Pythia. You knew Diokles forced her off the holy tripod… and you never told me." Their silence envelops me like mist rising from the bay. "You Hestos. And Brygos. Papa. All of you knew. He ordered her to choose: abandon me on the mountain to die—to be eaten by vultures—or forsake the sacred tripod as Pythia."

Sandals shuffle on the stone courtyard; a cough is stifled behind a hand.

The girl's piercing eagle cry shatters their silence.

Now they'll kill you.

I hear her words clearly as if she spoke them directly to me. I glare at The Child of the Clouds. She ducks behind Diokles.

The priest smiles at me—his eyes victorious—and lifts his staff high. "The god speaks. I hear his command in the Pythia's eagle call. She declares Apollo's will." Diokles looks from villager to villager. He drops his voice to a brittle whisper that carries like the breath of death. "The great god Apollo the Far-Darter says she must die for her trespass."

"No!" I glare at the stooped priest. "You don't understand the girl's birdsong. I do!"

"Apollo demands your death. You will not dishonor the gods and live."

His words are picked up and passed on by the priests standing closest to us, to the villagers, whisper by urgent whisper. "She must die."

"She's only a girl, a child!" Hestos shouts from Papa's side.

Papa rushes up and reaches his arms out toward me, but I stand tall and face down the villagers. Parmenides paces up the steps to stand beside me. I smile at him and shout so everyone can hear me. "The Child of the Clouds is not your true Pythia. She's an imposter. A barbarian who would seize the sacred power. Listen to me!"

"Apollo commands!" Diokles says. "The god commands. Would you ignore the god? Do as the god demands!" and waves for two priests to seize my arms. They press me tight between them.

My mind races. "Apollo where are you?" I shout with all my strength. "You did not demand my death."

The priests drag me away from Papa and Parmenides to the sacrificial altar. They push me backward across the bloodstained stone. The Child of the Clouds screeches another eagle cry.

"It is not the god's will! You did not hear Apollo's command!" I rip free and lunge at Diokles, but the priests pull me back and clutch me tighter.

"You lie! You lie!" My screams tear my throat.

They force my head sideways on the altar. I smell rancid blood and goat bowels loosed from fear. I watch in horror as a purple-robed priest towers before me with a broad sword clutched in strong hands. He stands, feet wide before me. Waits for Diokles' command. The priest nods to the young girls swinging the incense lamps. The chains rattle as each lifts her thin arm to the four directions. Laurel smoke threads through the golden sky.

"Apollo has spoken."

"No! It's not the god." My words choke out as a priest pushes me harder against the altar. "You lie!"

Another eagle cry raises a deep rumble that sweeps across the Sanctuary—the villagers' vow to destroy me.

CHAPTER FOURTEEN

YOU CAN'T KILL THE SONG

One priest holds my arms tight behind my back, while strong hands press my cheek against the marble altar.

There is sudden silence followed by a shuffling of villagers' feet on stone as the men move aside. In the gap, I see Mama weaving her way between them. How did she get into the Sanctuary? *No, Mama, they'll kill you too!*

The crowd pulls farther back, looking at Mama's scowl then down to their feet, the sky, the priest, and the altar—anywhere but at Mama's fury. Step by step, she walks up to me. When she looks from one priest to the other, they let me go and move back. As if they can't disobey the god's power that flashes from her eyes, they bow to Mama and back away from me. With shaking legs, I stand and hug her and look out over the sea of angry faces.

Parmenides lifts his arms in supplication, threat, a command to god and man. Papa lifts his.

Diokles straightens to his fullest height. With a firm, clear voice, he yells. "She is not allowed here!" He points his shriveled finger at Mama. "You are woman desecrating these holy grounds!"

"I was Pythia, Diokles!" My mother's eyes flare. She steps close to the priest.

"You are the Forbidden One!" Spittle sprays from Diokles' mouth. "You no longer belong in this Sanctuary."

"Beware, Diokles. Apollo holds sway in this Sanctuary. Remember well what happened the last time you threatened his Pythia."

"The fire started because of you, Hipparchia! *Your* sacrilege! *You* dishonored Apollo!" Diokles jumps at her and almost falls. But the priests catch him. He raises his staff as if he would strike Mama. I jump in front of her, and Parmenides seizes the shaft. The Oracle and priest stand, clutching the cane and staring at each other. There is a gust of wind off the Shining Cliffs; a cloud blows across the sun casting a shadow over the temple; a black crow soars from the peak of the temple pediment to land on the Rock of the Sybil. We wait. At last Parmenides releases the staff and moves to stand beside Mama.

He bows a deep, low bow to my mother. "I knew you were the Pythia the moment I saw you in the taverna. I never forgot you. Your beauty and wisdom sit softly on your brow. Your face still glows with Apollo's grace."

For an instant the god is with her still.

"Mama?"

"Thaleia, come home with me."

Without looking away from my mother, I sense the men step closer. Their anger surges like a storm-sea. "She violated the holy grounds."

"Apollo demands justice."

"She must die!" The crowd's outcry swarms over me.

"No!" Mama's face softens. "She's a child, Priest Diokles. A confused child. Let her father and I take her home. We will punish her."

"How can you say that? I'm not a child, Mama… and I'm not confused. The gods send me visions." I hesitate, waiting to see if she believes me. "You were Pythia. You *know*." The panpipes vibrate in my belt, as if they would leap to freedom like a snared lynx.

"Come home with us, Thaleia." Mama looks a warning at Diokles. Her voice is low and gentle, but her gaze defies the villagers to get any closer to me. Papa takes her hand.

"Will you obey the priest and his false Pythia?" I ask the men. Can I change their loyalties? In the villagers' hearts, there is only the way it has always been. If I try to unravel the thread of their safety, they won't tolerate it. They can murder me, banish me, but never allow me to seize a loose thread of the fabric of their traditions and pull.

That is betrayal of life's safe passage.

I have to convince them. "Diokles' uses your fear to control you! To claim power over you. Will you let him?"

Safe passage… except when you sacrifice a virgin to ensure fertility for your crops. The vision of Sophia murdered by the priest swells unbidden within me. The back of my neck tightens and my skin is alive with memory, sweaty and clammy as over and over Sophia's terrified eyes turn back to me.

"You want to kill me, because I defy your traditions? How do you justify slaughtering village girls in the name of those traditions? It must stop. I will be the one to stop it!"

For one stunned moment, they stand silent.

Diokles' scream jolts the men to action. The Sanctuary fills with their rage. They pry stones free from the sphinx statue base.

"Thaleia, you are not helpless. Do something!" Mama shouts above their angry cries. The men are no longer a potter, horse tender, shepherd, father, son. They melt together like a monstrous raging bull—eyes of fire and fury and power. I back away from the mob until my back touches the column.

"Apollo! God of light, help me! Pan, god of nature, help me!" My cry startles the doves. Their flapping wings echo off the stones. I blow high scattering notes that swoop across Apollo's Sanctuary. "I am Thaleia, daughter of your true Pythia."

The men press close with angry shouts, but I take a step toward them and shout. "On this sacred mountain, men erected our great temple. It faces east to the rising sun to honor you, Sun-god Apollo, and to the west to honor the god Dionysos and the coming night. Here in Delphi—center of all land and the wine-dark sea—I call upon you, our god Apollo the Healer, Apollo champion of all who would find the sun's light. Hear me!"

The Child of the Clouds peers around a column, lifts her chin, shrills and whistles what seems like all the birdsongs of our mountain: sparrow, lark, dove and night owl; her notes slip like a storm wind through trees. Her words assault me.

Die. Sacrilege. I'm Pythia. Not this imposter.

I lift my head and trill a fierce eagle cry in response.

An uneasy stillness once again descends on the Sanctuary. Every man looks at me.

Another cry cuts through their silence as I answer The Child of the Clouds.

I understand you. Your hatred. Your lies. I defy you!

The girl slips from behind the column and looks in stunned silence at Diokles.

He cocks his head and looks from his Pythia to me.

You can understand me? No one understands me… not the priest. Not even my own mother.

I scream another eagle cry.

Leave now! Never return.

The hummingbird—Pan's own messenger—swoops twice over me. In the whir of its wings, I hear Pan's voice—"Fire, sea, earth and sky honor you, Pythia. Thaleia, you are the true Pythia."

Pan? "No. What are you saying? Mama is the true Pythia." I shout my answer to the god, whirling in every direction to find him.

"Know thyself." The god's command echoes from the Shining Cliffs above us.

A sudden chill lifts the hairs on the back of my neck. *It all makes sense—the visions, my power to fight off Brygos, the reason I understand the child's birdcalls.* I touch the god's syrinx and move away from the altar and priests to stand at the edge of the temple step. I shake my head and look down man to man pausing at last to stare at Diokles.

"I am your true Pythia." I keep my voice low to restrain my fury. "The Child of the Clouds is an imposter!" I throw back my shoulders and shout across the sacred temenos. "I am your true Pythia!" Stepping so close to Diokles that I feel his shallow breath against my lips, I say, "You can't kill the song. It is Pan's song. It is the gods' song and the stars and sun and earth and wind. It is all of us. I am the chosen one who will sing its music so all can hear." Tears of relief fill my eyes. At last I said it. I claimed my destiny. "I am the true Pythia!"

The Child of the Clouds backs two steps away and then runs past the altar, priests, stumbling her path between the farmers and smiths and out the gate.

She's gone. Diokles has no power to deny me. He doesn't move or say a word.

The priests move aside as I join Mama. All around me, stones drop from their hands, stone hitting stone never sounded so sweet.

"I believed you were the true Pythia, Mama."

"I was… but no longer."

The bold sky calls to me. I force my eyes to focus and read the inscription carved into the stone portal above me: Know Thyself.

I remember Pan's blue eyes and falling into their whirling wind-vision.

A great calm buoys me. A wave of love as warm and enveloping as the summer sea, sweeps over me. My chest aches. He is here. I feel him all around me, protecting me in this Sanctuary. The flute's contours feel warm nestled in my palm.

I draw the panpipes to my lips and play. The Shining Cliffs, swallows and the earth's heartbeat fill me with yearning and a taunting desire that is irresistible, a power to dream. To speak the god's will. I am the stone and trees, the wind itself. Pan is the mountain. Now I am the mountain. I play as I've never played before. Stunned by the truth. I am Pythia. That is the reason Pan told me to return to Delphi. I am Pythia. I must guide them.

It's up to me to save them from the Persians. My thoughts sear me, while I play the satyr's flute. The notes ring with images of the Persian king, foot soldiers, the sea and Zeus destroying the bridge letting them onto Greek soil. My music pounds like a million invaders and fills me with power. I am the true Pythia. I will save Hellas. You can't kill the song.

Pan! The racing wind carries his low, counter melody. My melody dances around the temenos, cajoling and laughing. I feel my face flush with my effort to carry the thread of the satyr's melody.

"The girl called the god. There he is!"

Pan dances atop the temple roof. Our two melodies twist together like ivy vines. The ground trembles. Diokles' jaw drops open. The temple marble shudders and pulses beneath my feet. The old priest clutches his throat, gasping for air. Without stopping my playing, I turn to look in the direction the priest is staring.

"Look at the temple! The columns."

The temple pillars grow rough bark; sprout thick limbs and singing leaves. Four columns of Apollo's Sanctuary transform to sturdy oak trees.

The satyr laughs and dances and leaps on the roof tiles. His hooves clatter with a percussive rattle.

I throw my head back and laugh with him. *Is this your magic, Pan?*

The tiny hummingbird hovers, its pearl wings a blind blur. It lights on my arm and folds its wings against the sea-green feathers, tipping its head side-ways to stare into my eyes. I hear the bird's voice clear like spring water.

It is your magic, Pythia. It is your power. Soon you'll have your initiation as Oracle, your Night of Pan. Then no one can stop you. No one.

When I look away from the bird and back to the temple roof, Pan is gone.

My magic? I touch the broad stone pillars supporting the lintel of the Temple of Apollo now transformed from carved columns to towering oaks. Patchwork bark—like scaling skin of a fisherman's hands—covers the marble. I see the fluting beneath, as if Apollo's white marble changed to the riot of Dionysos' wild growth.

In disbelief, I stare up as sunlight sparkles through the oak branches. *I turned the columns into these trees?* Doves, their under-bellies soft white against a lapis sky, settle into the oak branches that twist away from the columns.

I sink to the stone tiles, lean back against one oak tree column and play once more.

The villagers drop to their knees staring from the oak columns to me to Diokles, their mouths open.

Slowly, I lower my arm and let the music fade. A shiver runs through me as I look at Diokles. His mouth is clenched as tight as his fists. He glowers at the men's bowed backs, raises his staff as if he would protest but remains silent.

Why don't I feel a sweet victory? Why don't I gloat that I defeated the old priest? It's not over. Diokles is not done with me yet.

I touch the oak bark.

Mama climbs the steps to stand before me.

"Even the Pythia can't summon this magic. How did I? Do you know, Mama?"

She sits beside me, leans back and smiles. Her eyes shine with joy.

"Gods and man unite on this sacred ground, Thaleia. The Pythia joins them. Only she can feel the god's breath and speak his words. The Pythia may call upon the gods for divine help."

"Have you always known I'm Pythia?"

"Yes, I knew this day would come, but I didn't want it to. I wanted to protect you." She lifts my chin and smiles. "I was wrong. No one can escape their destiny."

With a shift in the wind, the leaves turn white with Apollo's sun, casting bold shadows down the steps and across the villagers' uplifted faces.

CHAPTER FIFTEEN

31ST DAY OF APELLAIOS

KING LEONIDAS OF SPARTA

I start from my reverie to a great commotion—brass horns heralding, a clatter of many hooves and shouting outside the temple gates. The villagers scatter as a wild-eyed black stallion gallops up the Sacred Way and into the temenos. Stops just before the broad-stepped temple.

Diokles drops to his knees and bows to the man in shining greaves and horsehair-crested helmet. "King Leonidas!" Diokles shudders his greeting. "Noble king. No one told me you had arrived from Sparta.

"Priest." King Leonidas slides from a tall horse, his shield and short-sword rattling against the bronze breastplate. He storms the stairs two at a time, barely glancing at me or any of the men who step back, leaving a path for him to pass.

"High Priest…" the king stops his request and stares at the columns—the rough oak bark and sturdy branches sprouting from marble. "Great Apollo!" King Leonidas drops to his knees and stares silently up at Diokles who slowly pulls himself to his feet.

"Yes, great king. What is your request?"

I jump to my feet. "You would reclaim your power, wouldn't you old priest?"

Papa hurries up the steps and takes Mama's hand. Parmenides joins us and rests his hand on my shoulder. Mama, Papa, Parmenides and I stare down Diokles.

He frowns at us, but turns back to the king. "Have you come for an audience with the Pythia, blessed king?

"I need an audience with the Pythia. It is urgent." He looks around for the first time as if just realizing he interrupted some ceremony. "It cannot wait. The Persians are almost to Thermopylae. The Pythia must tell me what I should do."

"My king... of course." Diokles flushes red and looks around. "She awaits below in the sacred adyton."

I step into bright sunlight. King Leonidas glances over at me. Our eyes lock.

"King Leonidas, I am the true Pythia. I will question Apollo for you."

The moment I speak, I hear hissing like a thousand snakes. The king's face—mouth wide in astonishment, the priest lifting his cane—everything spins.

Clouds expand and swirl, forming indigo shadows and yellow scintillating outlines. I see currents of wind stir the air, sparkling lavender, rose and amber. It is so beautiful. I want to swim in the colors, wave my arms. The air is like warm seawater that swirls around me forming patterns repeated endlessly. Leaf, tree, rivers, rock-strewn shore.

The god fills me. To be consumed by a god! To be the god's Pythia. It is indescribable joy.

Words fall from my mouth. "Leonidas, King of all Sparta. Hear the words of the god. The strength of the bulls or lions cannot stop the foe. No, he will not leave off, I say, until he tears the city or the king limb from limb. Listen, for Apollo speaks."

I slide down, my back against the sturdy, oak-tree column. The sky breathes, its warmth enveloping me. Slowly, I regain awareness of Diokles, Mama, Papa, the men of the village who shudder in disbelief.

The god Apollo filled me. The god's words came from my mouth. As if struck by lightning, my arms and chest burn. My throat constricts and my mouth is dry like winter sand. I feel shaken but powerful.

"How dare you!" Diokles is the first to break our silence. "You dare to say you speak for the god!"

King Leonidas and Parmenides speak at the same moment. The Oracle of Elea waves his arm to silence the assemblage.

I force myself to focus on his words.

"Please, my king. Speak as you will." Parmenides speaks in a deep tone filled with confidence. Even the king quiets to listen. "We've all witnessed the power of the god today. The Pythia speaks your oracle."

"I will claim my prophecy." King Leonidas glances at the oak columns and then nods his head slowly to me. "I will return and present it to my warriors and ponder our path."

"No, the Pythia awaits. She… she did not yet speak your oracle…" Diokles stutters, trying to reclaim his authority.

"We all felt the power of the god," I say. Every eye stares at me.

"I am Apollo's true Pythia. Like my sisters before me…" I look over at Mama… "I unite mortals and Immortals. Here in this sacred Sanctuary, Apollo, god of healing and light, the god of song has spoken. Heed his words."

Parmenides raises his arms above his head and turns slowly to look back at the villagers waiting beneath us. "She is Pythia," he says, looking a long moment from villager to villager, his voice sharp and commanding. "She is your Oracle."

The chant is picked up and passed on by Mama and Papa standing beside me.

"This girl violated Apollo's Sanctuary." Diokles' long fingernails dig into my shoulder. "She must die!"

Planting my feet wide, the massive oak trees tangling their branches between the temple columns and fanning out behind me, I lift my voice to the vivid sky as if even the gods would listen. "No, Diokles. The great god Apollo, who brings both plague and healing to mankind, does not desire my death. I am his Pythia. He chose me to speak his wisdom to King Leonidas."

Man to man the people of Delphi ease closer me. As one, they lift their arms to honor the transformed columns, Apollo's power, and their true Pythia.

Wind rustles the brittle oak leaves, scraping living tree against the worn marble lintel. Hiding and revealing the carving: Know Thyself.

King Leonidas bows to me. "The girl speaks truth. I leave with my prophecy. I hear the wisdom of Apollo in her words. I must ponder the god's advice and understand how I may save my kingdom." He looks suddenly weary as he shakes his head and mounts the restless stallion. With slow, careful tread, he walks his horse between the gathered men. They part to let him pass and follow behind him like water flowing downhill.

A whinny from the king's dancing horse, the smell of dust and leather harnesses oiled by generations of young boys' hands… all of this fades as the procession of villagers winds back down the holy path followed by Diokles limping slowly behind.

I wait until they pass between the gate pillars.

I am alone.

I turn back to look at the great temple. While I stare in amazement, the oak trees glow and blaze with sharp light like Apollo's sun. I lift my arms in supplication. "Apollo, god of sun and song, god of plague and healing, I honor and thank you for your grace." The oak trees transform once more to stone columns carved by a stonemason's hands.

All that's left in the temple's emptiness is a rhythmic clang of the priests' bells as they pace down the Sacred Way. Only a scatter of footprints remains in the dust, work for the initiates later, boys hoping to be priests and eventually to hold the reins of power. They spend years sweeping away the footsteps of pilgrims every morning and every evening, sweeping kings' footsteps into a political air that could heat up or chill away to nothing by a single omen, an utterance of the Oracle whose every cry is interpreted by the priests.

Now I am that Oracle.

My house is my refuge until evening. Mama and Papa are gone, summoned by the council. Restless to do something, I can't stay inside another minute. With a water amphora as my excuse to leave the house, I head out to my favorite rock to scan the bay for the Persian fleet. Far off on the horizon, heat lightning flashes. Seagulls dip and soar, brilliant white against the leaden sky. Are they omens? Are the sunset blood and the storm Zeus' anger? Convinced the storm is a visitation by the gods, I whisper prayers to the windblown clouds. "Divine gods, help the Hellenes. Your Pythia will offer sweet libations to you—unmixed wine and spring water, barley and honey fresh from the hive. All this will I give to honor you if you will guide me. Show me the way to save the Greeks from King Xerxes' army." I kneel and rest my forehead on the cliff-stone.

Someone grabs my hair from behind. The wind betrayed me. I didn't hear anyone. A man wraps my hair tight around his fist and pushes my head hard against the rock. Sandaled feet circle close, kicking dirt onto me.

"You may have convinced those stupid villagers that you are Pythia, but I am your destiny, Thaleia. I will fulfill Apollo's judgment. Today you die."

I recognize Diokles' voice, angrier than I've ever heard it. A priest yanks me to my feet and pushes my face into the old priest's. His skin is rough. Hairs grow from his nose, and his breath smells fetid. He smiles and says, "It is a great honor to die for a god." The initiates surround me, many more than my wedding day. They're not taking any chances this time.

"How dare…"

"Don't…" The priest claps his hand over my mouth. "Quiet girl."

Wrenching my arms behind my back, he pushes me down the path to Kastalia Spring. A red sunray slices between the black pines, silhouetting rough bark and spiked needles. One priest clutches my arm tighter and grunts as he slips and regains his footing but doesn't release his hold.

They force me to stop at the edge of the spring. A dove calls her mournful cry. Calls again. Moss darkens the front of each marble step melting into the sacred waters, spring waters flowing from the Phaedriades rocks. Withered strands of yellow flowers drape over limestone along the stream's border, stark against the shadows of twisted, ancient laurels trailing up the rocky path beside the stream.

"Lift her chiton." There is a pause after his command. I hold my breath as the initiates look at the old man, but he waves his arm, his hand fisted and his brow scowling.

"No! Don't touch me!"

They pull my chiton over my head.

It's humiliating to stand naked before them. *I won't cry. I won't give them the satisfaction.*

Trembling, I scowl and turn from priest to priest. I cross my arms across my bare breasts.

Diokles stares me up and down and growls, "You must be purified in Apollo's sacred spring. Prepare yourself for the fulfillment of the god's judgment." His gaze is poisonous as a snake's.

My bare nipples tighten in terror.

I whirl away, but two priests seize my shoulders and push me down stone steps into the cold water. *Kastalia!* My memory jolts the moment my foot touches the water as if I become the girl of myth who fled Apollo's embraces. I feel the god seize her, grab her long, black hair and wrench her back to his bare chest. I feel her fear. In her desperate determination to escape, her arms and legs, muscle and sinew, become the spring. Kastalia's spirit and I blend as one. Together we lose human form and flow with the god's sacred waters.

We are free. We are lost.

"Spare me, Apollo!" With my shout, I am once again in my body, the water swirling around my thighs. I twist free from the priests' hands and try to reach the far side of the stone basin. One priest leans over the side and pushes me under the water.

I choke and struggle to swim across to the low, stone wall beneath the laurels, as far away from the priests' hands and stares as possible.

To escape the spring that is both sacred and defiled. This spring is Kastalia—all that is left of the girl. I shudder. She sacrificed her life to be spared Apollo's seduction.

I reach the wall, but the priests are there ahead of me.

Silent. Stern. Shoulder to shoulder they line the boulder wall above me leaving me trapped in the water.

"You cannot escape, Thaleia." Diokles' lips smile a tight grimace, smug and satisfied. "It is the will of the god. *Dios d'eteleietou boule.*"

"Is it god's will?" I stare at him a long moment, before I continue, "or is it your own, priest?"

"You trespassed in Apollo's Sanctuary, Thaleia. If the god commands, death is the penalty." He knits his brow; his eyes darken, but he doesn't move. He doesn't look away. "I will tell you this and you… will… listen. I am Apollo's right arm. *I* enforce the god's laws. And *you*, girl…" His words curl with hatred and disdain. "You broke with tradition. It is not for you to decide. Do you hear me? Do you understand me? I'll tell you for the last time. The Sanctuary is sacred. Females are not allowed. The penalty is death. I will not repeat this. Apollo decides your fate."

The initiates scowl at me and lean over the sacred water, but they do not dare set foot into the spring. Kastalia is my salvation after all. *Are we sisters then, Kastalia? Will your spring save me?*

"Is the will of the gods fulfilled? Or did you steal that power and only answer the pilgrims with your own words? Prophecies that have nothing to do with the gods and have everything to do with greed!" I swim into deeper water in the middle of the pond. My belly burns with heat that seems to warm the waters.

Thaleia. Thaleia. Kastalia's voice enflames me. *Defy. Apollo stole my life. Turned me into this spring because I defied him. But you, you can win, Thaleia. Defy.*

Diokles' voice cuts through her murmurs, shatters her words like ice shards falling to earth.

"Thaleia, do not walk the path your mother carved. Do not disrespect the gods. I control the temple. I interpret Apollo's prophecies! It will be easy to get you out of my way."

"Lies, Diokles. You never understood The Child of the Clouds' birdcalls. I do! She was a false Pythia that you manipulated for power."

I swim back to the steps that disappear into death-tainted water. "Don't threaten me." I hold my head high and walk up past the old priest. "Mama was the true Pythia. You ordered her to choose between the sacred tripod and me."

My anger wipes away their stares and my shame at my nakedness. "You ordered her to kill me!" I shove the old man with both my hands, and he stumbles backwards. "But she didn't. She wouldn't. You forced her to choose, and she left her god and the temple. She returned to the village with her baby and her husband." I whisper in the priest's ear. "She wouldn't abandon her child not even for the most sacred duty a woman can hold."

He glares at me.

"Now I am Pythia, Diokles. The god speaks through me. It's over. Your power is gone."

With his slight nod, three priests rush back around the pool toward me. They stop as one, an arm's length away. I smell their fear acrid as rotting sea slime and a bitter smell of the hunt from their loins. They could be three brothers, tall, amber-skinned, dark eyes staring and unsure. They avoid my gaze.

Diokles nods once again, a long slow bend of his head without taking his eyes from me.

I raise my arm to summon my power, but I waited too long, pushed too far.

The hook-nosed priest I saw murder Sophia in my vision rushes me.

There is a sigh from the waters behind me.

Each white-robed priest sparkles. As if I see it all in slow motion, they seize me and hurl me back into the spring.

Cold water sucks my breath from between my clenched teeth, as my head strikes a wall stone.

I sink beneath the spring's water, swept down to the mouth of the River Styx, the entrance to the Underworld.

CHAPTER SIXTEEN

DEATH

I am swept down, down through a cave below the spring to the Mouth of Hades. The great rock shifts.

I sink faster and faster into total darkness.

My body lies beneath the running water, wedged between step and mountain boulder. I see water sparkle above me on the water's surface, casting back clear sun rays that stream through storm clouds, caught and split by the Shining Rocks rising high above me.

No! I cry out for Pan and home. Memories swirl around me—the goat head lodged in the old shepherd's tree, staring with blind eyes as Sophia and I dance up the mountain path. Mama singing lullabies, while I drift away to a gentle sleep. Papa urging me to run away, run away. It's too late. It's all too late.

There is only silence.

And a sudden, blinding light.

I am lost in a sky of sparkling motes, lifting and dancing like thousands of butterflies or minute seeds carried on an invisible wind. My terror and loss are replaced with relief and joy. Bliss. As if the gods lift me to the clouds, the girl's body left deep beneath the spring water has nothing to do with me.

This is love. Absolute freedom from fear and pain. I am part of the floating colors, the silent dance. I am part of the joy. I am utterly happy. I no longer want to return to my body.

It occurs to me that I'm dead, but I don't care how long my body floats face down beneath the running water. Fleetingly, I think of Mama and Papa, Sophia, Parmenides… everything I've known and loved. But it is nothing compared to this feeling of complete contentment. My village, my world, seems far away—only a distant memory. It has nothing to do with this peace.

Until the day is gone, and I drift farther and farther from all I've known.

So, this is death? Let it be the end. Let it be over.

I don't know how long I drift in the timeless death current. Beyond time and danger. I am content to stay immersed, as if lost in the land of the Lotus-eaters.

Strong hands seize me. Pull me from the water, white and still. Have the priests found me? I resist, kick and struggle, but these hands are gentle. They lay me carefully at the spring's edge on rough-hewn stone. I smile to myself. There is a smell of goat and wild thyme.

As if I watch from a high perch above the spring, I see Pan lean over my body. He pulls strands of wet hair off my face. My ears ring with music of the winds, brittle like ice crystals from the north, sweet with incense and saffron from the east, the heat of Helios, a red-setting sun from the west, and from the south, sweet nectar of poppy and thyme and wild garlic. *Pan.* He pulls me close against his chest and kisses my brow lightly. I feel the warmth of his arms encircling me as if the earth protects me. *Where are the priests?*

They are gone.

Left me for dead.

Pan looks up alert. His back and leg muscles tense, as Parmenides strides down the path. As if he never knelt over me, the satyr is gone.

Pan, don't leave me. I try to tell Parmenides about the satyr, but I panic when I realize I can't. I'm detached from my body, helpless to cry out or move.

Parmenides lifts me into his arms. "Thaleia," he whispers into my hair. A wistful hope tugs me back toward my life, but cannot carry me all the way. Everything is disconnected.

A scream then another slices the night air. Torches flare ahead on the path, as Parmenides carries my body back up Mt. Parnassos to Delphi. The flames flicker, hidden behind trees. Another flare blazes momentarily visible but disappears the moment a keening lament snakes through the branches.

Sophia runs, stumbles as fast as she can down the dark path. "Thaleia!" She seizes my arm.

Dread cold courses through me. Her touch. There is nothing.

Her nails scratch my skin, and still I can't feel anything. Carried in Parmenides' arms, I am jostled and pressed against the Oracle's chest, but there is no sense of his soft tunic against my cheek, no feeling of strong hands clutching me close. Ahead up the dark path, I see torches waved by strong men's arms. Fire flares light a wall, a face, a shadowed doorway. And still I am distant and detached, unable to cry out or weep… only wait in the Void between an in-breath and out, snared and tangled like a Shade who sees life all around but cannot touch or sob or walk back into her life.

"She's dead! Thaleia's dead! The priest killed her! It was Diokles." Sophia shouts as tears flow freely down her cheeks. Her hair is loose from her braids and wild behind her.

May the gods curse Priest Diokles! His body left to be devoured by dogs. Bloody carrion for the birds. Help me, Sophia. Please help me!

The villagers call out to one another. Torches flicker, weave in and out of the trees ahead on the winding path. I observe everything from above, looking down as the Hierophant carries my body up the dark path into Delphi.

No. Pan saved me. That can't be my dead body.

My arms, legs and head hang limp, spill out of his embrace as Parmenides strides, each step forced and slow as if pushing his way through seawater.

I'm not dead!

Torches wave in the dark night. Villagers pour out their doorways.

The fire-flare lights their faces contorted with fear. Lamps are lifted, lowered and again held high. A woman's keening cuts through the confusion and panic. Screams and sobs sweep over me wave after wave.

I'm here. I'm here.

"Thaleia!" Mama screams. I barely recognize her voice, savage with sorrow.

Stunned, I watch the pantomime in the torchlight—mouths open and close. Mama's cries echo from the Shining Cliffs and bounce from wall to gate as if her terror could reach the Temple Sanctuary and awaken Apollo.

Mama, I'm not dead! I think I yell, but there is only silence.

I can't talk.

I can't move.

I watch the villagers gather around my body. *I'm here, Mama. Don't be afraid.* But I'm afraid. Has the old priest won after all?

"Parmenides!" Brygos shouts, his angry cry cuts through the confusion. The Oracle of Elea jerks aside to look at him.

"Parmenides, what did you do?" He steps close, towering over Parmenides who staggers with my weight.

The fisherman eases me from Parmenides' arms. He cradles my head like a newborn's against his broad shoulder, easily draws my body's shell to him. He faces Papa striding past the villagers toward him. I watch Brygos hold me and cringe with loathing.

Sophia collapses at his feet, sobbing uncontrollably.

No. I'm not dead, Sophia. I'm here. I won't abandon you. My body's eyes stare blindly into the villagers' frightened stares. They whisper around me like angry wasps. "Was it Priest Diokles? Did he murder the girl? She's our true Pythia. He killed her!"

One by one, my neighbors step back to let Papa pass between them. Sophia's grandmother Apollinaria raises her torch high and the others follow her example to light his way. Without a word, he gathers my body from Brygos' arms and walks back into the dark village to our home.

I feel safe in Papa's arms, warm and loved. I want to remember how it feels to live within my flesh and blood. "The gods finally claimed you, Thaleia. Dionysos took what's his to take," Papa says. His chest heaves. "I couldn't keep you safe. I failed. I've lost you." He presses his forehead against my cheek.

Dionysos? No, Papa, it was Diokles. He shoved me into Apollo's sacred waters where the god claimed Kastalia. The priest murdered me. Why do you blame Dionysos?

Suddenly aware that my body is gone, Mama runs after Papa. After my body.

I wait beside my body and Mama in the women's quarters throughout the long night, but restlessness seizes me with the rising sun, a yearning to walk my village streets, to find someone to help me, to touch me, to bring me back… or let me go. It's over. The priest couldn't kill me, but he might as well have. I'm caught here between life and death. Helpless to return to life or leave forever for the Underworld. I'm a Shade walking the mountain paths.

I walk a little uphill from the village. Walk? It seems as if I walk, though my body is no longer solid. My legs are a fog-cloud. My arms refuse to take form. They dance with motes of light, yet brush aside branches.

Am I alive? Am I dead? Great gods don't leave me like this!

I hurl a rock at a dead stump. It splinters the rotting wood. I scream and scream, but hear only a nearby stream and wind and somewhere a small rodent burrowing through pine needles. Will I drift forever between the girl I was in my village and this strange, bodiless state? Snatching up a poppy growing from a crack in the limestone, I try to crush it between my fingers, but my fingers can't destroy it. It shimmers with light, resting whole in my palm; it separates and dances with sun and earth. While I stare in horror, my hand also dissolves to particles of light. I jump up and throw the poppy to the ground.

But somewhere deep inside me, I understand that my body was always these sparkles of light.

It was always so.

I never knew.

I crouch to the ground and once again pick up the flower. I can't feel it against my skin. It has no weight or texture. I feel light and fearless.

Here between Life and Death, I know I have a choice. I can return to the sacred waters and the mouth to Hades. Just let go.

I want to. I want the quiet calm.

And my destiny? The Persians? Sophia?

I can't run away. The god Pan told me not to. I am Pythia. I won't abandon them.

I rush up the path. I know exactly where I'm headed: the clearing where I met Pan.

The wind howls. Storm clouds sit heavy on the Phaedriades. With no body to carry with me, I am the cold of the storm. I will myself up the mountain to find the satyr. Maybe he can tell me what the gods expect from me. A pine bough tears from a tree-trunk and crashes directly where I stand, but I am the tear of limb from tree. I am the smell of raw resin oozing from the torn bark, the sweet smell of pine and rain and mud. A feeling of growth and peace fill me. For a brief moment I feel the storm's power surge through me, and then I hear it—dancing between the raindrops, I hear Pan's flute.

Blessed Pan! I step into the clearing. Once again, there is no storm, no rain. Meadowlarks sing. The air is warm, earthy with thyme and sweet-flowing wine. I breathe a deep sigh and gulp a breath to fill my lungs with Pan's smell.

He sits on the ground with crossed legs leaning back against the old burnt pine.

"So, Thaleia, you found me."

The hummingbird circles his horned head, before it whirs its song around my head. I lift my translucent finger. The tiny bird lands on it.

Pan stands and holds his hand out in greeting, beckoning with a sweep of his arm for me to join him. The satyr smiles and his face fills with a glow, soft like moonlight across a calm sea. His arms and chest are sun-bronzed like hammered metal, oiled and glistening in the sun. But his eyes draw me close. Their blue is deeper, like summer sky now, cloudless, an endless path leading to Mount Olympos and the gods. They seem powerful and kind at the same time, as the god watches me.

"Welcome."

He sits once more beneath the tree. I sit before him, our knees touching. We lean toward one another.

The satyr grins. His smile warms me, races to my head and down to my belly. Pan lifts my hands and brings them to his chest then places his palm on my heart.

Help me Pan.

The earth is in his powerful hand, hard as mountain stone, but his touch is light.

Can you free me? Can you hear me? I look around. A songbird sings from a rock, half-shaded with tall rushes rippling in a warm wind, a cinnamon-scented breeze soft with mysterious sighs—the earth's breath and desire.

"Yes, Thaleia. You are not dead. That priest tried to kill you. I… well… sometimes the gods intervene. Now you may choose. You may stay here with me. Wander the mountain paths. Always springtime. Always life renewed or… I believe you have the strength… you may return home. It won't be easy."

The priest hates me. I place my hand over the satyr's strong hand and look into his eyes, fall into their brilliant abyss. A shock like a bolt of lightning shoots up my spine. I pull away and sit back on my haunches.

Pan smiles at me, at the bird and takes back my hand.

"Delphi is in great danger. As you know, the Persians are gathered at Magnesia, eleven days march from Delphi. They threaten all Hellas. And Diokles has bartered with King Xerxes; he offered to sell out Greece if the Persian King will allow him to keep his control over the sacred tripod. If the Greeks are destroyed, our civilization—the hymns and prayers and wise men like Solon—there will be no one to worship the gods."

Pan kisses the palm of my hand and rests his hand once more over my heart. He waits a long time, before he finishes his thought. "You are the only one who can help us, Thaleia. If you return, you may save Delphi, Hellas, even the gods. It is your choice."

I feel the warmth of the satyr's palm against my chest. Tears spring to my eyes.

How, Pan. How can I play gods' games? How can I save Hellas? Why am I the only one?

"You are Pythia. Pray to the winds, you said."

I shiver with the memory—vague but lingering—of shouting at the soldier, Diokles and Papa. *What did those words mean Pan? Do you know?* I'm not sure I want to hear his answer, but I must ask. I have to know.

"Three days ago the Persian fleet lost ten ships. A great storm arose suddenly destroying only Persian ships, casting them in great confusion. Thaleia, great winds destroyed ten ships. Will you still question? Do you still believe you are only a simple village girl?"

I want to believe this satyr-god. I want to lie back and let his warm words bathe me like sunshine on a late summer evening. I want to stay here forever.

Why don't the gods save the Greeks?

"The gods work through mortals. Apollo spoke through you to guide the Spartan King. Thaleia, do not question the will of the gods. We walk in mystery, beyond time. Listen for the gods' song in the wind rushing across high mountain crags. Walk with your mind calm and open. Believe you have the power to save your world. And you will."

How can Pan possibly expect me to save Hellas from the Persian invasion or save the gods? How can he ask me to help the priests? They hate me! Diokles will never allow me to be free. He won't stop trying to kill me, until he is rid of me. I look over at the old pine, burned hollow with only the bark shell remaining. That's how I feel. What is left of Thaleia who used to run wild up Mt. Parnassos?

I don't want to go back.

The satyr jumps up and holds his hands out to pull me up. When he throws his head back, there is mischief in his blue eyes. He dances around me so quick that the pines spin with my effort to follow his leaps and turns. His flute music laughs and mingles with his hooves' clatter against the earth.

I throw my arms in the air and whirl and laugh and cry. It feels like I fall up into the brittle sky.

I will stay here forever with you Pan!

There is only his flute music. The sun's warmth. I laugh with relief to never again have to face Brygos or Diokles, never again struggle against the destiny my village plans. *Forever Pan!*

As if a cloud blocks the sun, the idea that I could never return home stops me mid-twirl. *If I never leave? Never go back? I have to. I can't leave Sophia to face Diokles alone.* Without me there, it could be Sophia naked before the priest. A sword flashes in moonlight. My vision sears me like a fire-prod. Blood and terror and death. *Sophia!*

Pan?

The satyr stops before me and leans his head against my forehead. His curved horns tangle in my hair. His breath blows warm on my lips, as he stands so still that I imagine him a marble statue. The cinnamon-scented air is so thick I can barely breathe.

Pan, I can't stay. I have to return home.

He doesn't say anything, but there is a light in his eyes.

I want to stay, but… Sophia. I can't abandon her. I need to go back, Pan. And I will try to save Hellas. Pan, do you hear me? I don't know how, but I will try!

The satyr strokes his beard and nods, but he is silent.

I see my path in his wide eyes. He knew all along that I would help Hellas. He believed in me all along.

CHAPTER SEVENTEEN

"Some God Passes Here"

With that one thought, that one answer, I'm swept away from Pan. My spirit is swept along by the current of the sacred spring, trapped once more beneath the water.

I fall. And fall.

Down into travertine-walled stone. Cave walls. Dark and cold and water-sheeted stone.

I am surrounded by voices. Diokles calls me a stupid child. "Intruder!" shouts the Child-of-the Clouds.

My heart leaps and rips me from the dark waters.

Swept back to my home, I hover from the willow-branch ceiling, shiver as I watch my mother bathe my pale body.

Mama has dragged my bed to the center of our courtyard. She sops a rag in a bowl and washes my body's legs and arms with fig-steeped water. I'm still trapped outside my body.

My half-open lips are blue. My eyes closed.

What if I can't return?

Drops of water glisten in my hair as Mama gently pulls brown pine needles from the strands and from between my curled toes. I am not this naked body lying white, lifeless as cold stone, my chin lifted in defiance.

Pan, what do I do? How do I return to life?

Whispers from clinging Shades of the Underworld urge me to return to them. To let armies and village obligations go, to descend back to shadows and cool stone—free from Brygos, free from the invading Persians, free from my destiny.

Sophia's aunts sit on pillows, their backs against the clay wall and stitch together bread cloths and chitons for a shroud. My shroud.

Timon is huddled in the corner clutching a cup of wine, a blanket thrown over his shoulders. Sophia steps closer to my bed, and Mama gestures with one hand for her to help as she lifts my limp body.

My body hangs from her embrace, as she once again slips her wedding chiton over my lolling head, works it slowly over my shoulders and arms then presses her cheek against my hair.

"I made her an amulet to wear as Hades' bride." Tears fill Sophia's eyes as she hands a spun necklace to Mama. It is a woven spider web, made from soft strands of lamb's wool. Mama gently eases it over my head. The wool strands nestle against my chest, but still I feel nothing.

Pan, tell me what to do!

"Some god passes here. Some god passes here."

Slowly, I am aware of Apollinaria chanting over and over, her words a monotone.

It's the little things that bring us back, urge us to take that one step between boundaries, between the shadows of death and life.

A smile. A dream. For me, it is the chant and the smell of figs. All around me the smell of figs, sweet and luscious. Summer where there was only winter and Death.

Mama kneels beside my body. Sophia kneels next to her and touches the web necklace.

"I love you, Thaleia," Mama whispers.

In my dream state, I kneel with her side-by-side, smoothing, stroking the pale body, my body, on the bed before us, as if it is a gift left to bring us together.

"Dionysos, great god of life-eternal. Why did you claim her?" Mama sobs into my hair then brushes aside a damp strand caught across my lips. She touches my brow and cheek lightly with one finger.

With trepidation, I stroke my body's lips.

A rush of air, a command, sweeps me back inside my abandoned shell, back to the comfort of my own skin, my own breath. I feel it slip through me, warming my hands, my feet, calling me back. There is no other awareness, only my breath. My lungs gulp the air, air that for an instant is visible all around me, hanging like looped strands of drying wool. As I draw deep breaths, it fills my chest. Thick like honey, sticky as spider webs flung from the ceiling beams.

At first, I can't speak, but my eyes implore Mama. It is enough. She understands. The air clarifies. Mama and Sophia melt against me, sobbing on my shoulder. "Thaleia. Thaleia." Sophia calls my name in a cadence rhythm with Apollinaria. "Some god passes here."

Mama sobs and laughs. I cling to her. Her strong arms pull me close, and we both slide to the floor, laughing, crying. Sophia dances circles around us. A slight smile brightens Mama's face. There is something there, as if she knew all along. As if she had always believed I would return.

"Mama, hold me. Don't leave me. Don't ever leave me," I finally manage to say. I pull her even tighter against me, but my arms have no feeling; they seem as empty as moonlight brushing a midnight sea. She smells of barley tea and wine, her hair of the salt sea brine.

I am intensely aware of my breath warm inside me, filling my throat and chest.

"Thaleia!" Sophia gasps a choked half cry.

"Some god passes here." Apollinaria presses her forehead against the doorframe, pulls back, leans forward again, her white hair spreading across the wood grain. "Some god passes here," she repeats, her lips pressed tightly together.

Shaking uncontrollably, I look around the room. Sophia's aunts are huddled together, wide-eyed, staring at me. Brygos blows bursts of air through his open mouth. Hestos looks blankly at the floor.

Gradually, I hear rain, steady gentle drops on the thatch roof and the path outside the door, on Parnassos with its storm-worn limestone. I draw a deep breath and focus on the sound of the raindrops. Focus and listen. *I'm back—thank the gods—but my work begins now. Here.*

The next day, the tension in the village feels like air thickening before a thunderstorm, but Mama doesn't speak about what happened to me. I watch her, stay near, sensing she knows why the gods returned me, but I never ask her. I feel like the girl named Thaleia who grew up in Delphi is gone forever. I have no idea who is walking around in this shell of who she was. It's like the hermit crabs I used to watch. They'd outgrow their shell, pull themselves out of their old casing to creep across a sandy beach, until they find a larger home, a casing that was heavier and harder for them to cart around but large enough for them to grow into.

"Thaleia, it's me, Timon."

I hear him call to me, his voice faint, just outside our heavy gate, but I'm reluctant to talk. It is early the second day. With each step I take across our courtyard, I'm aware of the stone beneath my bare feet, the sea breeze on my face, my hair tangled, the braids from my judgment day half unbound… like me. One foot in my home. One in the god's.

I peer out the small tiled hole in the gate at Timon waiting for me to invite him in. He's so handsome; twenty instead of Brygos' thirty. Dark, thick hair… and his eyes—chestnut brown with sparks of hazel circling their black center, always searching and taking everything in like a wild horse. Not like Brygos at all.

"Come away with Sophia and me." His voice shifts from pleading to anger, when I don't answer. I try to focus on what he's saying. "Thaleia!"

Maybe that's it. If the three of us go away, it will save Sophia. Who am I kidding? It will save me. How would I feel living with the two of them?

I want to run away, just run far away with Sophia and Timon, away from Diokles, away from Brygos, but the gods unraveled me, like pulling a loose thread and yanking it through a cloth. They sent Pan.

Finally, Timon slips past me and walks into my courtyard. Shadows cast long behind him.

"Thaleia. I've been so worried. Are you alright?" Before I even know what to answer, he leans close to whisper. "What happened?"

There is wonder in his eyes. A timid hope to peer beyond death. "Why did Hades send you back?"

"I don't know, Timon." I sigh with relief at the honesty of my answer.

"Thaleia, come away with me and Sophia." His words come out in a rush. "We can go to Corinth—I have friends there—or farther, east to Ionia."

"No. I can't. I'm needed here. I won't run away."

His face shadows as if Thanatos, the death god, answered for me.

The morning seems to last forever. I find a routine: sweeping and scrubbing. But I'm too restless to stay indoors. Trying to feel comfortable in my own skin, I wander the rocky slopes above the village. Sunlight sparks and dances from the pines towering above me. I catch my breath when the boulder beside my path loses its substance, flows and sways like the laurel, lifting and breathing with the same wind that tugs at my hair.

I stare at the sun cresting the Shining Cliffs and try to pretend nothing is different. But the next few days after my return to my body, the mountain is mine, wholly, fully in a way I never before experienced. Not all at once. Not irrevocably—mine to claim at will—but in fits and starts with a completeness that takes me by surprise.

And when I wander back down off the mountain, along the village paths, Delphi is strange to me. Or am I a stranger to the villagers? I am ready prey for their questions, veiled whispered suspicions. I can only imagine what they think about my return to life. Even back in the safety of my home, they slow to peer into our courtyard. The old women come knocking, warm bread steaming under a cloth, goat's milk in a small amphora.

"Thaleia. *Kale mera*," my neighbor's morning call. "I have breakfast for you."

I move aside the flap to the women's quarter to a flood of sunlight, bright and clear after the storm. "I'm coming," I say and hurry to let in the village baker dressed in a purple chiton covered with a red *himation* smock, dusty from dragging along the path to my door. She pushes past me. Her plump cheeks are flushed. She urges me to take a platter with a loaf of bread still steaming and quickly places a jug of warm goat milk into my other hand. All the while, she doesn't look at me, everywhere but at me. Her heavy body is a whirlwind of motion, turning this way and that to look all around, pausing only a moment with a darkening flicker of her eyes as she catches sight of the shroud cast aside in the corner.

"So?"

She smoothes the wine-dark cloth of her robes with her palms.

"What happened, Thaleia? You know we've all been so worried." Her eyes dart to the door, to my feet, behind her to the street. "What is it like…" her voice trails away, as she studies her fingernails, turning her short fingers side to side to catch the light. She lifts a finger to her mouth, bites off her thumbnail and chews it while she mumbles. "You know…" and still she never looks at me.

I hear her words of compassion and concern, but it's a thin covering, a scum on the deeper pool of her curiosity.

"Thank you for the bread… and milk." I hold the jug high and guide her back to the gate, almost shove her out and close it behind her. *Nosy old fool.* What can I tell her? I don't really know how it happened. I was drowning in the sacred spring. Pan rescued me. That much I know. I shake my head. I could tell her a goat god told me I must choose. Great, I'll just tell her that I'm supposed to save Hellas from a Persian invasion.

I'll just tell her I'm supposed to save the gods. That'll go over really well.

I light the lamp at our home altar. "Warrior-goddess Athena, give me strength." I move a clay figure of Dionysos to one side—the flame flickering across his smiling face and adjust the larger figure of Apollo on the other side. "Great gods of Olympos, guide me. Give me the strength to follow my destiny."

Brygos walks in our courtyard gate without knocking, a fresh fish wrapped in cloth under his arm. For once he looks unsure. He throws his shoulders back and shoves the fish at me.

"And what if I don't want your fish, Brygos?"

"It's a gift. For you, Thaleia."

When I don't take the fish, he brushes my chin with the fish tail. "A gift for my betrothed. You must take it." He nudges the fish against my shoulder. The fish slips from the wrapping, its black eye stares at me. Blind. Dead.

Suddenly, all my pent-up rage explodes, and I see lights sparking between the two of us. "I don't want your stupid fish, Brygos. And I'm not your betrothed!"

"Just wait, Thaleia. You'll be sorry you didn't marry me when you had the chance."

I grab his tunic and push him back to the door and out onto the steps. Blood drips from the fish onto the fresh-swept stones. "I am not your betrothed." My voice lowers as I finally understand the truth of it. "It is not my destiny to be your wife, Brygos. Go away. Just go away."

What amazes me is that he does. He tucks the fish back under his arm, blood seeping into the loose-woven white cloth and walks away. Something in my heart wants him to look back, so I can yell at him again. So I can free the rage I feel strangling me. But he doesn't look back.

CHAPTER EIGHTEEN

A Promise

I sit cross-legged in the corner beside my stitched shroud and rub the soft cloth against my cheek. I died. *Died? What is death?* I'm here now… but what was it then? The dancing lights. Total peace. I remember clearly the feeling of not wanting to come back. Not wanting to return to all this… Brygos and the old priest. Pan and the destiny he says is mine.

It's too much!

Though it was beautiful and loving, when I floated outside my body, when I think back on it now, it terrifies me. I wrap my arms around my chest and listen to my heartbeat. Listen to my breath flow in and out; try to calm my mind so the terror will release me.

"Thaleia, it's me." Sophia pushes open my gate.

I rush into her arms and pull her into my courtyard. Arms stretched out before us, so we won't lose sight of each other's eyes, we spin in wild circles. Sobbing. Laughing.

"I thought I lost you forever."

"I will never leave you, Sophia."

At last, too dizzy to keep spinning, we run together into my dark room. When she touches my hair, I see myself through her eyes—

white and staring, laid out in the courtyard, while her aunts stitched my shroud. A shadow crosses her eyes. I understand. She's not sure.

"Thaleia, you were dead. But you're here." Sophia stands, shifts uneasily from foot to foot and just looks at me. "Is it really you?"

I yank the lambskin from the window to let in a golden light. The leather rips, where it was hooked over wooden pegs. Dust and pollen float lazily through the bright ray of light.

"It's me, Sophia. I'm here."

"Thaleia… I'm sorry I betrayed you to Diokles." Sophia pulls the soft fabric of her chiton up closer to her chin, clutches it tightly against her throat with both hands and stares at me. "What happened?" She paces to the door and back to face me. "He killed you! Diokles murdered you!"

I take her hands and pull her over to sit on the pillows before the hearth. "He told the priests to drown me. He wants to control the temple's wealth and power. He wants me dead."

"But Thaleia, you *were* dead. What happened to you? I saw Parmenides carry you into Delphi. How did you come back from the Land of Shades?"

I lean over and push cold ashes into a dusty mound. I can't look at her. "It was beautiful. So peaceful. Unlike anything I've ever experienced. I'm ashamed to tell you that I didn't want to leave."

"You weren't afraid?"

"Not then… it's more terrifying, when I think about it now. I might not have returned… ever." I'm shaking as I embrace Sophia. We are both silent for a long time. Each lost in our thoughts.

At last she pulls away, sets a nest of branches in the cold hearth and lights the fire from a candle burning on the altar. "What was it like?" She looks at me, her eyes brimming with tears. "What did you see?" She glances toward the open door. "Your body was here. I never left you."

"When we followed the flute music to the meadow, remember the storm stopped the moment we stepped out of the trees? Just the way I imagine the Elysian Fields."

Sophia strokes my back.

"Pan saved me. Diokles tried to drown me. I hit my head on a stone step when a priest shoved me into the Kastalia Spring. It was

Pan who pulled me out."

But I don't know how to explain the rest of it. My visions. My choice.

"It has to do with the spider screaming, your vision about the Persians, doesn't it? Is that the reason the gods brought you back?"

"Pan gave me the choice to stay forever with the gods or return to help the Hellenes."

"How?"

"I don't know. I only know I had to return to you. I stroke her cheek. "Sophia, you sent Timon. You asked me to run away with both of you. You would abandon Delphi, your mother… you would leave your home behind for me?"

"Come away with us, Thaleia. If you stay here, Diokles will kill you."

"I'm not the one we should worry about."

She sinks down into the pillow and looks up at me a long time. Twice she opens her mouth to say something but is silent. I can see she is finally listening. At last she says in a low voice, hesitant but calm, "The Agrionia again? It's coming up in just a few weeks."

"Yes. Promise me. Please, Sophia, promise me you won't go."

"Thaleia, it's crazy. Why do you keep saying I shouldn't go? I've planned on going for years. The last festival of Dionysos before I marry. You expect me to give up carrying the thyrsus, telling riddles, wandering the mountain all night pretending to look for Dionysos. And what about the wicker god they throw in the spring? You went last year. Now you're telling me I shouldn't go? I suppose you want me to stay home, but you get to go, since you didn't marry? Just like that? You'd leave me behind… again? I don't think so."

"No. No, Sophia, it's not like that. Let's make a pact. We'll both stay home. I promise. I won't go either." I hold my breath and wait for her answer. She is silent a long time. Time for me to remember a sword slashing through the night. "Sophia, please promise me." I squeeze her hand. She squeezes it back.

"Alright." She looks down at our clasped hands.

"Alright? You promise? *We* promise not to go?"

"Yes. Yes, I promise."

CHAPTER NINETEEN

JEALOUSY

Time has a way of passing despite our most fervent desires. I'd faced a priest, a god's choice, even death itself, and still the season crept from summer to autumn; the sun rose and the moon and the dog star found me wondering about my destiny, staring for a sign into the star-laden sky.

"Thaleia! Wake up!" Sophia whispers outside my window one evening early autumn. "An Athenian delegation is here! The Persians are through Macedonia!"

I throw on my winter shawl and follow the narrow goat's path with its turns between rocks and cypress. Sophia races after me up the back path to the Sanctuary. There is no breeze, no sound, only the mist that settles around me. Nothing seems familiar. With each twist in the path, each glade of pines or rocks jutting abruptly out of the clouds, there is only fear. The Persians!

I listen through the silence of the cold hoping to hear hoof against stone. I watch each curving branch as trees loom into view through the mist, hoping Pan will find me and tell me what to do. These are Pan's paths, his trees and stone. I can feel him in every whisper of fog through pine, every dove's call. This is Pan's mountain.

A slight breeze lifts the mist and suddenly Hestos' hut rises before us a short distance uphill. The shepherd sits on the front step, whittling a goat's head for a staff. He looks up from his work, stares at me with blind eyes as if they can see, as if all along he knew I would come.

I stop before him, panting and take Sophia's hand.

"Thaleia. Sophia." Hestos pats the step beside him. When we hesitate, he says, "Are you going back to the Sanctuary?"

"Yes, we heard an Athenian delegation is at the temple asking Diokles for advice," I say. Sophia glances at me, a question in her eyes but remains silent.

"Is it wise for you to return there, Thaleia?" Hestos says.

Sophia twists her hands behind her back.

I stare into the old man's eyes. It's hard to know where to look. Long, gray lashes frame them. They are milky white as clouds.

"Sit a moment with me, girls. Sit with a lonely old man."

I take the staff from his hands and trace the deep grooves and smooth wood with my finger and then sit beside him.

"Just for a moment, Sophia?"

"But Thaleia, the delegation…"

"I have to help him. We can't just leave him here."

Sophia sits beside me. The fog blows back in. I watch it mist between the planks of his goats' pen, where the listless animals huddle unmoving in the closest corner, squeezed so close together, they look like one amorphous goat, a dank muddle of wet fur, completely still and silent. Their stench permeates the air. Hestos rests his long fingers lightly on my arm to gain my attention then takes back his staff.

"Are you hungry?"

"There's no time, Hestos. The Persians forced their way through Macedonia. How many days' march is that? A week? Two at the most? You can't stay up here alone. It's not safe."

Hestos doesn't answer. He leans heavily on his staff and slowly pulls himself upright. We follow his stooped back inside. It takes a moment for my eyes to adjust to the flickering firelight burning low in the stone hearth to see what little the room holds: one shelf, hand-hewn, supported with two braces of laurel branches close beside the door. Three small red clay cups sitting alone there, carefully spaced, each turned so the handles face to the right, painted with crudely drawn grape vines. Another bench is placed to the side of the door. The damp wind blows through the cracks between the door's planks.

"I don't blame her for avoiding me, Thaleia. I was there when her mother died."

"What?"

"Your mother and I were great friends, when she was little. She was such a lively girl, so full of sunshine and mischief. I couldn't resist letting her run after the goats. She used to love to chase after the ones that strayed. Chase them right back to the flock. Wasn't long before she could outrun every one of them. I'd bring her back with me, when I came down the mountain in the evening and your grandmother would give me figs steeped in wine, a glass of cool water… but she just seemed to fade after they took your mother up the mountain to be Pythia. That day your grandmother was so proud… but so sad. She walked directly behind the priests—her strides long enough so she wouldn't fall behind, her head high. Tears streamed down her cheeks—she didn't even bother to wipe them away—just followed behind her daughter, stared at her back as if she thought she would never again see it, as if she needed to memorize its curve, the shine of her long curls casting back gold of the late afternoon sun."

Hestos whirls round to face me and for a moment the flash of anger in his eyes makes them seem alive. "How could Diokles tell the village that your grandmother threw herself off the cliff?"

I grab his thin shoulders. "You know what happened? Mama won't tell me."

He shakes his head. "Diokles blamed your mother. Told her that her mother jumped, because her daughter betrayed Apollo and brought shame to the family. I don't believe it for a minute. Your grandmother would never do that! She would never leave her daughter."

Mama! And her mother, the grandmother I never knew. The grandmother Mama never talks about! Did she throw herself off a cliff because her daughter was banished as Pythia? Or did Diokles kill her like he tried to kill me?

Hestos nudges a heavy pot of lentils off to the side of the hearth and pokes at the fire, until it flares.

"Thaleia, we can't wait! We need to go. He's not making any sense! Your grandmother tripped and fell, didn't she? That's what your mother told me."

"Hestos! Did you hear? The Persians are almost here!" I look to Sophia for help, completely unsure what to do.

The old shepherd pulls a moth-eaten blanket closer around him and runs gnarled fingers through his white hair and strokes his beard. "Don't know why I never asked her to marry me after her husband died." Hestos lifts the hem of his tunic and wipes tears from his rheumy eyes.

A memory of Brygos yelling fills me. *Ask your mother why your grandmother killed herself.* I grab Hestos' arm. "How did my grandmother die?"

Slowly, as if unfolding his limbs one at a time and testing their dependability, he stretches his arms, then legs and finally pulls away from my grasp and takes his mug from the stone shelf. He finds the amphora of cool water on the table by the door across the room then paces his way back avoiding every table and bench.

It's all I can do to sit still and wait for his answer.

He sips the water and then rubs the back of his neck.

My mind races. "Please tell me Hestos. Did the priest kill my grandmother?"

"Guess I never thought I was good enough. I chopped wood for her; swapped lamb on festival days for wine and brought her my best cheese… I loved that woman. I always wondered if I could have made a difference." Hestos drinks more water and speaks his words into the cup. "Just thought she would always be here."

He places the cup gently on the stone hearth; folds a crease into the wool blanket, smoothes it again and again as the soft weave resists his hand then looks once more toward me, his gaze missing a little, so he seems to stare over my shoulder.

I touch his shoulder. "Tell me Hestos."

Hestos' eyes widen and once again fill with tears. "Your mother was the best Pythia we ever had. Generals flocked to Delphi to seek her oracles." He turns his face to the fire, so the red fire-glow flicks angry shadows across him. "I didn't protect Hipparchia. I should have brought her up here… and her mother. And Icos."

"I know what you're not telling me. Mama was Pythia, until she was pregnant with me. She chose Papa. She chose me and… I think Diokles was jealous. I see it when he looks at Mama. I think he was furious that Mama left his temple because she loved Papa."

"It wasn't only Diokles who was jealous. It was the god Apollo. When he realized your mother carried another's child, he pursued her up the mountain. I saw it all. That was before the god stole my eyes. Apollo cursed me."

I fill his cup with warm wine, add honey. I wait.

"A strange storm raged from the bay below, sweeping like the Furies up Mount Parnassos. Apollo came to her with the ice crystals, caressed and taunted her as if he was the wind's heart and would claim her."

"Thaleia, let's get out of here. He doesn't know what he's saying. Completely fool-headed. The delegation is probably at the temple." Sophia tugs me back to the door. "Come on! Let's go!" I pull my arm free from Sophia and kneel before the old shepherd. He knows what no one will tell me. He knows how my grandmother died… and why.

"So much I should have done… but I didn't. Fear is a terrible enemy."

"You were afraid of Diokles?"

"That… and shame and ridicule. I let fear destroy my life. All I had to do was tell her that I loved her." The shepherd rubs his eyes as if trying to erase the memory. "Just tell her, before she died."

"What happened?"

"Your mother ran up the mountain. I can still see her weaving between black trunks of winter olive trees, hoping to confuse the god. Your grandmother raced after to stop her. Your grandmother was a fierce woman."

"Brygos said she committed suicide…"

Hestos nods his head a quick up and down of denial and rubs the back of his neck. "Maybe you already know, seems like all the village does, but I'm too old to care anymore. I loved her… your grandmother, only woman I ever loved, but she was married. I loved her years before her husband died."

I don't know what to say. The time I saw Mama and Hestos talking together, I knew. I've always known there was something between them. But I couldn't ask. Didn't want to know. Hestos loved my grandmother, even while she was married? Another village secret. Another shame no one shared with me. *What else haven't they told me?*

Hestos tugs the blanket tighter around his slumped shoulders. The fire flickers red shadows on his face. I feel Sophia's stare, as if the moment to not ask, to not know hangs suspended between us. *I have to know. I'm sick of all the secrecy… and lies?*

"How did grandmother die?"

Hestos turns away from the fire, straightens his shoulders and looks right at me as if he could see. And still he hesitates.

"Hestos?"

"Apollo swooped down upon your mother in the form of an eagle, breaking free from the storm. Your grandmother threw herself between the god and her daughter."

I jump to my feet. "She challenged Apollo?"

"The god's talons ripped the chiton off her back; his wing feathers cut like knives on her bare skin. All I remember is blood and her screams."

Sinking to the floor beside the shepherd, I try to imagine the frail grandmother I never knew. Try to see her forcing herself between the god Apollo and her daughter. "What did the god do?"

"I rushed to help her, Thaleia, but Apollo grew enormous. His eagle claws seized the mountain." Hestos pushes against the chair arms, so he can stand. The blanket falls to the floor as he limps to the hearth.

I am quiet, afraid to interrupt him.

"He wrapped massive wings around your mother. The god—filled with lust and jealousy and his rageful desire to possess his Oracle—pushed your grandmother off the cliff with one sweep of his wing." The shepherd rests his elbow against the mantle and leans into the fire. His voice is muffled by the crack and hiss of flames and embers, but his words are clear.

I don't want to hear, but I do. I want to turn my back and leave, never know the secret, but I sit completely still and wait for my life to change forever.

"He fled back to Olympos even as your grandmother struck the rocks. He left your mother to climb down the cliff to reach her mother; to hold her as her life's blood flowed over the rocks. There was nothing I could do to help either of them."

"Why didn't Mama tell me?" The truth of his words fills me. Flames spark as I poke the fire to life. "Apollo was jealous because his Oracle fell in love with a mortal? Why would a god be jealous of a mortal?"

"Ask instead why one god is jealous of another god."

"What are you saying?"

"It's funny. She didn't meet your papa until later. I'm sure she had told me she was pregnant before she met Icos. That can't be."

"Are you saying Mama was pregnant before she met Papa? That's crazy."

"The gods are jealous like men. We pray to them and honor their power and wisdom, but they're just like us with their loves and betrayals."

"You're saying Papa isn't my father?"

"It's nothing. Don't listen to me. An old man's memory is worthless."

Hestos' voice is almost lost in the fire's crackle. "Love. Love was your mother's downfall, Thaleia. Love and her own stubbornness. She angered the gods. May they bless and forgive her now. Diokles wanted her to abandon the child. Even though she was pregnant, he wanted her to continue as Pythia. She was that good an Oracle. As long as she left the infant to die, she would still be Pythia. She chose her love for you and your father over communion with the gods. Over the most powerful position in all of Hellas."

"Who is my father, Hestos?" I kneel before him and take his hands. If I could reach his gaze, maybe I could will him to tell me what he knows. But his eyes are cloudy white and will not divulge his secret.

"It is not my secret to tell, child. Ask your mother."

CHAPTER TWENTY

Black Blood Drips

This is crazy. Is it just an old man's ramblings?

Sophia takes my hand. "Your grandmother's death wasn't an accident."

I know only one thing: Mama abandoned the Pythia's tripod to save me. Now it's my turn to help. I must save Hestos. There's no time! I wrap one of his sheepskins over his bony shoulders and lead him to the door.

"Sophia, help Hestos back down to my house. Explain to Papa. Tell him about the Persians."

"But Thaleia, I want to go up to the Sanctuary with you."

"Please, Sophia! I need to go! I'll tell you everything I hear and see, but I must go, and we can't leave Hestos here."

Maybe it's the urgency in my voice, maybe it's because she ran away and left me on the mountain with Pan, maybe it's because she loves me, but Sophia carefully guides Hestos out the door.

He wrenches his body around to protest.

"Hestos, there's no time."

His shoulders slump, and he allows Sophia to lead him down the path.

I don't wait to watch them disappear. I race uphill toward the Temple. I need to hear for myself what the Athenian delegation asks Diokles.

I force my way up the back path through laurel and dead branches. The back goat path is steeper but more direct. My legs shake.

Rushing around the back wall as fast as I can, I hurry down the steps of the Theater of Dionysos. Breathless, I peer through the gate before running beneath the wide-stoned portal into the Sanctuary. A nobleman in rich furs stands with folded arms in front of the altar, a small garrison of soldiers flanking him. Garlands of braided purple laced with gold hang from his shoulders. Just before him—a step higher so he is as tall as the nobleman—is Diokles. The nobleman bows his head reverentially.

I strain to hear Diokles' words.

"That's what Apollo prophesizes, my royal one: O pitiful men, why do you sit here? Fly to the ends of the earth, leaving your houses and wheel-shaped city. Everything falls to ruins—head, hands, middle body."

"No! That can't be."

"The god has spoken, I tell you. The oracle is clear: Now your statues are standing and pouring sweat. They shiver with dread. The black blood drips from the highest rooftops. They have seen the necessity of evil. Get out, get out of my sanctum and drown your spirits in woe."

The Athenian sinks to his knees and clutches his bare head. His soldiers gather close, each weathered face stunned and disbelieving. Crushed by the Persians? They don't believe it. They won't believe it.

Diokles throws back his shoulders and commands. "Leave the Sanctuary and gird yourselves with courage to meet misfortunes!"

"Athens destroyed by the Persians? Never!"

Not Athens! They can't destroy Athens! Diokles is lying because he wants to curry the favor of the Persian king. Those are Diokles' words, the priest's betrayal, not the god's!

If only I could just tell the envoy that it's all lies. Diokles doesn't hear the god. He is playing for political power, manipulating. I have to stop him, but the Athenian would never believe me. Diokles would deny I'm Pythia. I need a plan.

I slow my steps as I approach my home. I don't want to tell Mama or Papa what I heard. Not yet. Diokles would have them murdered, like he drowned me. It's too risky. I need to think.

Sophia sweeps leaves from the courtyard and looks up the moment I enter.

"Sophia, come with me."

Hestos is asleep on a corner bench, a blanket draped over his shoulders. "You got Hestos here. Thank you."

"What happened?"

I motion to the spinning room, grab our spindles and enough wool to last the day. "Diokles told the Athenian noble that they should run away. He told him that Athens will be destroyed and there is nothing they can do!"

Sophia's jaw drops. She clutches her spindle and stares at me.

I shake my head in disbelief. "It's more lies."

"Why would he say that? Maybe this *is* Apollo's Oracle," Sophia says.

"The gods wouldn't turn their backs on Athens. No. Don't believe it for a minute, Sophia." I grab both her hands. "Remember the spider, Sophia? I didn't tell you—I turned the temple columns into oak trees. Apollo spoke through me. Through me the god gave a prophesy to King Leonidas of Sparta. Trust me Sophia. You of all people must believe me! Diokles' words are false."

"You heard the god? What was his oracle?"

"He said either a king or a great kingdom must fall. A city or a king will be torn limb from limb."

"Will Hellas be defeated by the Persians?"

"The Spartan king will have that choice. I trust King Leonidas."

I turn away and stare out the small window that opens to the back of my home with a view of cliff and the winding goat path that leads between crevices to high vineyards and Pan's clearing.

A man's form fills the window. I shriek and jump back.

"Thaleia, it's me… Parmenides. Quick! Let me in! I've brought the Athenian."

Two men stand just outside: Parmenides and the Athenian nobleman I saw in the Sanctuary. He crosses laurel branches over his chest. His eyes are dark with suspicion.

The Hierophant rushes around to the front gate, pulling the other man behind him. "You will see, Euthros. Please, come in and you will have your answer."

The man takes a broad step into my courtyard. Parmenides closes the gate quickly behind him.

I bow my head to the nobleman then turn with one motion to Parmenides. "Thank you for bringing him here. I didn't know how to help."

"Diokles told him Apollo foretells the destruction of Athens. But I convinced him to ask again. To return as suppliant with laurel branches to appease the god Apollo."

Before I can say anything, the nobleman questions me. His voice is trembling. "Are you the girl who they say spoke the oracle to King Leonidas?"

I nod.

"The same girl who changed the sacred temple columns to oak trees?"

"I am." I take a deep breath and wait for my destiny to twist its next turn.

The nobleman drops to one knee and holds out the laurel branches. "Grant us a better oracle for our homeland; respect these suppliant boughs which I hold. Otherwise I shall not leave, but will remain, until I die."

I look down at the man's back then stare at Parmenides.

"Know thyself, Thaleia," he says. "It is your time."

Once more a great calm fills me. A power to dream. To speak the god's will. Once more I am the stone and trees, the wind itself. I am the mountain.

Hear me Thaleia. It is time to speak my words. Hear me and speak them well.

My chest aches; heat flushes my face; my fingers tingle as if fire races up my arms and tightens my throat. A deep voice escapes me.

I make a second prophecy: Though all else shall be taken, Zeus, the all-seeing, grants that the wooden wall only shall not fail. Do not await the approach of horsemen or the arrival of foot soldiers from the continent. Turn your back and depart. A day will come at holy Salamis, when you shall face them again.

Sophia tells me later, as the day fades and I lie cradled in her arms, that I spoke these words as if in deep trance and then fainted. The Athenian rushed away with Parmenides close behind.

"Did Apollo speak through me again? Without the sacrifice, the sacred fumes? Without being seated on the holy tripod?"

Sophia brushes my hair, her eyes solemn. "He did, Thaleia. You said Athens must trust their wooden wall. Does that mean the wall around the Acropolis?"

"It's nonsense. It doesn't make sense. How can a wooden wall protect Athens?"

"You must believe. You are Apollo's Pythia."

"Did the god come looking for me? I don't remember anything. Not one word. And I don't believe any of it either."

"Trust Apollo, Thaleia."

Should I trust the god who murdered my grandmother? Was Hestos telling the truth? I keep my doubts to myself.

"The Athenian told Parmenides that one-and-a-half million Persian foot-soldiers destroyed Phthiotis and are already almost through Malis. Thermopylae is just ahead on their path of destruction."

A few days later, on the eleventh day of Boukatios, an autumn storm blows in and the Persian navy—over 1200 strong—reaches Magnesis. Where are our soldiers? Where is King Leonidas?

CHAPTER TWENTY-ONE

13TH DAY OF BOUKATIOS

NIGHT OF PAN

On black night Parmenides dresses me in deerskins and a crown of ivy.

"What must I do?"

"You must claim your destiny. You will be Initiate in the Cave of Pan."

"How?"

"You are virgin?"

Looking away from his gaze, I nod then force my eyes to meet his.

"Sacred union with the god Pan will reveal your divine power. This will be your initiation to womanhood and marriage. In your initiation, you will become Persephone—child of Demeter, wife and queen of Hades. You will marry the god, Thaleia. Only then will you truly be Pythia."

My initiation to womanhood—not the one I anticipated and dreaded for so long: my marriage to Brygos—instead I will have my initiation into the Mysteries. My Night of Pan.

He hands me a thyrsus—a staff twined with the carved image of a snake. He walks with me up the Sacred Way, before we cut off to follow the narrow path, seven miles—mile after long mile up to *Korykio Andro*, the Cave of Pan. As we had hoped, we are not noticed in the bleak night. Our torches sputter and flicker, drenched by sea-driven squall, but they stay lit.

My hair is plastered to my back. I shiver with the storm and with dread. I thrill with a strange new power that fills me more with each step I climb.

Just at the cave entrance stands a statue of the ancient fertility god—heavy haunched, squat, broad browed with erect phallus.

I straighten my shoulders and call out, "Pan? Are you here?" Parmenides and I wait. Nothing. No sign of the satyr-god. Only the rain sleeting down our backs.

We walk through the wide cave mouth then sweep our torches side-to-side trying to see into the dark shadows, checking for panther or bear, before we stick the flaming branches into wall stanchions. Dripping water echoes off dank walls. The air is cold, smelling of mossy stone and charred branches from long-dead fires.

Our torchlight flares against limestone boulders. For a breath, it stuns me how massive the cave is, at least the equal to twelve thyrsus high and maybe as much as twenty or thirty wide, a great gaping maw that howls in answer to the storm-winds. I hear laughter from deep shadows, far back in the cave… and what? There's power coming from the vulva of the cave, as if its womb is dark with life juices and blood, like my own life-change, the night the blood of my courses stained my sheepskin pallet.

"Back there! By that boulder. Do you see?" Parmenides nudges my arm with his elbow.

I peer farther back into the cave. A darker shadow shifts in the black crevice. The hair lifts on the back of my neck, as flute music swells around me. Parmenides hears it and pushes me to go alone toward the music. I sense another stands just beyond a phallic stalagmite. I grab my torch and lift it high above my head.

"Parmenides? Pan is there?"

There is a sigh like wind through river reeds, a breath that carries the smell of yeasty bread or hops. I step toward the living darkness. The musty smell is replaced by sweet narcissus and lupine.

"It is your time, Child. I will wait here for you."

"What do the gods expect from me? What will they demand? What will they require?"

"You are Initiate. You must discover your way without me at your side. Don't be afraid."

I move away from Parmenides and step around the stalagmite. My torch-fire warms dark rock edges. Only a few feet beyond, the walls fade into black. Above me is a quick flitter of bat wings. I cringe and duck back instinctively, wave my torch high above my head so sparks fly. Something moves just ahead. I can hear my heart beat fast and wild as if it echoes from the stone chamber. I try to peer into a dark gash in the stone. There is a step close to me—a staccato clatter—but I see nothing.

Three more steps are followed by a long silence.

The chamber fills with an alluring scent of honeysuckle and crocus. A cold draft sweeps my loose hair into my face and tangles it across my eyes. And in that wind, that moist breath, as if the cave itself sighs, I once again hear Pan's breathy flute melody, haunting and joyful, mingled with the percussive drops of water from the far darkness of the cave. Tears of joy fill my eyes.

As Pythia, Mama communed with her god. Tonight is my union and my divine power unleashed. I step to my destiny.

"Pan, are you here?"

My heartbeat races.

I crouch to fit through a narrow passage. Pan steps from the shadows. He seemed gentle and playful when I first met him that summer day. But in the dark cave, his hairy goat legs and horns—one cracked all the way to its base, a dirty gully disappearing into thick curls—unnerve me.

With nimble fingers, he traces my lips then leans his broad forehead against my chest. Leaning back, he peers at me. His face—only inches away from mine—is golden like the sun. His eyes reflect my own.

"Thaleia." Pan's voice is deep, rich as black soil. "Thaleia, tonight you are *Teleste*—Initiate."

The hummingbird, mother-of-pearl green with a slash of crimson at its breast, flits through the satyr's curls as if they are flowers.

Pan smiles at me. His tongue slips moist between full lips. I gasp as his smile floods me with warmth rushing from my belly to my face. Am I ready for this union? For a moment my muscles tense to take me away, out of the cave, away from the goat-man. But the satyr pulls me deeper into the cavern.

We stop beside a low sacrificial altar. It is a block of marble, rough-hewn like the cave walls. Etched on the sides are the words: Pan—Shepherd of all Nature. There are bloodstains in the stone bowl. I stare at the blood. Sacrificial blood.

At the sight of the dark stain, I feel light-headed and dizzy, consumed with a sharp understanding of the sacrifice. I reach out and grab Pan's muscled arm. He turns to me and seizes both my arms, lowers me to the damp floor. When he touches me, a vision takes me.

A goat kicks and bleats, pulls with sinewed legs sturdy from its days of rock clambering, while two women hold tight to its horns. An ancient priestess—dressed in deer pelts, her weathered skin painted red, pine boughs woven for a crown—slits the goat's chest. Warm blood splatters my face and tunic. Nervously, I lick my lips and gag. They are sticky, salty. I wipe blood off my face.

The younger priestess bows to me; lifts a necklace of goat knucklebones from around the ancient one's reed-thin neck and places it over my head. The ancient priestess extracts the goat's beating heart, places it in my hand and intones, "Daughter of Demeter, may you find power over the Lord-of-Many-Names who rules the Underworld."

The heart pulses, alive in my hand. Each throb fills me with a deep connection to every living thing. I feel the boulders the goat climbed, the grasses he ate and the sun on his back. With a great surge of compassion, we are one, this simple goat and I.

I know what I must do.

I place the heart back inside the cavity of skin and fur and curving bones rounded like the hull of a ship. With a pass of my hand over the wound, I heal the knife's incision. The goat licks my bloody hand.

"Thaleia?"

I hear Pan's voice as if from a great distance. Awareness seeps back, my vision of the priestess swallowed by the dark cave. I am lying on the stone floor, my arms wrapped tight across my chest. The satyr crouches on his haunches before me, his gaze a steady command. For a moment I hold my breath, caught between the goat's rebirth and Pan's strong body.

"I was Initiate in another life?"

"Many lives have brought you to this day. You have a sacred path to walk."

"I am ready to accept their gift." I stand. "I am a Healer, one who carries the god's light. I know that now. I understand."

"Sit a moment on the wide-danced stone, and I will cast your oracle."

I sit and touch the altar lightly with one finger then tuck my legs beneath me.

Pan sings an incantation: "Dionysos and Apollo, divine brothers of light and dark, Lord Hermes, lead the way!" He takes my hands.

There is a sharp pain, like stepping on a glass shard that jolts from my fingertips to my chest.

"In silence. In your heart, you must form your question, Thaleia. This night of your initiation, you may cast the knucklebones, these five *astragaloi* donated by a nimble-footed goat. They will reveal your path. Be clear, Thaleia. Be honest when you question the gods."

I juggle the five bones in my hand. *Poor goat.* I turn them like grist in a mill; feel the valleys and mounds in the bone. Before this night, I would have asked if I would marry for love. But all that is changed.

I silently form my question: *What is my destiny?*

I cast the five knucklebones. I hear each bone scatter, a distinct clatter of bone against stone.

"Hexas. Hexas. Tetras. Hexas. Hexas… six, six, four, six, six."

A slight smile dances at the corners of his eyes and lips. "An auspicious oracle, Thaleia. Twenty-eight. Apollo has spoken: With the help of Tyche, goddess of fortune, you will walk your path among the gods."

He pulls me to my feet.

A spider strand threads from my fingers. I sense my mother and the Pythias before her—woman-to-woman, Oracle to Oracle, each connected by the strand. I thrill with their power and love. Time swells and throbs as if the cave will birth me, cast me into a new world, where I am Pythia, Oracle savior of our Greek way.

Pan strokes my forearm, my shoulder and caresses my hair.

Lifting his syrinx, he plays a lustful tune—a song of wind in ancient trees, nymphs dancing naked through them… he dances circles around me.

Pointing his long finger at a cold fire-pit, flames leap to life. Our chamber fills with light and warmth. Smoke curls and fire dances to his melody.

"It's beautiful!" I laugh.

"You're beautiful, Thaleia."

I'm glad the fire casts red shadows across us, and the satyr does not see me blush.

He leans closer, his step a clatter of hoof against stone. He caresses my cheek then cups his hand behind my head, strokes my chin, sloping down to the deep hollow carved beneath.

"Don't be afraid, Thaleia." He holds out a thick, wooden bowl to me.

The satyr's brilliant blue eyes stare at me over the steaming bowl.

"Drink, Teleste-Initiate."

His command is both stern and cajoling. The cup brims with a bubbling liquid, golden as liquid amber fresh from a tree wound, sweet smelling with honey and nutmeg.

I hesitate a moment, remembering the drink Diokles gave me.

Sensing my thoughts, Pan laughs. "Ambrosia. A gift from Dionysos. You must drink."

"Legend says that if a mortal drinks ambrosia of the gods, she will die."

Pan smiles at me, and suddenly I don't care. I take the wooden bowl from his strong fingers and tip it, sipping the honeyed liquid. Overwhelmed at first, I want to hold on to something, anything to stop my head from spinning, but the only thing close enough to grab is Pan's shaggy thigh, and I'm afraid to touch it.

I stare, as his leg seems to blaze. His golden hair shifts, forming lines and patterns. A sweet fire fills my head and sweeps through my chest. I tear my eyes from the tangle of his hair and look around the cavern. The harsh cave-stone softens with a living glow. Walking over, I trace lines etched in the stone. A vibration tingles up my arm and into my chest. "These were drawn by the ancient ones, weren't they Pan?"

Pan smiles and joins me. The carvings are worn and faint, so I move my head side to side, trying to see them better.

The satyr's strong fingers turn my chin to look at him then he rests his other hand over my eyes so I can't see anything. Leaving my eyes covered, he takes my hand, stretches out my fingers and traces the design carved in the stone over and over. A circle on top of a triangle, two lines straight down, two lines on the side of the triangle, crooked so that an oval sits on top of them.

I don't understand and try to pull back from his hand covering my eyes. He presses his hand more firmly over my eyes and traces the lines again. A circle on top of a triangle; two lines straight down, two lines… a line drawing of a woman… a woman holding a baby. I pull his hand away and peer eagerly at the stone, lean so close my nose almost touches the stone, but Pan is wise. The lines you can see make little sense. They are worn away, just vague scratchings that are easily confused with the white veins of limestone.

My fingers see more clearly. I trace the lines again on the stone.

A sweet fire fills my head and sweeps through my chest. The ambrosia makes me light-headed and burns my stomach, but while I look around, I am overwhelmed with a feeling that nothing can harm me.

I look back at the wall dancing in firelight.

The triangles and circles carved into the stone come alive. Stick figure-carvings rock a babe in arms, kick a leg high and stomp the hard stone. It's as if these ancestors sing to me, urge me to do something: *We are all part of the human dance. Join in! Dance your dance! Birth a child and sing sweet lullabies. Anything. Anything but sitting back and waiting for others, holding back with fear and doing nothing to help.*

I laugh and whirl to face Pan.

Pan lifts the reed flute to full lips and breathes a melody. While he plays, he prances around me.

I stand completely still. I never understood how alone I felt. No one heard what I heard. Saw what I saw… always so alone. But at last I understand. I am Pythia, sister to all the women who came before me. Sisters who called the gods' oracles. Forged the connection between gods and mortals. I am not alone.

My chest aches from the music's force… as if it is my heartbeat. I want that power for my own. "Tell me what I must do!"

"I'm sure you know the myth of Persephone, Thaleia. Tonight you are kore-maid Persephone. As Teleste, I will tell you her story so you share her Mysteries. Hades, god of the Underworld, kidnapped Persephone and dragged her down to his dark land to be his wife. Her mother, Demeter—goddess of the seasons and fruit of the harvest—was enraged and turned our earth to perpetual winter. When I walked the mountain paths, wandered the high cliffs, all I felt was death. Cold. Endless winter."

Pan blows into his flute and plays the winter winds before resuming his story.

"Great god Pan, how was Persephone captured and dragged to the Underworld?"

"A bargain was struck with all-seeing Zeus, her father. He was the one who consented that she be Hades' bride. Struck with the maid's beauty as she wandered amongst meadows of crocus and narcissus, Zeus' brother, Hades, pleaded that she be his wife. And so it was Zeus the Loud-Thunderer agreed."

A vision of Brygos, my betrothed fills me. My father also gave me away. Suddenly sick and disoriented, I feel cold and clammy. The cave walls seem to close in on me. My vision darkens with a sense of foreboding.

"Winter months… gray months of Demeter's sorrow," I whisper, my head spinning.

Pan rubs his eyes. He looks tired, weary as any farmer struggling with drought and parched vineyards, cracking earth and dust, where fertile mud is needed.

I want to comfort him.

"After The Host-of-Many abducted Persephone, my mountain meadows never blossomed, the birds hid beneath brittle laurel, never leafing out with spring." The satyr shrugs his muscled shoulders and moves closer. His shaggy hair is soft against my arm. He smells of pine and summer dust.

"Demeter found Persephone after searching long months. 'Tell me you ate nothing in the shadowed halls of Hades,' the Goddess demanded to know of her daughter. But the kore was secretly given three pomegranate seeds by Hades. She could not leave the Underworld."

"Mama told me she comes up from the dark world every spring. That's why we have flowers and sweet grasses…"

"Seeing Demeter's great sorrow, Zeus intervened and allowed Persephone to live all but three months of the year with her mother on the wide-pathed earth."

Pan looks closely at me, strokes his beard, combing his fingers through a tangle of matted hair. "Three pomegranate seeds, that's all. But when swift-footed Hermes was sent to bring the girl home, three seeds required her to return to the Underworld three months out of the year."

"What are you saying?"

"Persephone has the power to come and go to the Underworld, but there is a price. The gods always extract a price."

"I am Persephone… and there will be a price."

The satyr pierces me with a look, a gaze that feels like a knife thrust in my chest. Just for a moment. A breath before his eyes calm. "When the girl returns to the Land of the Shades, her mother and the earth mourn. It is bitter winter."

The flames leap higher and flare in his deep-set eyes. "In those winter months another god comes to the Temple of Apollo, half man, half woman: Dionysos. This companion to the nymphs and the deepest song of the forest brings life… hope… rebirth to mankind."

A shiver races up my spine, a premonition that Hades and I will cross, that he will lead me captive to his dark realm.

"What is my place in this legend?"

Pan bows to me, takes my hand and pulls me toward him. "There was a prophecy thousands of years ago… my prophecy. Thaleia, you are chosen. The gods convened and chose you. We all agreed."

I swallow hard and try to gather my courage. At last I ask. "What is the prophecy?"

His answer, thunderous and deep, echoes in my mind as if the cave speaks his words.

"A beetle will crawl from earth-stone, no longer grasping the sun of immortal sun-god Apollo. Between its black pincers, the scarab will carry a child sacred to Dionysos, a girl who will bind mortals and immortals for time everlasting."

"They chose me." I only notice I am shivering when the satyr wraps his arms around me and presses my head against his chest. So quiet and calm, I hear his heartbeat slow and regular. His strong arms hold me, but they are gentle. They protect—not trap.

For a moment, Pan leaves to allow me a quiet moment to consider my prophecy. He steps to a shadowed crevice and lifts the top to a *kiste*, a sacred chest and then removes something so small I can't see anything in his closed fingers. "I waited many years for that child. I waited for you, Thaleia. The gods chose you to unite gods and mankind." He lifts my hand and presses three small objects into my palm, closing my fingers over them. "You are the Pythia the gods sought. With the help of the gods, you will stop the invaders. You will save Greece. You will save the gods."

I slowly open my hand. Three pomegranate seeds rest on my palm.

"Thaleia, you are the child of the prophecy."

Pan brushes hair from my eyes. Together we stare at the three red pearls. They roll, turn and swell, until they burst and pale green sprouts grow languid and twisting from each red kernel. Three trees grow in my hand. Miniature gray-brown trunks grow roots that dig into my palm, but I feel nothing. Slender leaves swirl and grow from my hand then sprout red pomegranates hanging like beating hearts from the drooping, miniature branches.

I watch in amazement as two snakes—brown of earth and blue of Apollo's sky—twine around the trees.

"The Greeks will prevail. They are rooted and strong like these trees, Thaleia. You will show them the way. You are the chosen one."

He smiles at me with a broad grin and lifts his pipes once more and plays. His smile is irresistible. I laugh. Pan spins on his right foot and leaps over the fire.

For an eternal breath there is no I, no satyr or the shadowed cave, there is only a moment of hope.

I am chosen to unite gods and mankind. I am Pythia. My mother would not abandon me to the vultures. She saved me. She knew. I am the Oracle chosen to save Hellas, to save Mt. Olympos and the gods. But how do I stop a million Persians?

As I wonder at the weightless trees sprouting from my hand, they fade. The solid, red fruit dripping from the twining branches in one moment grows transparent. The fire flares, visible through the silken branches, until the trees disappear like a raindrop sizzling on a hearthstone.

I touch the god's arm, but he doesn't seem to notice. With closed eyes, he sways side to side, lost in the song as it cascades around the stone chamber, bouncing from ceiling to wall and lifting the flames, forming brilliant patterns in the fire.

My breath is fast and shallow.

I step away from the god's closeness, shivering uncontrollably and bow slightly. "Great god Pan, sometimes this dreadful power is too much… like a god's breath devouring my life."

Pan steps past the fire, pulls me down, until I sit once again beside him.

He lightly touches his forehead to my knee before peering up at me. When the satyr cradles me, his muscled arms comfort me. His shaggy hair is soft against my arm.

The satyr takes my hand and kisses each palm.

"You are Pythia. It is time to welcome the Divine, to claim your power as Oracle like your sisters before."

I take his head in my hands and kiss his forehead.

The satyr's honeyed breath blows soft from his full lips on my brow and each palm. He rests his strong hands on my head. Power from the god and the fertile soil—the earth's song fills me. Cradled between earth and god, the firelight intensifies and my awareness shifts, lifts me until I am no longer Thaleia, a girl empowered by a god. Every part I thought was mine. Arms and legs… everything I thought was my flesh alone, melts into a cloud of light, starlight, sun, moon… we are one like salt dissolving in a cup of water. I am enshrouded by the earth's breath, a brilliant evanescence of motes of color and feeling and joy… and yes, love. My feeling of communion with this god intensifies as I lose the girl and become the Pythia, the divine messenger.

With great tenderness, he rests his hands on my shoulders. Squeezes once and then turns away. His long fingers reach three times into the fire. The flames dance and flicker around his hand, but his curly hair does not burn. He does not flinch. With grace, he plucks three poppies magically from the fire then kneels beside me. Blossom by blossom, he tucks the flowers behind my ear.

I close my eyes. My body sings with a new power.

The poppies burst into life, twist and multiply, until my hair is a storm of green stems, a filigree of leaves and blooms. Blood red in the brilliant firelight, like the deepest sunset or sacrifice, they tangle in my black hair.

"The Greeks will prevail. They are rooted and strong like those pomegranate trees, Thaleia. You will show them the way. You are the chosen one."

He smiles at me with a broad grin and lifts his pipes once more and plays.

I throw back my head and laugh.

Pan spins on one hoofed foot and leaps over the fire.

He is gone, disappeared into a back crevice of the cave, before I draw another breath. I touch the poppies dancing like Medusa's snake-hair.

The gods chose me.

Clutching the tiny pellets, afraid they'll drop; I slip back to the outer cave, grab my thyrsus with my left hand, so I can press the seeds to my palm and thrust the shaft into the air.

"Great god Pan!" I shout then lift my feet with quick dance steps.

The poppies twist, curl and leap as I pull the panpipes from my sash and play a wild dervish.

"Thaleia!" Parmenides stares at the writhing poppies in my hair.

"Dance!" I laugh. "Tonight is truly my Night of Pan! Follow me to the Temple. We will descend to the sacred adyton. There I will claim my heritage, my destiny. Apollo will tell me how to save us from the Persians! Dance, Parmenides and rejoice!"

The Hierophant waves a torch over me, sweeps his hand through the smoke, so it swirls around my head.

CHAPTER TWENTY-TWO

14TH DAY OF BOUKATIOS

YEARNING WILL CARRY YOU TO THE GODS

Dawn follows us across Mt. Parnassos as Parmenides and I retrace our steps, scrambling down the goat path. The storm lifts and brave stars struggle against the light of the setting full moon. The sun rises with Apollo's chariot of fire-gold, casting blood red off the Phaedriades, glancing like burnished bronze from the shining cliffs.

We hope to steal unnoticed back to the Temple, but the village is in an uproar. Men surge just outside the Sanctuary gate with hoes and long lances, sharpened short knives thrust through wide leather belts. Women are gathered. Steaming bread loaves and jugs of wine, cheeses, and dried grapes in large baskets hang from their shoulders. Crying babies and toddlers cling to their mother's chitons or curl safe in cloth slings draped across women's milk-filled breasts so as not to be trampled.

The hook-nosed priest—Diokles' right hand man—accompanied by several soldiers—gestures and shouts orders to the crowd.

Why is the priest with soldiers?

"Xerxes is at The Hot Gates! Two days' march away! He's reached Thermopylae!" The blacksmith pushes his way through the villagers shouting and inciting.

"There's a million, two million!"

"Hide the treasures! Hide your wives and children up the mountain!"

"Parmenides, there's no time. We have to get into the temple without Diokles' priest seeing us. Quick, follow me. I know a way."

I motion for him to follow me back up to the Theater of Dionysos behind and uphill from the Temple, into a rough-hewn tunnel for the actors in the bowels of the stage. It leads between the theater and the dressing room. The passage is narrow and damp. We grab burning torches from stanchions; the flames flicker a faint light on blackened walls as we race through the tunnel.

At last, we emerge through a small door into a storage room filled with masks and armor, human-sized wings of seagull feathers as well as shields and lances for the actors to enact the satyr plays.

"Well, Thaleia, it was your idea to come back here. Now, what do you plan?"

"In the adyton, you must guide me in *Hysechia.* In the Great Stillness, Apollo will find me. In the Great Stillness, Apollo will guide me." I hope I sound confident to the Hierophant. "I need your help now, Parmenides. I've heard you are the greatest Oracle to ever study the healing art of the god Asklepios. I want to heal all Hellas. Wash away her fear. Assure her that the gods will guide her generals' minds, the women's brave hearts and her warriors' strong arms."

Parmenides strokes his beard and nods. A smile lights his eyes. He spins on his heel, tossing his wool shawl over one shoulder and strides out the door.

I hesitate. Do I dare return to the Sanctuary?

I am Pythia.

Initiate into the Great Mysteries.

I touch the poppies in my hair and take a deep breath as I follow Parmenides out the door into the courtyard. Beyond the Cyclopean Gate, villagers shout, but the Sanctuary is quiet otherwise, too quiet.

There are no birds. Last night's storm passed, puddles fill gashes in the paving stones, reflecting the sturdy columns. The air feels thin, rarefied like they say high Mt. Olympos is. Air fit for the gods to breathe. I stare at the Oracle's receding back and run across the open space. My sandals echo in the empty silence with my shallow breath. "Apollo, greatest Healer of all, protect us!"

Parmenides runs up the temple steps.

I stop at their base and look at the fluted columns remembering them as towering oak trees. My flesh shivers with its memory of Apollo's oracle filling me.

Above me are the carved inscriptions: Know Thyself and opposite it on the other lintel, the large letter **E**. The carvings are stark, sharp-edged as if newly cut. I should hurry, but I feel like there is something the gods want me to understand. **E**—the fifth letter in the alphabet—five for our five senses. It claims my attention. Demands that I understand its meaning. Maybe Parmenides knows.

A footstep, sandal-leather against the worn marble, startles me and I whirl, squinting my eyes against the bright sunlight.

"Who's there?" I ask at the sound of footsteps.

It is only Parmenides coming back to join me.

"Are you alright? Why did you stop?"

"Why did Pan grow these poppies in my hair?" I lift one stem and let it fall.

I point up at the carved epsilon. "I think they have something to do with that **E**, Parmenides. What does it stand for?"

Parmenides looks back over his shoulder. Shouts outside the gate rise and fall like a stormy sea. "It's crazy to stop now…"

"I have to know!" Grabbing his tunic, I turn him back to face me. "I don't know why, but I have to understand this."

He looks at me in silence. Touches my poppy-hair. Cups his hand beneath my chin and says, "**E** stands for *ei*, 'to be' or some say it means 'Divine is… Divine is everything.'" He waits to see if I understand… as if we have all the time in the world and the Persians aren't just beyond our borders.

My legs want to run into the temple. Away from the shouts and fear outside the gate. I desperately need to do something to stop the invaders, but I know I have to understand this. Somehow I know that this is the key to my destiny.

So I wait.

I ignore the commotion and my own fear and try to focus and understand. "All our senses—sight, hearing, smell, touch and taste—our entire consciousness lives in that ocean that is Divine Being—**E**?"

Parmenides throws his arms in the air and beams the broadest smile I've seen. "Yes! We believe we are separate from the gods. We believe we are alone and that only the choices we make determine our destiny. We… are… not… alone. You must remember that Thaleia. *You* are not alone."

I turn away from the Hierophant unable to look him in the eye. "If there is no separation between us and the gods, why can't everyone hear the spider and see visions like I can? Why am I different?"

"Everyone *can* to some extent, Thaleia. They just don't pay attention. Magic comes on the wind to all of us. A spider weaves its web in our doorway, and we walk past without really seeing it. Maybe on that day there is a call from Pan's flute. You chase up the mountain to find the god. *You* don't ignore his call. Another might think it is only a dove in a tree."

Parmenides rests his hands on my shoulders. "Another might not hear the flute at all, might only be worrying about whether some boy loves them or whether the laundry is dry yet or if the soup is cooking too fast and sticking in the pot."

"So, no one is separate from the gods?" I look down at the marble step, embarrassed to ask my next question. "I'm not special then?"

"You *are* special, Thaleia. You were born with the power to see and hear what others do not. The link between gods and mankind is closer than you think, like two sides of one coin. Most don't see it or feel it. That **E** is there to tell us—Everything is! Not everything *was* or *will be*. Everything is *now*. But to see this, we must calm our minds like an ancient sea, undisturbed by wind or storm. Come with me."

Parmenides runs up to the sacrificial altar, pulling me behind him, shouting as he runs. "Right now you're worried about the Persians invading Greece. Are they here now?"

We stop on the highest step. He turns me to face him. "Is a vision of wild-eyed horses and fierce warriors filling you with fear?"

I tense and nod, unable to answer.

Parmenides strokes my back. His touch calms me.

"Be brave, Thaleia. You are not alone. Still your heart. You will never hear the god's voice when you are afraid. Look within and learn." Parmenides sweeps his arm through the sparks dancing from the sacred fire. "Remember when you died?" His voice drops lower.

With his last question, I am swept back to the complete joy I felt when I died, to the absolute certainty that I was not alone. I begin to understand. Diokles, Mama… even Brygos… we are not separate from each other. Love is the fabric of the eternal Divine, and I am woven into its pattern. If I want to heal Hellas, then first I need to heal myself. And to heal, I must let go of rage and anger.

Forgive.

But forgive Diokles and Brygos? That is the hardest of all.

I look up at Parmenides' patient expression and whisper, "I must forgive. Let the gods heal through me. No fear. No hatred. Will you teach me? Show me the Mysteries, the healing?"

"You finally understand." He smiles and wraps his arm around my shoulders. "Hurry!"

We run through the large main hall of the temple.

I am not afraid.

Down a narrow stairway.

I am not alone. I will save the Greeks.

A long, low corridor stretches before us. The stones lining the wall are massive, stacked without mortar, stained with seeping water where moss clings. A few wall torches are still lit. We turn the last bend and shove open the door into the secret adyton deep beneath the temple—the omphalos chamber, the bowels of the temple.

Candles burn around the edges of the small room. A few torches light the rough walls. The stone chamber is no wider than the village millstone with rough-hewn walls. The navel of the earth. This is where Mama was Pythia, where she communed with Apollo and cried out his prophecies—this blackened hole, rife with half-burned twigs torn from laurel and myrtle, left to decay on the damp floor. All the tales I've heard in Papa's taverna; all start here. The close air is cloying with sweet-smelling steam.

With one stride, Parmenides crosses the narrow chamber to a three-legged seat, the legs carved from smooth branches stripped of their bark.

The Pythia's tripod!

Beneath the blackened, leather seat, a carved mound—shaped like a beehive—releases sweet smelling smoke. It hisses from a cleft in the stone floor and drifts around the tripod legs.

Just beyond is the gold statue of Apollo. Its onyx eyes seem to follow me.

I start to feel light-headed from the fumes.

Parmenides guides me by the elbow to a shelf carved into the wall, covered in soft lambs-wool, wide enough for the Pythia to rest on. He pulls a small vial from his waist sash.

"Drink this, Thaleia. It will lead you into a deep sleep. In the Great Stillness you will find a path to help Hellas. The god may come to you as a black dog, as Asklepios the healer or even an eagle with strong talons… Apollo… but do not fear."

The drink is bitter and stings my throat. My eyes water.

Parmenides paces the chamber, whispers and cries out metered incantations, hexameter rhymes that carry me far from the temple. "Your own yearning will carry you to the gods, Thaleia. Know thyself."

I lie back and close my eyes. I immerse myself in dream, in breath, in the whisper of gods' voices as they swirl around me like *thumos,* the breath of life.

"Help me Apollo, God of Healing. Please help me." As I utter this plea, a vision…

The Persians march across our sacred land. An army so vast with camels and horses, camp followers of cooks and blacksmiths, whores and desperate villagers with no home to return to, no one to turn to but their torturer—King Xerxes.

In my dream I stand before the stone omphalos, carved like a woven basket and cry out once more, "Help me, compassionate Apollo, divine healer of mankind! Please, show me the way!"

As if the god's invisible hand sweeps aside the dust and despair, I see a spider web strand from each of my fingers, my toes, my head and shoulders—a great web sparkling with dew and light.

Parmenides' chants come from a great distance. *Toi pant' onom' estai.* Its name shall be all things.

I fall deeper into sleep and dream.

Mama steps from the space within the writhing weave, her thin frame formed from earth's mist swirling around me. She stretches her bronzed arm toward me and rests her fingers on my knee as I sit on the Pythia shelf. There is completion in her touch.

"Mama, where are we? How are you here with me?"

"As Pythia I learned to walk outside my body… to walk beside my god."

Her voice catches. There's something she's not telling me. Fear and anger swell in my throat like bitter bile. "The god, Mama? Hestos told me…"

"I wanted a home for you in the village, but the gods found you, claimed you for their own." Her voice is as brittle as the wing of a dragonfly—The Forbidden One, the banished Pythia who left her god to raise her child. "But Brygos. He knew. He found me wandering down to the village stunned and alone. It was after…"

"After? What happened to you, Mama?" I stand before her, hoping she will finally tell me what happened that day high on the cliffs when my grandmother died.

"I was out of my mind. I told Brygos I was pregnant. I told him who the father was."

"You told him about Papa? Papa was your lover, while you were Pythia?"

"I don't know why I did. He was just a young boy. He'd been Diokles' errand boy. Used to bring sweet figs and sometimes wildflowers, while I recovered from the god-trance. I had to tell someone. But later. He made us promise you would marry him… or he'd betray my secret."

"That's why you betrothed me to him? Because he knew Papa was my father? Everyone knows that. It doesn't make sense."

"He threatened to tell the villagers the truth… I didn't want that. I wanted a peaceful life for you. A normal life."

"The truth? What is the truth? Is it true what Hestos told me?"

She drifts away, her form smaller and smaller as it fades into the shadows.

"Don't leave!"

I focus on her voice and summon all my will. I have to know. "Hestos said the god Apollo murdered your mother. Pushed her off the cliff. Is it true? Mama, Apollo destroyed Kastalia. Did he kill my grandmother?"

Her voice is fractured and distant, but her words feel like a knife in my chest.

"The gods are selfish."

There's movement out of the corner of my eye, just a flutter of deeper darkness in the corner of the small chamber, a shadow looking back at me.

Apollo! The god looms massive before me.

His scream shatters the steam and smoke. His form obliterates the towering statue of Dionysos. He pulls Mama by her hair, jerking her back into the chamber. She struggles and kicks but cannot break free from the god.

"She betrayed me!" He dumps her on the high tripod.

The air between us sparkles. Black cracks flow across the floor away from the tripod, a shadow river winding its twisted path to me. With a sudden rush, his wide-eyed face lunges at me. "She betrayed me! She was my Pythia. I cherished her. In divine communion, I gave her prophecies to guide the mortal world. She betrayed me with *him*!"

Apollo points across the room as if Papa crouched behind the stone tomb for Dionysos waiting to be condemned. Yellow light shimmers around the god, licking his head and shoulders like hungry flames, until his form fractures into dancing sparks. His muscled body dressed in white silk with long golden hair flowing over his shoulders, melts until he is everywhere and nowhere, like the scattered dust of life.

Each a spark of the god.

A god seeking revenge.

I feel the god's breath on my neck. The room smells of decaying eggs.

"You are the Pythia's daughter." His voice is dark and cruel. "You are proof of her lies and deceit… her betrayal." His voice hisses in my ear.

"Will you kill me like you did my grandmother? Like you did Kastalia?" It's all I can do to form my words.

Mama slumps in the sling seat, the white vapors billow around her, lighting her arm hanging lifeless down toward the earth's maw. The sickly glow is restless, hungry. It lights a leg, an arm and her closed eyes. In the fumes, she is neither young nor old, only a woman used up, discarded by her god, left exhausted and drained.

Rage rises in me as I look at her. "Will you murder my mother?"

I raise my arms. "I am your Pythia! You will not harm her!"

The adyton fills with a tiger's low growl. It rumbles and echoes off the stone walls.

Easing closer to the tripod, I grasp Mama's foot to feel for the pulse of her blood.

She's alive.

"Apollo, all honor I bring you. Sweet hecatombs will I burn in your honor and the fat of two bulls will I dedicate to you."

Smoke billows from the fissure beneath the tripod.

Gulping, I gasp for breath as the air in the chamber thins, loses its yellow shimmer then settles back into shadow and white steam. It's terrifying to face a god without form. His power is everywhere. It pounds like a thousand goat-skinned drums inside my scull. Each strand of vapor seeping from the earth's cleft is a hissing viper dedicated to the god… to his wrath. I am surrounded and overwhelmed by the god's rage.

"You can't kill the song! It is ancient. It is rock and stars and, yes, even more terrible than tigers. It sings from twining ivy and the sea. It is life's song that unites every living thing… even gods and mortals. Even you, great Apollo, cannot kill the song of the kosmos."

With a dark cry, Apollo transforms into a ram, vast, white, his four horns twist around themselves, swirl circles, until they stretch away from the ram's curls to form two twisting snakes. They wrap around Mama, pinning her arms against her body. One snake tail flicks and tangles in her long hair, caught on the brittle, shiny scales, so that each pull of the tail jerks her head side to side. Like a helpless doll manipulated by the god.

I lunge at the godly-ungodly snake, dig my fingernails into the snake-coils and scrape off scales, pull the coils from Mama's arm and the tripod seat. Distracted, the snakes relax their hold on Mama; drape their tails over her shoulder and across her lap. Two heads turn, black eyes glare at me. Mock me. Once again the god dissolves to mist and shadow.

I'll never defeat the god by force. *What do I do?*

As if in silent answer to my question, the blind shepherd's words form in my mind. "Fear is a terrible enemy."

My senses tell me the god is gone… but he is here. **E**—Divine is. Without end.

How do I see him? How do I convince him not to kill us?

"Your mother lied and deceived me." His voice shatters off the stone chamber, so loud that I cover my ears and fall to the floor.

"Forgive, great Apollo. Forgive your Pythia. Forgive my father. Do not let your hate destroy your wisdom and your power." I stand up and turn in slow circles. If only I could see him, confront him.

Swirls of smoke and fumes—bitter and acrid, sweet as cinnamon and honey—surround the tripod.

I reach up and take Mama's limp hand… and it hits me—the chain of Pythia's from moonrise to sunrise and again to moonrise. I remember the dancing figures carved in the Cave of Pan. I saw them better, when my eyes were closed.

I close my eyes and reach into the mist with my other hand. Fill my heart with a yearning to make whole, to step beyond all fear, to touch the god and see him fully.

I speak Pan's prophecy for the god to hear. So Apollo will remember his vow—

"A beetle will crawl from earth-stone, no longer grasping the sun of immortal sun-god Apollo. Between its black pincers, the scarab will carry a child sacred to Dionysos, a girl who will bind mortals and immortals for time everlasting."

I drop to my knees and lift my arms in supplication.

"Apollo, you are the god who heals our wounds. Healer, heal your own! Heal your hate and jealousy. Forgive and heal. Your Pythia did not deny you for power or revenge. She followed thumos, the heart of the kosmos. It was love that took her away from you and to my father. It was love that created me… and my destiny. It was the song of the universe. Forgive and heal, great Apollo."

My eyes fly open when the god's hand takes mine. It is strong and warm. It is gentle. I feel his other hand also wrap around my small hand and squeeze, before he lets go.

Mama smiles down at me.

The mist and fumes and smoke fade away. I hear the god's voice, brittle and clear. "I will honor my vow to the child who binds mortals and immortals. I honor you, Thaleia, my Pythia. You are brave. You are wise. Together we will save Hellas."

I jolt out of my dream.

The stone shelf is beneath me. I look over. Mama is gone. Vapors lift and twist beneath the sooty tripod seat, hissing and sighing.

Parmenides still paces the chamber in front of me, whispering and crying his metered incantations—"the mares they carry me far as yearning can reach…" He stops mid-verse and stares at me, a long hard stare.

"The god touched you? Did he tell you how to save Delphi?"

Before I can answer, pounding feet and shouts and metal against stone causes me to whirl toward the doorway.

Diokles, The Child of the Clouds, and armed soldiers burst into the sacred chamber. And Brygos!

"How dare you!" Contorted with rage, Brygos rushes me through swirls of white smoke.

CHAPTER TWENTY-THREE

THE DEATH-HAG—*KERE*

Vibrating with righteous fire, I leap to my feet and face my attackers.

A victorious smile slashes The Child-of-the-Cloud's face as she screeches the eagle's cry—

At last! This time we have you! Stupid girl. You won't get out of this alive! My power is secure!

Her words thresh my anger. White heat surges from my heart and down my arms—a desire to protect Parmenides, a fury to get even with this obnoxious creature adored by the priest. *Diokles! You drowned me…but I'm alive. Strong. Just try to destroy me this time!*

Enraged, I spin motes of light from my fingertips and whirl a red maelstrom above Brygos' head. The look of triumph on his face vanishes. I can taste Diokles' fear, as bitter as bile in my throat.

"Are you afraid of me, old man? You? A priest?" My anger pushes him back.

"Seize him!" Diokles points to Parmenides.

I shape my anger to form the *Kere*, handmaiden of Hades, daemon of death—a woman of red, vaporous flames. She waves thin, undulating arms. Viscous strands of the hag's hair flow down her back. A deep hood covers her face.

Parmenides is just beyond, his face white. "No! Don't, Thaleia!"

I point at Diokles. The daemon lunges at the priest, like a wind swept from the River Styx, the black torrent rushing dead souls to the Underworld. She sweeps over Diokles. He screams. Writhing as searing fire licks his face and shoulders. The fire-hag's hair, long, undulating flames wrap around his body. The Kere is transparent… not yet fully realized. Blazing and taunting but not burning the priest.

I keep my voice steady. "You can't have Parmenides."

Diokles' dark eyes dart fearfully between my hands and the wrinkled crusted fingers of the Kere. Her red robes thicken.

The Child of the Clouds runs to shield the priest. Before she can reach him, the Kere sweeps over her. She traps the girl. Flaming robes singe her hair. The Kere's fury explodes. The chamber smells of rotten meat.

The fake Pythia shrieks the eagle's battle cry, shrill and bold.

As the death-hag wraps her arms around the girl, the child's white hair tangles with the hag's flaming robes. The fire engulfs her. Her screams are sheer terror, beyond animal or human.

Diokles takes one step toward the girl, before he turns away and points one long finger at Parmenides. "Seize him!" the priest says. The soldiers lift the Oracle bodily and carry him out the door.

The Child of the Clouds writhes a dark silhouette inside the flames.

"Parmenides!" I rush after him, but the flames force me back.

The stench of the girl's burning flesh is awful.

"Thaleia, stay true!" Parmenides screams. I can't see him, only the soldiers' backs as they shove him up the stairs.

"Parmenides!" I rush after the priest, but stop, frozen in my flight by another eagle's cry—a death screech.

Help me! Thaleia, please help me!

"Why should I help you? You deserve to die!"

The wood door and frame are ablaze. I throw myself through the wall of fire. The air is thick with smoke. Tears sting my eyes. I choke and gasp. The smell is horrible. Two steps at a time, I race after the soldiers.

From the depths behind me, another bird call, a bird of dark night—the owl. ***Help me!*** Her cry echoes wall-to-wall, shatters into screams. ***Thaleia! Don't abandon me!***

"Parmenides!"

It's dark on the stairs. They've grabbed all the torches, but I hear bronze armor crashing against the stone passage. Shouts from the soldiers. And beyond—faint and fearful—cries from the villagers.

Thaleia, help me... the girl's cry is weak.

Then silence. The silence is worse. I sink to my knees. Parmenides' words fill me. *You must forgive, Thaleia.* If I let her die because of my rage, I am no better than she is—a false Pythia.

I whirl back.

The adyton looks like the Underworld. Monstrous and huge, the daemon caresses the girl with flaming arms. With a scream, I rush through her. I tear my dress over my head. The panpipes clatter to the stone floor as I wrap the girl's body with my chiton, holding the fabric over her mouth.

The Child of the Clouds crumbles in my arms.

So thin. So frail. How could I hate this little girl? It's the priest! Not her. Diokles controlled her. Used her.

I clutch her slight body to my chest. All I see is fire. It's as if the flames are alive and want to devour me, but I feel nothing.

Pushing through the Kere, I run to the far corner of the room and lay the girl on the sleeping shelf. My tunic wrapped around the child catches fire, but hugging her close, I quell the flames.

Whirling back to face the Kere, I snatch the panpipes from the floor. My melody is the sound of rushing water like the Kastalian Spring coursing across worn stone. Water flows from the tripod, down to the stone floor, rises to fill the sacred chamber... to my ankles, my knees.

"I am Pythia, daemona. You will be gone!"

The black water laps cold against my thigh as it rises, filling the chamber, almost covering the shelf where the child lies unconscious. Pan's song is gone. This is *my* power. *My* song. Neck muscles tight with concentration, I focus on the Death-hag. When I believe I cannot bring the water higher, or the child and I will drown, the daemona's robes sizzle, fade and sink, until she disappears into the flood. The Kere is not stronger than my music.

And still I play. Willing my song to push back the rising water, I imagine raging rivers running off a mountain, down limestone cliffs. Plummeting. Cascading.

My melody is the rising sun, morning light to sweep away dark night. The flood waters recede through cracks in the wall, leaving the sacred chamber as if I never called forth the Kere, never summoned the saving waters.

Turning back to the girl lying on the ledge, I pull the scorched cloth from her face, lift her limp hand and feel her wrist for a pulse. Nothing. Her face, black with smoke, is blistered and raw.

I stare at the girl's closed eyes and draw a deep breath. *I've murdered a helpless child.* Shaken and drained, I sink to the floor. Part of me listens for any sound from the stairs. There's nothing. Parmenides is gone. The Child of the Clouds is dead. *I failed. Pythia? Healer? I killed a child and could not save my mentor.*

Despairing, I open my hand to stare at the three, red stains on my palm. *I am chosen. The gods devise their own plans.* The girl's pale face is livid with red welts; her lips swollen. *And this poor girl? Apollo, here in your adyton you see your pythias… one manipulated by your priest… and me? Have you abandoned me?*

I sit back on my haunches and spread my arms wide. "Will you betray me now?" The dank chamber fills with light and warmth. The wet floor steams and dries. With a surge of hope, I'm filled with the power I felt my night of Pan, when the nature god spoke my prophecy and gave me the pomegranate seeds. The rough wall behind the maimed child shadows with girls—generations of pythias going back to ancient times, to the time of the Python. They are my heritage. They are my strength.

My fingertips tingle. I lean over the child's lifeless body. *A spider web strands from each of my fingers, my toes, my head and shoulders, connecting me to The Child of the Clouds.*

Her chest lifts slightly with one sigh, shallow, not soon followed by another. She sucks in a deep breath and opens her eyes.

I take both her hands and help her sit up. Our eyes stay locked one to another. Sister to sister.

I loathed you. Her dove-call trembles.

"I hated you."

You saved my life.

"I called the Death-hag. I killed you."

But you brought me back... how? She rests her hand on top of mine. ***Why?***

I'm not sure what to say. I hug her gently to me. As I hold her in my arms, it all makes sense. "If I hate, if I allow rage to turn me into a murderer, if through revenge I would justify your death? Then I would dig two graves… one for you… and one for me."

She stares at me and then untangles her thin limbs from my arms and whistles a delicate sparrow's call. Her joy surges through me. The smile that fills her face bursts into a cry of the mountain eagle. ***You saved me, Thaleia!*** But she grimaces with the effort and pain.

I hold her at arm's length and look at her. The girl's skin is scorched white like a dried underbelly of a dead fish. "Holy Apollo, Asclepius the Healer, help me," I say and rest my fingers lightly on the top of her head. But I don't wait for help. I can't wait. Closing my eyes, I take several deep breaths and will myself to return to the Great Stillness.

All her burns disappear.

Her face is once again pale and smooth as Parian marble.

The Child of the Clouds' breath comes deep and steady. She takes my hand and tilts her head back to sing the mournful song of the dove.

I hated you. I wanted you dead.

The dove song soars, bounces around the adyton.

I was wrong. You understand me. You are the only one.

The chamber shudders with deep, echoing calls of owls.

And I can help you. I know why they took the Oracle. As ransom to King Xerxes.

I jump up.

Throbbing air pulsates with owl cries, filling my heart with the girl's message—***I'll go with you. I want to help you, Thaleia.***

I feel the beat of bird cries in my chest. The girl's song gathers full in her throat, an owl's territorial cry. I lean into the hope her song carries. ***You are the true Pythia.*** She touches my shoulder. Low, comforting calls of a nesting dove bring tears to my eyes. ***Thaleia, you are the true Pythia. I'm not. I never was.***

Facing her, I trill the call of a mountain sparrow. I pull her pale figure against me. Skin to skin, we have nothing to hide. Together we stand in the stone-hewn chamber, sweet smoke wafts from beneath the tripod.

A quiet dove call is her answer.

"They intend to take Parmenides to the Persians?" I say. "I don't know the way to Thermopylae."

Pan's tiny hummingbird, wings fluttering as fast as a winter wind, flits past my face as if answering me.

In a chest beside the stele to honor Dionysos, I dig out a yellow ceremonial gown and throw it on. I grab my shawl from the sleeping shelf, careful to cover my poppy-hair.

Pan's tiny messenger flies up the steps.

I don't hesitate. I run after it. The cry of a falcon chases behind.

Thaleia! Wait! Let me come with you!

I stop on the second step, immobilized by the dark. In my moment of hesitation, she is next to me. Her long fingers light on my arm their touch as gentle as a moon-ray. It's her silence that sweeps away the remnants of my anger—nothing left but cold ashes dusting from the loathing I had felt for her, when I first understood her birdcalls, her desire for power, her determination to be rid of me.

My hand—flushed from my battle with the Kere—covers hers easily. "Stay here. Heal."

I run up the steps after Pan's messenger. The cry of a falcon chases behind.

The hummingbird twists and flits out the Sanctuary Gate and between armed villagers. It's pandemonium. Men shout orders to servants to gather swords and armor, sacks of grain. Women run with large amphora back and forth to the cistern for water in case of a long siege. Children scramble beside them clinging to their mother's chitons. The young ones laugh; the older are solemn with fear.

"Thaleia!" Sophia calls me. There's something about her shout that stops me dead in my tracks. "The Persians, they're at the pass—Thermopylae. King Leonidas is there with 7000 hoplites, but no one believes he can stop King Xerxes."

Without hesitation, I run back down to Sophia and grab her shoulders, look her square in the eyes. "They have Parmenides."

Her wild eyes fly up to search my face. She clutches my arms, her mouth open with unspoken questions.

I'm silent at first. How can I explain? I summoned a daemona… almost killed a child. What can I tell Sophia? I ask the first thing that occurs to me. "Sophia, they'll cancel the Agrionia, won't they? If the Persians are this close, they'll surely cancel the festival."

"No. They couldn't. They wouldn't dare offend the gods, now of all times." She looks around at the frantic villagers. A young girl, trying to carry a jug too heavy for her, stumbles. Oil seeps from the cracks and trickles down the path. She gives the mess one desperate look and runs away. "Thaleia, they can't cancel the festival. If we lose all fertility of our crops… the Persians are just outside Phocis pillaging and stealing the stores of grain for their soldiers. Diokles couldn't possibly cancel Agrionia."

She's right. We both stand silent before the truth of her words. I drop my arms to my side. "But you won't go? We promise each other that we won't go?"

Sophia nods her agreement and then stares at my yellow priestess robe. She rubs the fabric between her fingers and looks up at me. "Thaleia, where are you going?"

I look back up the hill hoping to spot the hummingbird, anxious to go after Parmenides. Sophia catches my look.

"You're going to the Persian camp, aren't you?"

"I won't lie to you. I have to find the Oracle."

"Let me go with you."

"No."

Anger flashes across her face.

"Help Mama and Papa. Please, Sophia. If the Persians break through... Delphi may be abandoned. The heathens are only a day's march away."

I hug Sophia again. "If I'm not back..." But I can't finish. I choke on my words. "Help them, please?"

Between us there's secrets and laughter—dancing days when we were children together. Gone. Destroyed.

"Please Sophia. Promise me you won't go to the fertility festival if it happens while I'm away."

"I promise."

Without another word, without another look back, I run as hard as I can. Pan's tiny guide swoops two times over my head and darts up the twisted path, rests with folded wings on a pine branch, then leads me all the way to the Cave of Pan. Apollo's sun casts a red flare off the Phaedriades, the sheer cliffs glinting like armor in the dying sunlight. With a swoop, its feathers brilliant from the setting sun, the tiny bird flies into the cave.

I stumble in behind and collapse beside some amphora stacked off to the side. There's water and dried figs and wine left by the celebrants. I stare a long moment at the bird. It lands on one of the torch stanchions and stills its wings. The last time I was here... the memory of my initiation washes over me.

"Pan, are you here?"

Silence. Darkness with no scent of thyme or goat. No hint of the satyr's power.

I pour oil on a pile of twigs and build a fire in the same back recess where Pan led me to my destiny. The cave is cold and damp. I run my fingers over the carvings and whistle a soft sparrow call.

CHAPTER TWENTY-FOUR

16TH DAY OF BOUKATIOS

THERMOPYLAE

Walking all day and the following night beneath large oaks, the moon scattering and dancing between clouds, I sing the birdsongs I heard from The Child of the Clouds, distracting myself as sparrows and doves and crows black as Hades answer me and follow as I scramble higher up the stone crags.

But it's much farther than I thought. The sun is bold as I follow the small bird across the plateau between Mt. Parnassos to Mt. Kallidromos and descend the steep, oak-strewn hill to the Gates. My legs throb with exhaustion, my feet are blistered, when I finally see smoke rising in the distance from sulfur springs. It feels like I will never reach them.

At last, just as the sun is about to set, I see the sea angry beneath limestone cliffs—the blood-red sea of the Gulf of Malikos surrounding tree-studded Euboea Island, lush and green beyond the narrow pass.

But I still have to make it all the way down the mountain. I stumble to the travertine hill just above Thermopylae after another moonlit night. Two days. Two nights. Each step is anguish.

As I limp down the rock-strewn hillside, round a last bend in the path, I hear a man shout and another answer, angry spiteful words surrounded by a vast silence as if thousands hold their breaths and wait.

I pray they didn't hear me stumble through the scree. With slow steps, I creep behind a large pine and peer down the path.

I'm not prepared for what I see.

Two armies face off in the pass below. An ancient crumbling stone wall—the Phocian wall built to stop wars between Thessaly and Phocis—stands between them. There are thousands of Greeks in full armor with long swords and horse-hair-crested helmets, their proud chests clad in bronze breastplates, shins covered with metal greaves. They form one great phalanx, a shield of warriors—beyond them is a vast sea of Persians. Long lances thrust skyward, mounted warriors on massive Nisaean horses, restless camels, led by the black-hooded Immortals. As far as I can see are wave after wave of humanity—soldiers, women, camp followers, and slaves.

The sun clears the mountain, its rays sharp shards of light. Bronze Greek shields cast back the dawn.

As if one massive beast, both armies scream. Greeks pound fists against bronze shields. Persian drums throb. I feel like I am Hellas, her rocks and dirt threatened. Guttural cries assault my ears. A million swords clang against bronze shields. The army's breath is a whisper of rage. Sandaled feet shuffle in the dirt and the dust of camels, elephants, warriors and one proud king sting my eyes and nose.

Down the hill I see two warriors facing off, shouting at each other. Their last cries carry up to me on a war wind.

"Be prepared to die! Our arrows shall block out the sun!" A Persian messenger threatens, his voice low as he steps close to the Spartan hoplite.

"Then we shall have our battle in the shade," the Greek laughs. Turning on his heel, he walks away from the Persian. His words are passed from soldier to soldier, and a ripple of proud laughter follows him as they part to let the Spartan through.

A strong arm grabs me from behind. I cry out, but a hand clamps over my mouth, silencing me. I kick and struggle but can't break free, can't see who it is. A knife blade presses against my throat.

"Cry out, Thaleia, and it will be the last sound you ever make."

I catch my breath. Brygos! His voice. His smell.

He forces me to face him.

"Did you miss me?" He smiles broadly. "You traveled a long way to find me."

Persian soldiers surround me. Why are they watching Brygos as if he's in charge?

A soldier wraps a hairy arm across my chest and drags me backwards uphill, as if I am a sack of barley, my heels scraping across rock and scree, and at last pine straw and back into dense trees. I struggle at first, but it's useless. The dark man squeezes tighter, crushing me against his wicker breastplate. Ridges of reed against reed dig into my back. It's hard to breathe. When I give up trying to get free and go limp, he tosses me over his shoulder and trudges on. I can't see anything but the ground.

The morning barely lights the old pines, their bark black and mossy, the ground soft with loam and decaying needles. The air smells like a crypt.

The soldiers don't talk amongst themselves. The woods are filled with creak of leather straps against swords, grunts and guttural curses in their strange tongue. *Where are you taking me?*

We reach a clearing on a hillside, just past a dark copse of pine. The soldier dumps me on the ground. A stone cuts into my shoulder. I gasp and clamp my hand over my mouth. Brygos kneels beside me, jerks me to sit and presses his knife once more at my throat. He whispers in my ear with a foul breath reeking of sour wine. "Look, Thaleia. It's your beloved. Aren't you glad we brought you to see him?"

Parmenides! I hadn't seen him in the tree shadow at first. He's slumped over, his head bowed. Blood oozes from a cut at his neck. His skin is pallid, bleached white like abandoned fish bones.

"What did you do to the Oracle?!" I jerk my arm to pull myself free, but the knife presses deeper into my throat. The sound that escapes from Brygos is more like a growl than my name. I stop struggling.

"He is our ransom for the Persian king." His eyes take me in. I shudder with their caress. "And now, Thaleia, I have you. As I always knew I would. As I always planned."

"King Xerxes will kill you."

"No, the king will give me power and land… and you, Thaleia." He touches my cheek with his left hand.

I draw myself up to stand tall and stare back; hold his stare without blinking. He stands with me. Doesn't try to stop me but keeps the knife pressed to my throat. "You saw what I did at the temple, Brygos. You saw the death-hag. I summoned the Kere. You cannot hold me!"

His knife arm trembles, but he does not draw the knife away. The blade-tip cuts my throat.

"Gods! I command you! I am Thaleia, the Chosen One! I summon you, Death Hag! Destroy these men!"

Brygos gasps. With one breath the soldiers draw breath, a breath I hope will be their last. We wait.

"Divine Zeus! Did you hear my command?" My head feels like it will burst. My ears ring. The air sparkles and spins. Birds are quiet.

"Zeus? Apollo? Do you hear me?"

There is no lightning or resounding thunder. There is no Kere. Far below us, I hear screams of the dying. Sword against sword. Cries from those shoved off the narrow path to crash far below against sea cliff, jutting stones from an angry, storm-tossed sea.

"Pan, you told me I am chosen. You told me I was the only one who could save all Hellas!"

I am surrounded only by the laughter, relieved, loud laughter as Brygos pushes me across the mountain away from the Greek army, shoves me past Parmenides. The Oracle is awake. Awake and furious. *What did I do wrong, Parmenides?* His stare leaves no doubt. He is not pleased with me.

"So, what Thaleia? Now you think you can command the gods? Such *hubris*! Such pride will be your downfall, my bride."

"I'll never be your bride, Brygos. And if you're so brave, why aren't you down there fighting with the Greeks. You're a traitor!"

I don't struggle as the soldiers lead us, half-dragging Parmenides, north across the mountainside. *Gods what do you want from me? Pan told me to choose, and I did. You brought me back to save Hellas from the barbarian invasion. You told me I was to save the gods! Why did you abandon me?* My answer is the creak of leather against wicker breastplates, men's laughter and lances pounded against stone and log and dead leaves. There is no answer from the gods.

Scrambling around boulders and thick brambles endlessly, at last I see the Persian King far ahead—King Xerxes high atop a hill sitting on his marble throne, storm clouds silhouetting him.

Parmenides stumbles down the path; his deep-sunk eyes stare at his feet. The blood from his wound has soaked his tunic through. Between one step and the next, he looks up at me with anger.

Parmenides, the gods betray me… now you?

I want to take his hand and help him, but the soldiers push me along winding rocky precipices, backtracking several times from paths that end without warning at sea cliff. At last, the trail broadens and traverses down the sandy hill, until we stand before the dark king sitting on his throne high up marble steps. Persimmon-colored banners fly against a threatening sky.

He ignores us, when we walk up, and talks in loud, commanding tones to several advisors who've spread a goatskin map across his lap. While they point and gesture to the sea, I study the king's face—a long nose and high cheekbones, black, curly beard and thick wide eyebrows slashing across a domineering face. I can't decide if his deep-set eyes speak of fear or fury… but they speak of power. His shoulders and tunic drip with gold chains and filigreed bands wrapping his crown, seated low on his forehead. He's flanked on either side by warriors, black-hooded Immortals standing as still as carved statues; long lances pointing to the sky.

Brygos shoves me from behind. "Bow to your king! Even Priest Diokles honors King Xerxes. He ordered me to bring Parmenides to the Persian king for tribute. Now, bow to the emperor of all Asia and soon the entire world!"

I shiver at the mention of the old priest's betrayal.

"Bow, Thaleia!"

My face is shoved hard against the stone step. I don't look up, but I hear a messenger run up to stand beside me.

What is he saying? What's going on? He sounds worried… no, he sounds afraid! Something about King Leonidas. What happened?

I don't dare look up. I am alone. The gods abandoned me. Greece will fall to barbarian hands.

"Thaleia," Parmenides whispers beside me. He moves closer in the confusion. "Thaleia, the Greeks are winning. They are slaughtering the Medes and the Cissians. We're beating them back, Thaleia!"

I steal a sideways glance. At least he's talking to me. I thought he might never again. His face is still pale, caked with blood and dirt, but his eyes glow.

One of the Persian soldiers shoves Parmenides. He stops whispering and just looks at me as if willing me to understand. My heart swells with hope. There is a chance. The Greeks still can gain victory. Under the cover of shouts and commands and heated questions from King Xerxes, I whisper, "How can you understand what they're saying?"

"My family was from Phocaea. The Persians forced us from our home. I understand some words passed down to us. But what matters is that we're beating the Persians!"

The soldier kicks him. He sucks in a sharp breath and is silent.

Can it be true? Is King Leonidas defeating a million Persians?

CHAPTER TWENTY-FIVE

17TH DAY OF BOUKATIOS

DEATH AT SEA

A murderous wind blew strong all night long. We spent the night in an oxen-hide tent tied to a sturdy center pole, rawhide thongs around our wrists and ankles. Every time I drifted into a sleep—more like death than rest—storm winds rumbled off the sea. I dreamt of the Kere. In my dream, she turned on me. Her fire eyes glowered. When her flaming arms seared my skin, I jolted awake. Over and over, until at last I forced my eyes to stay open and my mind alert to the guard's breath. I prayed to Zeus to help us. Morning came, and I was still awake, stiff and sore.

"Why couldn't I call the Kere, Parmenides?" All night I'd wanted to ask the Oracle.

I feel like such a fool. Why did the gods ignore me?

Our backs lean against the rough bark left on the pine-rod, so we face the tent sides like spokes in a wheel. He doesn't answer. "Parmenides, are you awake?" I ask louder. The soldier sitting cross-legged at the door flap turns and scowls at me, barking a command.

I am silent a long time. But I have to know. "Parmenides, why did the gods forsake me? Why didn't it work?"

"Thaleia, no one commands the gods. What did you think?"

I don't know how to answer. I summoned the Kere. I healed The Child of the Clouds. I am exhausted. I didn't sleep much. All night I heard and smelled… no, I felt the restless energy of war. It was a smell of anger, doubt and brazen courage. It was a smell of young men sweating all night with the fear that this would be their last night.

Was it my last night?

"Parmenides?" I say, not sure I really want him to hear. "I summoned the Kere. I healed the girl. There's power in my hands. She was dying…"

"No! You did not! The gods called the Death-hag. The gods healed The Child of the Clouds. You were only their vessel. Why do you think the Pythia must be purified at the Kastalian Spring, before she can speak Apollo's oracle?"

I feel the rope tighten, as Parmenides twists and tries to turn toward me. "The gods speak through you, Thaleia. They heal *through* you! We are all part of life's web. If we touch or break or even blow our warm breath on a strand of the web, then our breath touches each one of us. This is true, Thaleia."

He is silent a long time. Too long. I don't know if there is more. I don't know if he is so angry with me that he will not continue, but at last he does.

"Hear me, Thaleia and remember this well. Your yearning may tremble the web." His voice deepens. "But the gods *are* the web. You may be a drop of water as it spins in a powerful vortex; spins and whirls, until you feel you will burst from the power of the whirling water. But the gods are the vast sea in which that whirlpool forms."

Once more he is silent.

He's ashamed of me. He believes me a fool.

"You don't command that sea, Thaleia." His voice is softer and kinder. "But now you must forgive yourself for your hubris—that pride of yours—and hope the gods will as well. This is no time to feel sorry for yourself."

We sit a long time in silence. Wind beats against the tent sides, so they crack and flap like waves against a sea-cliff.

"Parmenides, may I ask you something?"

"Anything, Pythia."

Relieved the Hierophant still honors me with the title of Pythia, I sigh.

Strong fingers clutch my shoulder and turn me. The guard crouches before me, face to face. He's maybe five or six years older than I am, but weathered with sun and wind. His turban wrap sits low over his forehead, just above strong eyebrows and eyes black as a night sky… furious eyes. His language sounds guttural to my ears, but it's clear what he wants: Don't talk.

But there's something else in his gaze. Surprised and fascinated, I can't look away. I'm drawn to his dark intensity. His delicate hands… not what I'd expect for a soldier's hands. And there's something about the way he looks at me. It makes me want to reach out and touch his hand. With that thought, I see us lying side-by-side; a wide-running river flows nearby. I am warm and content. I am loved.

Confused by my feelings, I lift one hand and sweep it past his startled face. The spider web strands from my fingertips, snaking to his hair and narrow shoulders. Maybe I can discover who this barbarian guard really is.

I smell jasmine and see him dressed not in a soldier's uniform, but soft robes of lavender. He stands beside a broad river and stares first into the rushing water then up at a blameless sky. Two river birds fly overhead. In love, the young man thinks. And that love is a beautiful thing. An arrow flies like a black tear through the blue sky and pierces the male bird. He falls dead at the young man's feet. Limp and lifeless in the river mud, while the female bird circles above and screeches helplessly. He looks around and sees a hunter lower his bow. Filled with rage, he speaks. These words, though spoken in his foreign tongue, I understand.

"You will find no rest for the long years of Eternity
for you killed a bird in love and unsuspecting."

I come out of the vision with an idea for our escape. I look once more at the soldier squatting before me, so filled with rage, but now I know his gentle core—a poet's heart. I soften my gaze and hold his stare and wait, until his eyes widen. His tight grasp eases. At last he lets my shoulder go. I can feel Parmenides watching, twisting around the tent pole, but I never take my eyes from the guard.

"What is your name?" I ask softly. His eyes look confused. He stands up and steps back, staring down at me. "My name is Thaleia. What is your name?"

He hesitates for a moment, time for him to blink and raise a slender finger to his own chest. "Valmiki. I am called Valmiki," he answers in perfect Ionian Greek.

"You speak Greek?" He frowns but doesn't explain. "Valmiki? That's not a Persian name. You're not from Persia, are you, Valmiki? Where are you from?"

"India." Pride flashes in his eyes, and he straightens his shoulders. "Son of Sumali. We lived near the Vipasa River in northern India."

"Why are you fighting in the Persian Army? Why are you soldiering for King Xerxes?"

"We Persians come from many lands—not only India but Egypt and the Levant, as far away as Africa. The King forced many to serve him."

We are both silent. Both thinking of the million Persians facing King Leonidas of Sparta. Both thinking, undoubtedly, of wives and children left behind whether Greek or Asian.

"Let us go, Valmiki."

He stares at me in silence.

"We can help you. Let us go."

"I can't. King Xerxes would have my head."

"You must let us go. I am Pythia, the Oracle of Delphi. Apollo will honor you and protect you." *I'm no longer sure that's true, but he doesn't need to know that.* "Let us go."

Valmiki steps close, towering over me. "Why should I believe you are the Oracle? Prove it, if you are the Pythia."

"Pull my hood down." His eyes are bemused. *What must he think I have in mind?* "Just do it."

He steps close and slowly draws my wool shawl off my hair. My hair writhes like Medusa's snakes.

Valmiki jumps back.

Now. Repeat his words to him. Prove you are an oracle. Show him your knowledge. Convince him to help.

"'You will find no rest for the long years of Eternity, for you killed a bird in love and unsuspecting,'" I repeat Valmiki's couplet.

The guard drops to his knees and bows his head. "How? How do you know the beginning of my poem?"

"I am Pythia."

Behind my back, Parmenides sighs. The rope tightens around my waist as if the Hierophant is pulling away, but I focus on the young man.

"You're not a soldier. You have the heart of a poet. Please, for your sake as well as ours, for the sake of the gods… set us free."

He stands very still, crosses his arms. A crease furrows his forehead.

What else can I say? How do I convince him? An answer whispers in my heart and without taking time to think, I continue. "You were not always a good man, Valmiki. When you first grew hair on your face, you had a wife. Soon two children. But you had no way to feed them, so you robbed innocents. You murdered for gold. Now is your time to redeem yourself. This is your chance."

I can see he's shocked, but he quickly unties us. *I want him to come with us. Why? There's no time to waste.*

I smile at Parmenides then at Valmiki. "Join us?" When he nods his assent, Parmenides grabs my hand. He pulls aside the skin tent flap and peers out into the morning.

I smell smoke from dead campfires and mist from the sea. But the morning is already alive with a clatter of war and men's low voices giving orders, laughing with a humor not felt, coughing.

We slip behind the tent, unnoticed and watch as Persian warriors with long lances pointed skyward march through the encampment in tandem step. They pound clenched fists against black-shrouded chests. Each masked face stares straight ahead, ahead to the battle against the Spartans. Ahead to death. They shout a war cry as if one beast.

"The Immortals! The Immortals!" A shout rises around us fierce as pride.

Valmiki stands over us pretending to guard us, while soldiers flow past either side of the tent. Theirs is a thirst for blood. For power. For victory.

Their war song sweeps them past us. It is an old song, ancient and decayed like crumbling temple columns. A familiar song. I heard its whisper as the soldiers seized Parmenides in the Temple of Apollo. It is a song without fear, but also without hope.

"Now." I urge Parmenides and Valmiki to hurry up the steep hills away from the Persian camp. The mountain air is charged. Black clouds, dangerous clouds foment a death squall, whipping the shadowed Bay of Malia far below us. I feel the heart of the storm gather around us.

I fly up the mountain, as if the wind lifts me up. Is a god's hand helping me escape? But Parmenides clutches his side and is soon far behind. Valmiki and I stop and wait, crouching behind some sage. We're not concealed enough for my wishes. Valmiki heads back downhill, wraps his young arm around the Oracle's shoulders and practically lifts him up the mountain to reach us.

"Look!" Parmenides points back to the bay. The wind brings color to his face. His wound is an angry welt. Blood cakes on his cheek and down his neck, a black stain on his tunic.

"Parmenides, your wound."

"It's nothing. Look." He pulls his cloak around him and points again. Far below, storm-tossed on the bay, are Persian penteconters: broad, sturdy warships. There must be over a thousand. They are spread as far as I can see from the narrow strait between land and Euboea Island. Just before them, tossed in high seas are our brave Greek *triremes*—at most two hundred.

"The Persians are attacking by sea as well as at Thermopylae."

I drop to one knee and raise both arms to the storm clouds. "Poseidon! God of the deep sea and Zeus, Thunder-bearer! Help the Hellenes!" My prayer is a cry into the teeth of the storm.

The sea-swept winds rise. Heavy rains wash my up-raised face. I gasp as Persian ships round the backside of the island; emerge like some sea-creature slipping from the island-shadow. "No! Look! The Persians!" Four hundred or more Persian ships sail around Euboea Island and surround the Greeks from two sides.

We stare in horror at their warships.

"I'm going to the shore. I have to help them."

"No, Pythia. All is in the hands of the gods. You cannot control the Greeks' destiny."

I smell hope dancing away between the pelting raindrops. The will of the gods. Am I to stand here helpless and watch while the Greeks are destroyed? There's a stirring in my chest. The hairs lift on the back of my neck. Poseidon's anger is in the storm. I squint to see the ships clearer through the slanting rain.

Power surges through me. I am Pythia. I am the wind path that connects the gods and mankind.

"Storm winds! Great Poseidon and beloved Aeolus, Father of all Winds, if you will allow it, let me see through this storm. I will burn sweet hecatombs to honor you, if you will help me now." I shout to the leaden sky. Fire fills my chest.

The ships grow huge, shivering from wave crest to black wave shadow. I watch, fascinated, horrified. The ship seems so close that I reach my hand out as if I could touch the painted eye on the penteconter's prow. Squinting against the storm, I concentrate on that one Persian ship, its red form tossing in the wave froth, churned and carved by Poseidon's rage. I can't tear my gaze away as a giant wave hovers, suspended over the ship. It crashes against the penteconter's wooden planks. Persian faces contort with fear. I see them clearly between one tumult of towering water and the next.

At the ship's foremast, a woman faces the waves. With astonishment, I realize she is the ship's captain. She shouts commands to the young sailors. I hear nothing but see her mouth stretched wide, demanding, exhorting, screaming.

I tighten my eyes into thin slits trying to see through the storm. Every muscle in my back and arms tenses. I feel ropes slip through the frantic sailors' grasp. I cry out in pain as the ropes cut and burn my own fingers. "Poseidon! Let me suffer this pain if it means the gods will help the Greeks."

The wind shifts, turns against the attacking Persians to become a following wind—a death wind.

"Save the Greeks, divine Zeus!" I shout against the storm winds.

Will death take the Persians or the Greeks? Who will the sea destroy?

Another shout from the Persian captain, and they drop their wind-full sails. Lines are cut in all four hundred boats. Rudderless penteconters are dragged helpless into the black waves. I am filled with the god's wind. Zeus heard my plea.

The gods reverse the wind. They shove the Persian ships and force them prow-down into the towering waves. Parmenides clasps his hands together and raises them to the sky. With a shout, he throws his arm across my shoulders. "Thaleia, the gods heard your prayer."

I dare to hope.

I dare to believe.

Persian ships crash into each other and are shoved against the island's rocky shore, while our own smaller Greek triremes bob and lift unharmed in the narrow strait of water between the pincers of Persian ships.

I watch as Persian faces twist with fear, their mouths raging against the god's wind. Each wave, larger than the last, pulls them under, hurls them off the crest, frothing and slipping into the black trough then spits them out again. Wave after wave after wave. Four hundred Persian vessels flounder, capsize, then sink, buried beneath the cold water.

I can't look away. My senses fill with wet hemp and wood and lost cries of young sailors. They shout to their gods, cries drowned by towering waves.

All four hundred ships sink beneath the storm waves.

I shake my head. There is a chill in my bones. Cold so gripping, I feel like I sank to the sea's bottom with the drowned Persian sailors. Seagulls soar and swoop through a golden light shaft, flash past like ghosts of the drowned sailors.

I collapse to the muddy ground. The wind fades. The squall quiets as if it never was, but the sea—now calm—reflects the sun, the brilliant shaft of light like a celebration: Zeus, Apollo and Poseidon savoring their victory, clasping godly hands, victorious hands that destroyed four hundred Persian ships.

I'm spent. As if the gods' power swept through me like a wildfire, I feel purged but devoured.

"Parmenides, the Persian Captain was a woman."

"Artemis," Valmiki answers.

"The goddess of the hunt? Apollo's sister?"

"No. King Xerxes named a woman sailor by the name of Artemis as admiral of his fleet. I've heard stories of her skill and bravery."

"She's lost to the sea."

"Thaleia, there's no time." Parmenides says and pulls me to my feet.

We rush uphill, scramble over stone and fallen pine, until we can go no farther. Behind us the cries of seagulls fade, until they are only a whisper in the fraying winds.

Parmenides grabs his sides and bends double.

"Are you alright?"

He doesn't look up, just nods panting and wheezing for breath.

It feels like someone is watching us. I try to clear my mind from the storm and the sailors' deaths. I listen for Persian soldiers. Are we being followed?

CHAPTER TWENTY-SIX

18TH DAY OF BOUKATIOS

THE SPARTAN THREE HUNDRED

"Let's rest here. We can hide behind these boulders." I pull Parmenides' wet hair away from his face.

"We shouldn't stop yet, Thaleia." Parmenides peers back downhill. Rain once again spatters the stone around us, scraping rough branches together. It's beautiful, but this way is too well known. It could spell our death.

"You need to rest, Parmenides. I don't hear anything. Just for a moment." I take his elbow and lead him farther uphill off the path. Valmiki follows us. We sink down behind a large, barren rock.

The air is eerie, as if something alive, a beast that will claim us. We crouch behind the limestone boulder and struggle to catch our breaths.

"What was that?" I hold my breath and listen. There is a rustle of needles a short distance down the path. A sigh as if Death follows us up the mountain. I shake my head. I feel surrounded by a black will to destroy.

I don't need to look.

I know who's following us—the Persian Immortals.

This back trail leads to the Spartan camp! The Greeks will be surrounded!

"This way, Captain!" I know that voice. It's Brygos showing the Persians the secret back path, so they can surprise the Greeks and attack the Spartans from the rear. His greed. His lust for power will betray us all.

Death is in the air. Every breath I gulp is stale with its bitter taste. My mind races with images of bloodied Greeks, wailing wives clutching orphans to their breasts. I can't shake the vision. I grab the Oracle's hand. Valmiki rests his hand on my shoulder. We struggle straight up the mountain, keeping massive oaks and boulders between our escape and the Persian Immortals.

When I can no longer hear the rustle of armor and scrape of boot against the mountain, I signal for us to traverse our way back to the path. We have to stay ahead of them. We must warn King Leonidas and the Spartans.

We stop when we find enough silence on the path behind us that we can bend double and try to catch our breath, try to ease the pain in our sides and legs. Parmenides stumbles and collapses to the ground. "Go on without me." His voice is weak. A dark shadow crosses his face, but he waves a dismissive hand at me. We crouch down beside him. The gash on his neck, opened fresh with his exertion, oozes bright red blood.

"Parmenides, you are Healer. Can you heal yourself? You're losing a lot of blood." He doesn't hear me. His eyes are glassy and unfocused from so much blood loss. I press my gown against his face to try to staunch the blood. He winces.

A branch snaps down the trail. Valmiki and I pull him back to hide behind an ancient oak, old as the sky, its bark rusted with lichen.

Two Persians come into view. They scan the hillside with restless eyes, their gazes sweeping past our hiding place. We hold our breaths. My hand is on the Oracle's leg as if I can will him to stay quiet, to not moan with his pain. He has a wild look in his eyes.

The soldiers are less than a stone's throw away—heading straight toward us.

Suddenly, I am intensely aware of heat in my hand resting on Parmenides' thigh. It seeps up my arm like sap in a tree, expands my lungs and rushes all at once to a piercing flare between my eyes. I don't move or breathe. The air around us is breathing for me. A deep sigh slashes the storm clouds and whirls invisible strands of heat around us. Calming my heart, I breathe in and out. I sit completely still, aware of a tingling in my fingers. *Tendrils grow from each finger and wrap pale green shoots around us—the Oracle of Elea, the Indian poet and the Pythia of Delphi.* My power rises in me like solid stone, as if my body is the mountain, cracked with sacred springs and night winds. I breathe in and out again but do not move. Closing my eyes, I will myself to urge the power from between my eyes, down my arms. The heat surges from each finger into Parmenides. He opens his eyes. They are calm. A careful smile lifts his lips. Neither of us moves.

The Persians are three steps away. As if outside my body, I sense how they must see us: a tangle of ivy vines, dark and wild and unpassable. They veer aside, heading back downhill. They are gone. Silently, I bless Pan for all he taught me about trees and sacred springs, the power they possess, flowing like nature's whispered song waiting for us to listen.

My hair brushes the Oracle's pale cheek, when I lean close to feel if there is breath escaping his parted lips. His eyes are glazed over, his lips half-open. "Parmenides?"

Valmiki kneels beside us and rests his ear on the Hierophant's chest.

When I squeeze the Oracle's fingers, they are limp. I breathe deeply and focus on the burning point between my eyes, willing Parmenides to live, to breathe, to come back to us.

My hope is to find that quiet place where I can heal this wise man. Instead, with dizzying speed and a whirling, spinning of sky and trees, we fall into a tunnel of absolute darkness. We are held as if an unseen hand carries us down into the earth's bowels. My ears fill with a churning sound like water rushing over boulders or wind between ancient trees. And something else. In the black void, I become aware of shifts of light—gray against black.

More terrifying—there are cries and sobs in that rushing wind.

Death Shades, hero's wraiths, some young, others withered with age—all eager to return to the earth's trees and light—brush against us as we fall. They cling to my skin, like tendrils of a spider web. Their frail whispers weave around our plunging bodies, still dense with blood and skin and bone.

"Look at me. No, look at me. Save me! Help me!" Their thin pleas surround us like spray from the sea.

I squeeze Parmenides' hand tighter, but there is no response. Stone walls fly past, slick with mold and slime as if we've fallen through the earth's crust.

Is Parmenides dead? Has he swept me down with him to the Underworld?

I came to this dark world once before. As initiate to Death. As guest of Hades. This time I come as intruder to rip aside the veil between life and The Lord-of-Many-Names.

The air grows hot and thick. I can barely breathe. Far below, I see a river snaking its way between stone and mud banks. Fire flares and ripples on the surface of the raging water. We fall closer and closer. The heat sears my skin. I cry out, when my feet plunge beneath the flames. My knees. My thighs.

Parmenides squeezes my hand. *You're alive?* His voice fills me, like warm tears washing over me. "Thaleia, Hear me. The Fire River's not real. Death and the Void do not exist!"

I want to believe him, but my feet, my calves, my belly are on fire. The heat is unbearable. My skin blisters. The smell of burned flesh and sulfur makes me gag. I scream.

But Parmenides' voice stays calm and insistent. "Can you feel my hand? That is real. Your fear makes this land of Death real."

But the flames? The stench of rot and flesh and the earth's foul breath?

Parmenides clutches my hand tighter. "There is only Being. Life. Squeeze my hand, Thaleia."

"I can't. I can't feel your hand. Parmenides!"

Shades brush against my face. "Give us blood. Give us our lives. Help us."

The Oracle's body falls limp beside me. "Parmenides!"

"Blood" the Shades answer.

Flames seethe and roar around me.

Parmenides says something, but I can barely hear him as his voice drifts away with the Shades. "Trust me, Thaleia… yearning will carry us… eternal longing of life for life… you must not be afraid."

His body floats off, his strong torso fades to gray, mingling with mist and Shades, moans and cries, until there is little left of him. His strong jaw and black hair and fine robes—nothing but a tattered sail left years in the salt wind, frayed and limp.

Panic tightens my throat. The heat is unbearable.

Parmenides' voice fills the chamber, echoes from the stone walls. "Trust the gods. They determine my destiny. Not me. Not you."

These are my mentor's last words: *Trust the gods… but I don't. Apollo killed my grandmother. I dare Hades to claim Parmenides!*

I should never taunt the gods.

A face thrusts from the flames, shoving aside frantic Shades. A god's black face, as if etched in stone—The-Lord-of-Many-Names, Hades, god of the Underworld. He turns his massive head side to side through flames and cries, shadowed by smoke like a half-remembered nightmare. He startles and whirls around to face me. His broad chest is encased in a gold breastplate. He reaches for me with muscular arms. His fierce eyes flare with anger.

"Intruder, who are you? Who is your family? From what rocky soil are you birthed?" His voice roars.

"Thaleia, daughter of Icos. Pythia of Delphi."

I point to Parmenides growing fainter in the mist. "I would claim my mentor, the wise Oracle…"

Without warning, the god's face, as if disembodied from his body, rushes me.

I throw my arms up to protect myself.

He opens his mouth to scream. Reaches out to throttle my neck.

My every muscle tenses for his assault. In that instant I remember. No, I know with a dark certainty. The only hope I have: I must not be afraid.

The King of the Dark is inches before me. I feel his breath, his powerful rage, but I force myself to lower my arms. I want to fling them wide and accept my destiny, but can only open them part way. At the moment the god would devour me, I spread my arms wider as if I would embrace his fury.

"I am not afraid!"

The god vanishes. The moment he would cover me and claim me, that instant I force my arms open… the god disappears.

There is only one way to return to the land of the living: follow my heart. Valmiki. A desire to be safe beside the poet with the sun hot on our bodies fills me with such longing that I think I might retch. Shades cast shadows on the rough stonewall. Are the hewn stones closing in on me?

"Give us blood. Give us life and we will show you the way to return to the Land of the Living."

I focus on the light far above me. Only a frail tendril defying the mist and black chaos that wants to suck me deeper into earth. I imagine floating away from the flames and rising out of the stone tunnel.

The fire river recedes and with it the heat and stench. A knowing fills me as I drift closer to the shaft of light, helps me release my fear: Earth and Heaven grow their roots here in this bleak Underworld.

The light touches my face like hope.

Out of sulfurous mud. Slime. Powerful oaks and sweet narcissus all grow from the Earth's dark core, I remind myself and lift my hand to the light.

My chest aches as I remember Parmenides. A memory of his deep voice deep brings tears to my eyes. *You must travel all through all there is. There is no chasm between Life and Death, between the gods and man. Trust thumos—your heart will tell you who you are: Pythia. Daughter. The girl who joins mortals and immortals.*

The Shades' pleading voices fade as I drift upward toward sunlight and away from dark despair. Staring at my uplifted hand, I imagine the pomegranate tree reaching for the sun. Enveloped by a whirling sound like water rushing into the Kastalia Spring, I rise beyond the shadow-filled dark toward the morning sun.

There's a subtle shift, and I am once again behind the boulder. Valmiki kneels beside me, rests his hand on my knee. Our eyes darken and hold. He removes his hand and lifts Parmenides' body, so the Hierophant's head rests in my lap.

"No mortal is allowed to leave the Underworld," he says. There is fear in his voice.

I crumble. Drop my head to my mentor's chest, resting my cheek against his heart. My fingers clutch the earth. "Parmenides, I'm sorry." There's sulfur in my hair, its bitter smell reminds me of the Shades.

With a deep breath, I sit back and stare at the poet. Black and gritty mud oozes between my fisted fingers. I tear at my breast and rip flowers from my hair, keen a wild lament. *I failed you, Parmenides. I don't deserve to live.*

When my sobs calm to short gasps, Valmiki takes my wrists and holds my hands against his chest, draws me up so we are face-to-face. He stands still and quiet. He waits.

"You can't kill the song. Parmenides' song. And the gods'. *My* song." My voice sounds distant to me, as if I left it behind in the earth's bowels. "He always said Life and Death are just a Veil… but he's gone."

I trill a sparrow's song. There's an answer from a brown bird in a nearby bush. "I left him there." Pan's hummingbird swoops over my head, sunlight casting off the emerald and red feathers.

The tiny bird touches my cheek with swift wing strokes. Warmth rushes through me.

Valmiki stands and paces around the jagged rock, scanning uphill and down, before coming over to touch my shoulder as if he would bring me back. "We need to warn the Greeks that they are betrayed by Brygos." Valmiki stares beyond the boulder as if expecting the Persians to appear.

"But we can't just leave his body here. If we leave him, the Persians will find it. They'll…"

Valmiki puts his hand over my lips to stop my words.

In silence, I turn to the ivy thicket I created to hide us from the Persian scouts. I will tendrils to grow, until they writhe and clutch the boulder and smaller stones, a thick blanket of vines woven around the Hierophant's body. Until he is invisible even to us.

When I take Valmiki's hand and run, I feel strong and wild. I pull us down the path, while the day's light fades. Faster and faster, desperate to save the Spartan king.

"Stop!" A soldier leaps in the path before me. He's Greek from Phocis, the mountain region surrounding Delphi. I recognize his accent.

"We are not your enemy, Soldier. I am Thaleia, the Oracle of Delphi daughter of Icos. We've come to warn King Leonidas!"

"Why should I believe you?" the soldier shoves me aside and faces Valmiki, eyeing his Persian uniform, he points his lance straight at his chest. "What are you doing on this mountain?"

"You've been betrayed. We need to warn King Leonidas," he answers, his voice is deeper than I've ever heard, imbued with new authority.

I try to hold my tongue. Men only want to talk to men, but I can't stop my words. "Please! The Immortals are marching the back path to surround the Greek army."

"Stand aside, girl." the soldier towers over me, so close that I smell onions on his breath.

Valmiki steps up to stand beside me. "She speaks the truth. The Immortals discovered the trail you guard. We must warn the king."

"Who is it?" A man shouts from the shadows. For a moment, I'm afraid Brygos has found us, but it's not my betrothed.

An older man, with a white beard and stooped back faces Valmiki, his hatred as he stares at Valmiki's wicker breastplate with Persian insignia fills me with fear. My saliva is bitter in my mouth, when I move away from Valmiki and stand close before the old man.

A shock of recognition passes between us, only a brief moment of acknowledgement, a sharp pain in my chest and a look that tells me instantly that this is a seer. One who knows, a man not easily fooled. But I also know that he is my friend.

"You are a seer?" I nod my head out of respect and kneel. In supplication, I grasp his knees.

"Yes. My name is Megistias. I travel with Leonidas."

"We must speak to your king."

With his wrinkled hand, he pries my hands from his long, dusty robes and lifts me to my feet. "Child."

A thrill passes through me in the brief moment he holds my hands.

"Let them pass." He frowns at the guard standing directly behind me. "She is the Oracle of Delphi… one of the wisest oracles in all Greece. Let them go. Now!"

The soldier bows his head and steps back.

He knows me. Honors me.

Relief sweeps through me. I didn't know how frightened I was, until my fear was lifted from me. "The Immortals are not far behind us, Megistias. The Greeks will be surrounded!"

"I know. That's why I waited here for you. I've seen it in the sacrifices."

"King Leonidas, you are betrayed!" I drop to my knees in the king's tent. He extends his hand to me.

"Stand, Thaleia. I remember you. You spoke my true oracle. Stand and tell me what you know."

"Brygos, a fisherman of Delphi, showed King Xerxes the Anapoea path over the mountain ridge between Mt. Oeta and Mt. Trachis. They're close! You will be surrounded."

King Leonidas turns his back, paces to a camp table—two planks across water barrels—and snatches up a goblet. He gulps the wine and pounds the vessel back on the table. "By the gods!" But almost immediately, his face calms. He walks back to stand before me. Lifting my hands, he holds them for a long while. "You told me child: He will not leave off, until he tears the city or the king limb from limb. You told me. And now should I be surprised? The god warned me. You warned me!"

"What will you do?"

"You must warn Delphi. I'll hold them here at the pass as long as I can, but you must save Delphi and the treasures. Thaleia, you must save Apollo's Sanctuary. Far better for the king to die than the kingdom. I would save Sparta. I would save Athens. I seek *kleos andron* for myself—a hero's death. It is far better to die immortalized as a brave warrior than to live a long, inglorious life. I will claim my glory—the gods willing—and my song will be sung generation after generation forever. It is the death I have always wanted. My whole life has led me to this day. In my moment of death, I will be equal to a god." He bows his head and touches one finger to his forehead.

"King Leonidas, withdraw. You will soon be surrounded. There are over a million Persians!"

"Hellas—our democracy and our lives as free men—all are in my hands. I know this is a battle we may not win. I will return to Sparta either with my shield or on it! I will not run away. Warn Delphi! Warn Athens! Warn the free world, Thaleia!" He lowers his voice. "We will hold them here at Thermopylae as long as we can. Now go."

The king passes us as if we already left and yells commands. "Assemble the army. They must all leave. Now! My Spartan three hundred will fight by my side… and the Thebans. They will stay to fight beside us."

"As will the Thespians, King." A scarred soldier—neither young nor old, but battle-wearied—steps forward from the tent shadows. "We will fight beside you. To the death if the gods so decide. We stand beside you, my king."

"And so it will be, my friend. May the gods bless you and your family. Assemble the troops! Now!"

"Thaleia?" Megistias moves close to me—a young soldier with a long, beardless face and thin shoulders at his side. Determination gleams in the boy's eyes as he waits beside the Seer. "Thaleia, this is my son."

"Megistias! You also!" King Leonidas shouts and strides over. "You must leave. Travel with this girl. Keep her safe."

"With all honor, my King, I will not abandon you. I will not leave your side." Before the king can answer, Megistias turns back to me. "Thaleia, please, take my son with you. He is young." Megistias faces his son, such sadness in his gaze. "He is brave and strong and will bear many sons to continue our line."

"I won't leave you, Father. I will stay here with you."

"No, my son, return home. Raise fine children and tell them to honor the memory of their grandfather. Keep Thaleia safe. She is the Pythia."

Tears fill my eyes.

"My king, order my son to go."

There's a shout outside the tent. "The Persians! They've gotten past the Phocians on the mountain pass! The Persians are close!"

We run outside. Greeks shout to one another, running in every direction. Some fleeing, others putting on their armor. The air is electric like Zeus' thunderbolt, dawn white with rage and fear.

One thought fills me. Save Leonidas. Save the Greeks. Our feet pound the path. We never stop. The shouts from the camp fade. We don't stop running, until we reach a high pass. From our vantage point, we can see the Thermopylae Pass with an eagle's view.

Below, the Spartans move farther out from the old wall, taunting the Persians, destroying the Persians. They retreat pretending to flee—only to entice the Persians into a trap, a slaughter. The brave Spartans push forward again and rise like a rogue wave to force the Persians back. I see black-clad Persian bodies fall to their deaths off the cliffs into the sea.

But the Greeks are outnumbered. When Persian soldiers hesitate, other Persians shove them from behind and whip the fearful up to the front line. Volleys of arrows rain down on the Spartans, who lift their shields to save them.

"Where is Leonidas? Has he already fallen? Where is he?" Megistias' son asks.

King Leonidas leads his men to a level space far beyond the wall, away from the narrow pass and into a broader field. There is a flash of lance and sword.

"The King! King Leonidas has fallen! The king is down!" My cries fill the blood-orange sky as if they could thunder down the mountain and rescue the fallen warrior. But I already understand that it is too late. My prophecy fills me. Maybe if I hadn't told him a great king or a kingdom must fall… maybe if he hadn't heard the god's prophecy, he would not have sent the other soldiers away. No, all is the gods' plan. I could not have changed Leonidas' fate. He will claim is immortal glory. Even the gods will honor this hero.

Four times the armies struggle back and forth, the king's body the prize.

The Greeks did not save their king, brave Leonidas who gave his life to save his kingdom.

The King is dead.

I cover my face with my hands unable to watch, but soon draw them away.

Persians advance from the opposite side, from the Greeks' rear. The warriors close in. The Spartans gather as one body on a hill and face down their attackers. They fight with sword, teeth, and hand-to-hand combat. They fight to the last man. The Persians surround them. As I watch, horrified, unable to help, unable to look away, a shower of arrows brings their end, their shade. Death corners the last of the three hundred Spartans.

King Leonidas was Hellas. What will the Greeks do now? He was Herkules' ancestor. It was King Leonidas who unified us. We were a bunch of warring city-states, kingships and newborn democracies at war for generations. He brought together Sparta and Athens, Corinth and the Macedonians. Though he was king in far-away Sparta, in some strange way, King Leonidas was the taproot that clung to Parnassos and kept us all anchored.

I mourn the loss of our greatest warrior. And king.

CHAPTER TWENTY-SEVEN

19TH DAY OF BOUKATIOS

DELPHI BESIEGED

I straighten my shoulders and turn away from the carnage. We can't stop now. There is no time to mourn. It will take us all this day to reach Delphi and most of the night… if not all the night. Valmiki and I with Megistias' son run as long as we can. At last we collapse, huddle together and pull our cloaks close. A dense fog walks up the mountainside from the sea, cold and damp, obscuring the path down to Delphi.

My dreams are filled with blood and war-cries. Swords, arrows and stealth. The advancing Persian army in the mist. Just as I awaken from a fitful sleep, there is one last dream. An image so horrifying it flees the instant I open my eyes: An arm slashing down. A scream and blood. Frightened eyes stare back at me. They are not the Spartan king's or any of his soldier's. They are Sophia's.

We arrive in Delphi at sunrise. A cloud sits low, like wave froth gathered from the sea. It smells of crab nets, damp and salty, caked with sand. The streets are empty. Where is everyone? Mama? Papa? Sophia? I need to warn them. But there's no time to look. Maybe they already heard the Persians broke through at Thermopylae. Maybe they are hiding.

As if of one mind, we run up the Sacred Way toward the Sanctuary of Apollo.

Like some evil apparition, the priest Diokles—flanked by twenty or thirty Greek soldiers—appears out of the mist. He looks older, a red shawl draped over his head, his white hair wild and tangled poking from beneath the loose weave. And his eyes… they rage at me with pure hatred. The soldiers must sense it, because they keep their distance from him and glance at him cautiously as they point long lances at us.

"Let us pass, Diokles."

He smiles, but his smile does nothing to soften the fury in his eyes.

"The Persians broke through Thermopylae! King Leonidas is dead! They're almost here! Listen to me!"

I stare at Valmiki and hold out my upturned palm. The pomegranate tree. I need the tree to grow once more in my hand. There is a tingling there like a song or a wind from the sea. And music? Pan's melody, very soft and low, singing in time with my heartbeat. I feel certain no one hears it but me. I don't look around. I stare at my palm and will the tree to grow.

First a seedling then a sprout that thickens to trunk and limbs and at last—I smile—at last the red pomegranates hanging from delicate limbs.

Diokles steps back. He looks around, desperate as the soldiers prostrate themselves in the dirt, eyes cast down, arms stretched before them.

"They honor me now, priest. Your day is over. Your power is gone."

This is no time to gloat. I hear muffled shouts, but they are far up the mountain. Probably at the temple.

Valmiki and I race around the betrayed priest and up the Sacred Way and through the Cyclopean Gate. The temple columns jut like teeth through clouds then disappear into the swirling fog. The Sanctuary is filled with the men of Delphi—Papa and Hestos and Timon off to one side just by the steps. Bells clamor, insistent and sonorous, ringing their endless warning: The Persians are upon us. They are almost here. King Xerxes. One million Persians.

"Pan?" I squint hoping to see him. Something moves inside, behind a column. Is it the god?

A sudden silence descends on all of us.

In the distance, we hear a persistent *thrum* like a heartbeat. Soldiers' feet pound our Greek soil. We all hear it.

Everyone erupts at once.

"Should we hide the treasures?"

"What about us? Our wives and children? Should we hide in the Cave of Pan?"

"Ask the Pythia!"

Dark storm clouds roil. A wind like a god's breath, sweeps aside the fog.

The men are silent, their faces tight and anxious.

The villagers hold their breath as one, as the wind stills.

Persian drums throb closer and closer.

I fling both arms to the storm clouds. "Great gods! Our fate is in your hands. Will you save the children of Delphi? We will forever honor you with the fat of bulls and sweet libations, if you will guide us now. Give us a sign."

There is a roar as if a fire rages deep inside the temple.

Mingled with the roar, a hiss like water thrown against red-hot iron. Silence. Then heavy grinding—stone against stone.

I hold my breath.

The air smells of rotten eggs. Yellow smoke billows from the temple, foul and bitter smelling. A massive serpent head emerges, red tongue tasting the wind like freedom, white teeth flashing sharp. Before I know he's moved, Valmiki is by my side and clutches my hand. The villagers hide behind treasuries and columns and the Rock of the Sybil.

"Sacred Python!" My cry is joy. My cry is gratitude.

I step closer.

The serpent eases beneath the temple lintel. It has sea-green scales, shimmering like ocean water over stone and red eyes on either side of its monstrous head that swings side to side, glaring around the Sanctuary. Long talons, black as onyx, curve from its knuckled fingers.

A scraping sound, like Hephaestus, the blacksmith god raking fire-red iron over coals, honing and pounding it with his hammer… this godly echo fills the temple.

Its tail is wrapped around the statue of Apollo!

The Python swings its head to face me and flares fire over my head followed by billowing smoke, rank with a smell of rotting meat.

Apollo's statue towers over us, as the Delphians slowly re-emerge from hiding.

I don't hesitate. Two steps at a time I run up the last steps and stand beside Apollo's great statue, burnished gold and sixty meters high.

I whirl back to face the villagers. "People of Delphi!"

The Sanctuary fills with the Python's hiss and the wind's howl.

Diokles has snuck back into the Sanctuary and takes two steps toward me but freezes when the Python rears up swaying over his head.

"Hear me! I am your Pythia. We must ask Apollo for guidance!"

The blind shepherd raises his cane with both hands. "We turned our back on her mother. Listen to Thaleia!"

"The Python is a messenger from Gaia, the ancient earth goddess. She brings with her Apollo, her own conqueror. Together they offer us guidance and wisdom. We must listen!"

The villagers surge up the steps, shouting and screaming my name, pleading for me to help.

I follow the Python back into the temple.

I take the steps two at a time as I descend to the adyton.

Grabbing two crossing branches, I pull myself slowly up onto the tripod.

I fold my hands carefully in my lap. Cross my legs. In the air before me are twining pythons—one brown as earth, one blue as sky.

"Apollo, guide me. The Persians are here. They will murder us all and claim your sacred temple. Tell me what to do, wise Far-Darter."

My heart swells with Apollo's command: *Trust Apollo. He will take care of his own.*

Pan's melody weaves through the god's words as if I see them etched in the smoke.

Trust me child. I will take care of you.

It is exquisite. It is hope. *Trust Apollo. Trust the god.* It is the god's love.

In a daze I climb down from the tripod. Walk slowly back into the sunlight. Look down as they wait—the ones who love me.

I look up at the gold statue of Apollo towering over me then back down at the waiting villagers. Will they follow Apollo's command?

CHAPTER TWENTY-EIGHT

KNOW THYSELF

"Trust Apollo. He will take care of his own," I declare the god's prophecy. Whispers then shouts carry up to me.

"What? What did the girl say? What did the god command?"

"Trust Apollo! He will take care of his own," I shout. And I know; I feel the truth of my words: Trust Apollo.

I turn to the carvings—Know Thyself and the giant **E**. At last they make sense. I trust the god. I trust my destiny.

What do they shout?

"We won't hide! Keep the treasures where they are! Hold your children and tell them—Trust Apollo!"

"The god has spoken!"

"Thaleia declares the god's prophecy!"

"Tell your wives! Tell your children! Today is a day in history!"

"Apollo has spoken!"

They swarm around me. I run down the temple steps, down the Sacred Way through our village.

Persian drums tremble the morning sky. There! I see a glimpse of flashing lances, glinting in the pine grove just outside the village. I know what I must do. Storm winds catch the poppies in my hair.

They flare red against the threatening sky.

I plant my legs wide on the Sacred Way and face the invaders. A dust cloud hides them, but the ground rumbles with horses, camels, chariots and soldiers.

"Pan!" As if he was there all along, waiting for my call, the god stands beside me.

King Xerxes' gold chariot rumbles closer, pulled by white Nisean horses and surrounded by the Immortals. Their feet stomp our Greek soil in cadence as they pound lances against their chests. Clarion horns blare.

Pan smiles and lifts his syrinx with a nod to me.

We summon storm clouds with our music. Massive oaks grow in cliff-stone where there had been no trees shadowing the pass the Persians must enter. There is a rumble of distant thunder, as if the wrath of Zeus protects the Delphians.

The storm blows through my music. Carries it up and away, fills the angry sky with the struggle between Greeks and Persians. Another lightning flash and a rebounding thunder roll, so close it rumbles in my chest.

The voice of Zeus!

The satyr and I play and dance. Our flute melody weaves around us. "Zeus!" I cry out and play a song of earth and sky. "Poseidon, shake this sacred Greek soil!"

The ground beneath us rumbles.

Persian drums *thrum.*

Pan drops his flute and cavorts around me. I close my eyes and play Apollo's sun and the dark earth-depth of Hades. I play the wind and the heart of every Greek who walks this land from father to son to mother to daughter back hundreds of generations. I squeeze them tight while white lightning flashes and thunder rumbles off the Phaedriades. I do not open my eyes, when the rocks scream above me as an earthquake shatters the cliffs.

At last they fly open when I hear screams.

The Persians stare with horror at the cliffs as boulders crash in the road before them.

Though I can't understand their words, it's easy to understand their terror. They know the gods are the cause of the earthquake and storm. The sky and earth split asunder, because they violated Apollo's sacred precinct. The gods curse them for their sacrilege.

The dirt way beneath me shakes and groans. I'm thrown to my knees. Sharp pain courses my spine as my knee hits a pine stump and my flesh rips. I grip the panpipes tighter and summon the gods with every fiber of my will.

Help me now, Poseidon the earth-shaker. Apollo, save your sacred temple from the invaders.

My music fills me. It bounces off huge boulders that fall away from the mountain and scatter the Persian army.

It is pandemonium. Soldiers scream. Horses whirl in panic, crash their chariots against one another, tangling hooves and powerful bodies. The drivers are thrown beneath bucking legs and shattered wheels. Foot soldiers race downhill, trying to outrun the massive boulders cracking free from the mountain, but are crushed.

Pan lifts me by the elbow.

I lean into the powerful winds but never stop playing. I am filled with the god's music. Jumping atop a boulder, I allow the music to tremble and shriek, to swell with the earthquake and storm… all the gods' power. As if the earth herself rises up to defy the *barbaroi* army.

A mountain summoned by a girl's flute destroys the Immortals—those Persian warriors who claimed they would never die by a Greek hand.

The King's horses bolt and run away from Delphi, dragging King Xerxes' chariot behind.

One million Persians flee, never to return.

Pan bows before me.

"We stopped them, Pan. Zeus, the god above all gods, Zeus the storm-gatherer helped the Greeks."

Pan's smell of garlic and thyme softens to honeyed-sweet wine and columbine. The scent deepens as he smiles ear to ear.

I touch his beard with my fingertips and cup my hand over his cheek. Tears of joy course my face. "Zeus listened, Pan."

"Thaleia." His voice is a mountain cry, warm as summer sun. He lifts my fingers to his lips, holds them there a moment, before he jumps high with a deep laugh and leaps from boulder to rocky rubble.

The satyr is gone.

My heartbeat slows and waits. I want Pan beside me. I hear his flute distant and high on the mountain.

The Persian army is only a dust cloud far down the road, a trammel of horse-hooves and screams.

I lift my flute and play.

Just below on the path villagers hug, jump up and down with uncontainable joy. Women fall into one another's arms and chant. "We are free. The gods saved us from the Persians. Saved the free world from King Xerxes."

Sea-blue, red, and yellow scarves wave high above the dancing and laughing men and women and children. They cry, linking arms to circle and whirl in ancient dances. Men thrust both arms skyward to the gods. Their joy shouts and sings, lifts skyward with strong arms or joined work-worn hands.

"Thaleia! Oracle. Our Oracle. Our Thaleia who speaks to the gods."

I hear their shouts from the square below me. "The gods are great!" Halfway up the trail, Papa drops to his knees and prays. He leaps to his feet and flings his arms toward me. Tears pour down his face. "Zeus and Poseidon saved us. And you, my daughter, brought the gods to us."

Mama runs up laughing and stands beside him. She shouts, "Thaleia, my daughter, you are the child of my blood. My heart overflows."

I did it! I vanquished the Persians. I drop to my knees and raise my arms.

No! It wasn't me. It was Zeus and Poseidon and blessed Pan.

When I stand, my feet feel rooted to the rock beneath me, now solid. Gods and man defeated the invaders. *It is my prophecy fulfilled. I joined mortals and immortals.*

Sophia runs up screaming and laughing, tears pour down her face. She throws her arms around me and spins me in wild circles. "You did it! Thaleia, you stopped the Persians. They're gone!" She kisses my cheeks and brow, hugs me tight again. Her eyes shine with pride and wonder. "They ran away." She shakes her head and laughs a deep cry of joy and release.

The villagers chant and laugh as they dance along the Sacred Way toward me. "Thaleia. Our Oracle." Their shouts are unending. They sing and circle-dance steps as ancient as our Greek love of freedom rooted in the earth.

They'd forgotten. They followed Diokles who stole their hope. They let him dictate to them the will of the gods.

His words were false. He said he spoke what the gods wished.

He lied.

Where is he now? Did he leave Delphi?

I shake my head to dispel the thought of the old priest. Today victory is ours. We looked into our own hearts and found the god's words there, nestled like newborn birds waiting to break free from brittle shells. It's too easy to be afraid. Too easy to let the priests take control.

I jump into the air with a shout and dance my way back down the mountain. I play a new melody.

Future generations will call it Thaleia's Song.

The celebration lasts all night and into the next day. With more exuberance than any other year, the villagers shift their celebration of the Persians' defeat and move on with the Agrionia—their festival to honor Dionysos and the fertility of crops and children of their loins.

All day I dance, laugh, shout with the villagers in their joy, but I want to be up the mountain with Pan. I slip away as soon as I can and run up the path. The evening's beauty calls me, bathes me in a warm sunset glow that spills over the mountaintop.

I see everything with new eyes. The mountain feels alive—the Persians are defeated—stones and trees and the wind sing my praise.

"Praise the gods, not me," I laugh. "Poseidon and mighty Zeus. Praise Pan."

I step into Pan's glade. His hummingbird buzzes three times past my face and hovers before a poppy hanging over my forehead. It sips sweet nectar before flitting from poppy to poppy.

"Hello, little one," I whisper, so I won't startle the tiny bird. "It seems a long time, since I first met you here, since Pan told me I needed to choose. I guess I made the right choice." I laugh and the bird flies to the pine-shadows at the edge of the clearing.

I lean back against the charred pine. I want to feel the sunrays, humid with salt-brine from the sea, to be with the mountain stone and winds, to wait in silence for Pan.

A black beetle, large and shiny, slowly climbs the hills and folds of my chiton, scrambles to pull its armored body up my leg, and finally, after a couple of attempts, climbs onto my knee. I pick up the scarab, its tiny legs swimming uselessly in the air and put it back in the hollow of my lap. As soon as its legs touch the soft cloth, it starts the ascent again. You are stubborn, Child of Egypt. No wonder the Egyptians say you are the god of re-birth, of all that is immortal.

"Pan, where are you?" I shout. I don't really expect an answer.

I jump to my feet at the sound of hooves clattering against rock. The familiar smell of garlic and sweet-musty wine fills the glade. There is a throaty laugh then the trill of Pan's flute.

"So, you arrive triumphant, Pythia!"

The beetle clings a moment to my chiton before falling to the ground on its back. Its twig legs flail frantically to turn the shiny body. I bend over, hoping to hide my blush and scoop the scarab up gently, holding it lightly between thumb and finger. Its legs are running before it touches the ground, when I set it right side up.

I straighten. Pan stands directly in front of me smiling.

"Pay attention, Pythia. You may find the gods in a sacred temple. You may find them in storm-cloud and mountain cliffs. And, yes, you may find them in a scavenging beetle that burrows for treasure in foul excrement. Behold, Thaleia! Your work is not over. Look and understand."

With Pan's words, I see a vision: *A young girl, seven or eight years at most—her chest still without bud, her limbs lithe and sprouting from a fragile body—walks with dignity up the broad steps to the Parthenon Temple in Athens. With arms stretched before her, the girl carries three honey-cakes on a red platter.*

She places the offering just inside the temple shadow then steps back.

Standing stiff with crossed arms, tight-lipped and pale, she waits for the great serpent, the temple's guardian, to accept her offering. If the huge serpent eats the cake, then the goddess Athena still abides in her temple, still cares for the citizens of Athens and will protect them from the invading barbarians. If not…

Time passes in the vision. Is it hours? Days? There is no time in the Dreamworld.

Flies cover the unclaimed cake.

Greeks pound planks, wooden doors—every piece of wood they can find to barricade the great temple on the acropolis.

The honey-cake is never eaten. Athena has left her sanctuary.

Priests whimper in the dark temple shadows. Flaming arrows fly into the sanctuary, burning barricades and the ragged robes of Athenians too poor to flee the city, too drunk with the hope that the goddess Athena will keep them safe in her temple.

While the Persians' arrows assault the citadel, the sacred olive tree dedicated to Athena burns until nothing is left but a charred trunk.

Black-clad Persians scramble hand-over-hand up sheer cliff walls. Bodies of desperate priests and beggars fall from the precipice as men hurl themselves off the steep cliff to escape slavery or death at the end of a Persian spear.

There is nothing more. Flames and screams fade to blackness and silence and the deep blue of Pan's eyes.

He smiles a broad smile and dances three times around me, cavorting, laughing, playing a melody filled with joy. His laugh fades as he jumps from rock to rock and disappears in tree-shadow at the meadow's edge.

Stunned, I sit in the deep grasses and play a slow melody on my panpipes.

I lay the pipes in my lap; hold my breath and look around the meadow hoping to see the satyr.

Rubbing my eyes, I stare at the beetle stumbling through the grass. It turns to look at me. A shaft of grass beside the scarab transforms to the charred olive branch outside the temple in Athena's sacred sanctuary.

A green shoot—already supple and sprouting two leaves—grows from the black tree stump.

A TASTE OF

BOOK 2

OF THE

ORACLE OF DELPHI

TRILOGY

CHAPTER ONE

B*ring Sophia back? Where's she gone?*

Shivers crawl across my flesh. I hide behind the doorframe and watch.

Papa goes to gather a clay platter covered with cold chicken, boiled eggs and soft goat's cheese in the crook of one arm and another mug of wine for himself. He settles heavily on the bench then chooses an egg and peels it.

"Sophia will join the other maenads at the Agrionia," Papa says quietly, taking a gulp of wine. "It's necessary. It insures fertility. Of the fields. Of our women… but she is just a child!"

Mama crosses to the other side of the table, so she stands behind Papa. She rests a hand on his back. "Should we tell Thaleia that Sophia's gone up the mountain or wait… Sophia will probably be fine."

"Wait for what? Wait for the damn priest to apologize for his sacrifice of an innocent girl?" Papa pushes against the table. It tips then rights itself, but the eggs and cheese and wine crash to the floor.

Mama glances toward the door to see if the noise woke me, but she does not move, does not raise her voice as she speaks with the insistence of winds falling off the mountain above them.

"Wait… until… you… can forgive."

"No!" I run into the room. "She promised she wouldn't go."

I look around the room at their stunned faces.

For a breath I am empty. Nothing matters. Not the Persians. Not King Leonidas. Not the Greeks. If they kill Sophia with their vicious traditions, they all deserve to die.

The night devours me as I race through the village, some homes lit brightly with oil lamps and candles, the day's celebration still continuing; others dark and closed. My breath is ragged, but I don't stop running.

I'm past Hestos' goat pen… the animals crowd against the railing and bleat for me to release them… I rush up the back path toward the Cave of Pan. It's so dark beneath the pines that I can't see where my feet land, but I push myself to run faster.

Just ahead a torch flares. I hear laughter—girls calling in nervous excitement to one another.

"Dionysus, are you here?"

It's not Sophia's voice, but I chase after them.

Three girls, all dressed in fawn skins, sit by the cave mouth, casting knucklebones to find their fortune. Their faces are hard as marble, and they don't look into each other's eyes as they throw the goat bones onto the dirt brushed clear between them.

"Where's Sophia? Have you seen her?"

"She said she knew where she'd find the god."

A tall girl, the goldsmith's daughter nods and points into the darkness farther uphill.

"She said she was going to look for Dionysus up there. Something about a dream stone. Sophia said something about…" Her eyes widen in terror. I whirl around to see. A priest rips my torch from my hand. Strong hands seize the girl's arm, but she jerks free and runs off. I can't see in the black confusion of screams and torchlight and running girls. The priest grabs my shoulder, rips my chiton. "Thaleia." The threat in his voice is dark and vicious.

I pull free and run for the dream stone, run like I've never run before. Leap onto boulders and down into gullies wet with moss and spring water. My foot slips, and I almost go down, but behind me I hear the ragged breath of several men. I throw myself up a rock face and grab roots jutting from scree and rubble, scramble higher and higher.

"Sophia!" I'm near the clearing and our stone. It's just before me—white and gleaming as the moon clears the cloud cover. A girl jumps up, ghost-like in the moon's shimmer. "Sophia!"

"Thaleia, look out!"

The hook-nosed priest catches up to me and grabs my sash, but I run harder and pull him along. Against the white stone, I see a shadow loom: his arm, the thrust and strike, a bitter edge of bronze. I drop down, just as the priest slashes with his sword. It skitters against the stone as I throw my body to the side. The blade jolts off the rock and slices my thigh, but I roll clear. He crouches over me. Raises his arm to strike again.

Time slows. The sword flashes in moonlight. Its shadow lifts.

Sophia jumps on the priest's back, wraps her legs around his torso and bites his shoulder. He rolls his body and with one motion swings his right arm to strike her.

Slow and calculated, filled with one desire—kill to honor the god.

"Sophia! Look out!"

She jumps clear and runs away, scrambles up steep rocks grabbing the cliff stone, panting and pulling herself up. She turns back to peer behind her.

I feel the night wind against my face. Sophia's frightened eyes stare through me, the priest in yellow robes with black hair chases her. I hear his harsh breath, feel his thirst for sacrifice. "Sophia run!" Do I scream? She doesn't seem to hear me, only scrambles uphill with all her strength, clawing stone and gnarled trees.

Rage propels me. Empowers me. Time slows to moment by moment. I run after the priest. A cry tears from me, when the priest grabs my hair and jerks my head back. Sophia grabs his tunic just as his sword flashes in moonlight. At the last moment, I jerk free. Blood fills my vision. Sophia's blood and terror and death. Hoping to kill me, he strikes Sophia.

I rush the priest. His eyes widen with surprise. I shove him as hard as I can with both arms. He screams and falls backward off the rock ledge. His cry shatters like rock splinters, sharp, cutting… until there is only silence and the night wind.

I kneel beside Sophia and cradle her in my arms. Her blood is warm against my skin. It soaks her black robe and my yellow one, warm and sticky. There's too much blood. "Sophia." A moan escapes from her lips' tight line. Her eyes are half open but unfocused.

"I won't let you die, Sophia. Even if you travel to the Land of the Shades, I will find you. I will bring you back."

Her eyes lock with mine. "Pray to Hermes for my safe passage, Thaleia."

Her fingers grasp my fingers and release. *Divine Apollo the Healer do not claim her. The priest wanted me. Not Sophia. Don't take her. Take me.*

I slowly lift my arms and strain my neck as if I can reach to Mt. Olympos with my will. I take a deep breath and try to control my anger.

I rest my head against her cheek. A fire stirs in my palm. "I will bring you back, Sophia." I try to summon the pomegranate tree once more. Passing my hands over her head and along her body, I pray. "Heal her. Please, Asklepios and divine Apollo." Sophia's face is blank, white as winter snow. My throat is tight.

There is only silence. The night waits with me, but the god does not answer. Once again I pass my palms across Sophia's heart.

Nothing.

With one breath she is gone.

I kiss her forehead and crush her to my chest. "Apollo, hear me. Take me. Not Sophia." The night is silent and empty. Time expands, until the stars above us would crush me. I'm the god's servant. What good is that? Sophia's body is heavy in my arms. My tears bathe her quiet face like a sacred purification. Memories wash over me: Sophia at her betrothal, beside me at our dream stone pasting Timon's name in flower petals, running from the priests in the Sanctuary. And on this night mountain.

Down the mountain I hear shouts, a scrabble of feet on rubble. "Sophia, I promise. I will go to the Land-of-the-Shades and bring you back."

Several priests rush us panting and shouting.

"We need the girl's body to offer to the god," Diokles says. They surround us. The priests step aside to let Diokles pass.

I stand and block their way. With two slow steps, I move close before Diokles. Our gaze meets and holds eye-to-eye. Emboldened by my silence, Diokles motions for the priest to lift Sophia's body.

Though her blank eyes stare at me, I move aside and let them carry her past. She must go through the death ritual, so she is not caught between our worlds. I have to know she travels to the Land of the Shades so I can find her. I will wait, until the ceremony is accomplished.

They carry her body back to the temple.

I follow like a shadow behind and wait outside. I turn my head to heed an owl's call and listen to the wind, hoping for a message from a god. The night fills with the priests' incense-laden chants. I sit cross-legged on the bottom step and wait for Pan.

The night sky fragments to red shards of dawn, and still I wait without moving. It's silent inside the temple. The chants and scattering melody of finger cymbals and tympani long since faded. I don't want to move. Her body is inside. Covered with laurel and pine? Scented with frankincense? Cinnamon? I won't go in to look. In my heart I understand that she's gone. I understand what I must do.

Slowly, I unfold my stiff legs and stretch. I walk beneath the wide portal; pace the Sacred Way down to Delphi, past the cistern and bake oven—the silent path soft and gray with the early light. Pine needles whisper together in the morning fog. The sibilant rush of Kastalia Spring draws closer. Beckons me to the River Styx—mouth to The Underworld.

I stand before the Kastalia Spring. I am here. Rushing waters and wind barely conceal the whispers of the dead caught in the current of the River Styx. Filled with rage, I kneel beside the sacred spring. "Gods, you claimed my life before. Now I would claim Sophia's." Sobs mingle with the racing water. "Sophia!"

There is only wind all around. And birds, shadow vultures casting their wide wings in this unseen wind. It blows through me, and I am chilled and afraid. My body is gone. There are shades here in the wind—the men who went before. And women wailing in childbirth, moaning to leave behind their child. And when they are gone, there is no one to give sweet milk to the babe; no one to plead and throw themselves at the father's feet in supplication if he decides the child is to be abandoned.

They are all here.

But not.

And then Sophia is with them. She flows through me. She is in me, but I am not. We are both this black wind. I would cry, but I have no body to cry with. I would reach my hand to her and pull her back to the world above, to the trees she loves, wild laurel, sweet smelling along the River Pappadia.

But she is inside me, and we are both this dark, ill wind. Nothing is—not stone nor tree nor a soft poppy. There is only the three-headed dog Kerberos, slobbering between sharp teeth, guarding the god-gate to the Underworld.

I must go alone to find Sophia, to bring her back to the Land of the Living.

COMING SOON

FROM

CURIOSITY
QUILLS PRESS

ANCIENT GREEK ALPHABET

Want to have fun with your friends? You can use the Greek alphabet to write notes to one another—a perfect secret code! Ιτ λοοκσ λικε θις!

Here's the alphabet with both the upper and lower case letters:

Upper & Lower Case:	Name of Greek letter	English
Α α	alpha	A
Β β	beta	B
Γ γ	gamma	G
Δ δ	delta	D
Ε ε	epsilon	E
Ζ ζ	zeta	Z
Η η	eta	Sounds like long A
Θ θ	theta	Th
Ι ι	Iota	I
Κ κ	kappa	K
Λ λ	lambda	L
Μ μ	mu	M
Ν ν	nu	N
Ξ ξ	ksi	We don't use this letter
Ο ο	omicron	O
Π π	pi	P
Ρ ρ	rho	R
Σ σ	sigma	S
Τ τ	tau	T
Υ υ	upsilon	U
Φ φ	phi	Ph (F)
Χ χ	chi	Somewhat like our H
Ψ ψ	psi	We don't use this letter
Ω ω	omega	Long O

ANCIENT DELPHI CALENDAR

1st semester

- Apellaios
- Boukatios
- Boathoos
- Heraios
- Dadaphorios
- Poitropios

2nd semester

- Amalios
- Bysios
- Theoxenios
- Endyspoitropios
- Herakleios
- Ilaios

GLOSSARY

- *adyton*: Secret, sacred chamber reserved for Oracles and Priests. See: http://www.wikipedia.org/wiki/adyton
- *Agrionia*: An ancient Greek fertility festival to honor Dionysus usually celebrated by women at night. Originally included human sacrifice. See: http://www.wikipedia.org/wiki/agrionia
- *amphora*: A container (usually ceramic) used in ancient times to store and transport wine, grains, etc. See: http://www.wikipedia.org/wiki/amphora
- *Apollo*: Greek Olympian god of oracles, healing, music and light. Son of Zeus and Leto. Twin brother to Artemis, goddess of the hunt. See: http://www.wikipedia.org/wiki/apollo
- *Asklepios*: God of Medicine. Son of Apollo, raised as mortal boy by centaurs (half man-half horse beings) who taught him the art of healing. See: http://www.theoi.com/Ouranios/Asklepios.html
- *astragaloi*: Knucklebones of a goat used for divination and prophecy. See: http://www.ancientgreektoys.gr
- *barbaroi*: To the ancient Greeks: Anyone who is not Greek. Though it sounds like our word barbarian, it signifies any stranger. See: http://www.wikipedia.org/wiki/Barbarian
- *Bardo*: A state of consciousness between life and death See: http://www.wikipedia.org/wiki/Bardo
- *Bouleuterion*: A building inside the Sanctuary at the Temple of Apollo that housed the Council of Citizens. (Boule) See: http://www.wikipedia.org/wiki/Bouleuterion

- *Carneia*: Sacred festival celebrated in Sparta. The reason Leonidas could not gather troops and could only take his personal guard to Thermopylae to confront the Persian invasion.
  See: http://www.wikipedia.org/wiki/carnea
- *chiton*: A simple draped garment often of wool or linen worn by ancient Greek men and women.
- *Cissians*: Part of Persian army under King Xerxes. The Cissians and Medes were part of his advance guard in the Battle of Thermopylae and suffered heavy losses
  See: http://www.ancientgreekbattles.net
- *Cyclopean*: A type of masonry found at the Temple of Apollo Delphi, Greece: Wall stones so massive that legend stated that only the Cyclops could have been strong enough to set them in place.
- *daimon/daimona*: Spirits who were often messengers between mortals and immortals. Could be both evil and good
  See: http://www.mythindex.com
- *daouli-drum*: A cylindrical drum with two heads.
  See: http://youtu.be/xVjxs6wf2JA
- *deliver earth and water*: This is an ancient phrase that means to surrender. An army would symbolically gift earth and water to a conquering army.
- *Delphi*: One of the most sacred places in the ancient world. Located in Phocis, north of Athens, Greece. Supposedly, the place the two eagles sent by Zeus-one east and one west-met. The exact middle of the earth.
  See: http://www.wikipedia.org/wiki/Delphi

- *Dionysus*: A god also known as Bacchus, the god of wine. He is much more: a god of rebirth and all vegetation. Child of Zeus and Semele. See: http://www.theoi.com/Olympios/Dionysos.html
- *Dios d'eteleietou boule*: A Greek phrase that means: And the will of the god is fulfilled.
- *Elea*: A town in southern Italy colonized by Ionian Greeks. Birthplace of the wise healer Parmenides
  See: http://www.wikipedia.org/wiki/parmenides
- *Far-Darter*: Homer refers to Apollo as the Far-Darter. (called an epithet) This can refer to his prowess with the bow but also to the god striking down mortals with the plague. It might also pertain to his ability to see into the future.
- *flax*: A plant (with blue flowers) used as a fiber crop to produce linen cloth dating back to ancient times.
- *Gaia*: Earth Goddess. The great mother of all. Very ancient.
  See: http://www.theoi.com/Protogenos/Gaia.html
- *greaves*: Armor that protects the leg.
- *Hades*: God of the Underworld. Brother to Zeus and Poseidon, Demeter, Hestia and Hera. Husband of Persephone. (Whom he abducted with Zeus' permission.)
  See: http://www.wikipedia.org/wiki/hades
- *Helios*: A Titan sun god. Also god of oaths and sight.
  See: http://www.theoi.com/Titan/Helios.html
- *Hellas*: The Greek name for ancient Greece
  See: http://www.wikipedia.org/wiki/Hellas

- *Hellespont*: A narrow strait connecting the Aegean Sea to the Sea of Marmara. King Xerxes crossed the Hellespont on a bridge built of boats and tied together with flax ropes to invade northern Greece in 480 BCE.
  See: http://www.wikipedia.org/wiki/Hellespont
- *helots*: Spartan slaves.
- *Hera*: Queen of the Olympian gods. Wife of Zeus. Goddess of women and marriage. Known to be extremely jealous of his amorous ramblings.
  See: http://www.theoi.com/Olympios/Hera.html
- *hexameter*: Poetic verse that is constructed with six "feet," comparable to six measures in written music.
- *Hierophant*: A holy man, interpreter of dreams and sacred mysteries.
  See: http://www.wikipedia.org/wiki/Hierophant
- *himation smock*: A cloak worn over a chiton.
- *hoplite*: Citizen-soldiers of ancient Greek city-states, primarily armed with swords and shields
  See: http://www.wikipedia.org/wiki/hoplite
- *hubris:* Over-weening pride. A sin punished harshly by the gods.
- *Hysechia*: The Great Stillness. A meditative state often led by a priest or healer.
- *Kale mera*: "Good morning." in Greek.
- *Kastalian Spring*: The sacred spring near Delphi, Greece where the Pythias were bathed before delivering their oracles in order to be purified for the god.
  See: http://www.wikipedia.org/wiki/Castalian_Spring

- *Kerberos*: Three-headed dog that guards the gate to the Greek Underworld.
- *Kere*: A female, vengeful death-spirit. Daughter of Nyx, goddess of the night.
- *King Darius*: Persian King defeated at Marathon by the Greeks 490 BCE. Father of King Xerxes
  See: http://www.wikipedia.org/wiki/battle_of_marathon
- *King Xerxes*: Persian King who fought against the Greeks and the Spartan 300 at Thermopylae 480 BCE.
  See: http://www.wikipedia.org/wiki/king_xerxes
- *kiste*: A small box that holds sacred artifacts.
- *kleos andron*: The immortal glory and fame of a hero.
- *kore-maid*: An unmarried maiden. Persephone was the archetypal kore when she was abducted by the god Hades and forced to be his queen in the Underworld.
- *Korykio Andro*: The Cave of Pan located about seven miles up Mount Parnassos above Delphi, Greece.
- *kosmos*: Greek spelling for cosmos: the universe.
- *kouroi*: Archaic statues of Greek boys or simply male youths.
- *kylix*: A cup to hold wine.
- *Land of the Lotus Eaters*: An island near north Africa, mentioned in The Odyssey when Odysseus and his men were blown off course.
  See: http://www.wikipedia.org/wiki/Lotus-eaters
- *libation*: A ritual pouring of wine, olive oil or sometimes just water to honor the gods, often in the name of someone who has died.

- *maenads*: Women followers of the god Dionysos. Liberating, dancing celebrations took place at night in wild locations like forests or mountains.
  See: http://www.wikipedia.org/wiki/maenads
- *Magnesia*: A region in central Greece, southeastern Thessaly
- *Marathon*: Location in mainland Greece of a seaport where the Greeks defeated King Darius and the Persians in 490 BCE. Legend says that a runner ran from Marathon to Athens to announce the victory only to collapse from exhaustion and die. This is the beginning of our modern marathon race.
- *Medes*: An ancient Iranian people, part of the Persian Empire.
- *Megistias*: Seer for King Leonidas mentioned by the historian Herodotus.
- *Menin Theou*: Greek: "Wrath of the gods!"
- *Minyan family*: A proto-Greek culture possibly from the early Bronze Age. (2800-1900 BCE)
- *Mt. Parnassos*: A high mountain of limestone in central Greece that towers above Delphi.
  See: http://www.wikipedia.org/wiki/mount_parnassus
- *Olympos*: A high mountain in northern Greece and the supposed home of the Olympian gods.
- *omphalos*: This stone (that looks like a beehive) was located in the adyton of the Temple of Apollo in Delphi. Legend states that the ancient goddes Rhea fed this stone wrapped in swaddling clothes to her husband Kronos when he intended to eat his lastborn son Zeus. (As he had all his other children.) By tricking her husband in this way, Rhea saved her son and eventually all her children.
  See: http://www.theoi.com/Gallery/T6.1.html

- *Pan*: Ancient nature god. Half man/ half goat. The archetypal god for all the satyrs and a companion of Dionysos.
  See: http://www.theoi.com/Georgikos/Pan.html
- *papyrus*: A plant commonly found in Egypt. Often used to make paper and rope.
  See: http://www.wikipedia.org/wiki/Papyrus
- *Parian marble*: A beautiful stone found on the Greek Island Paros and often used for sculpture.
- *Parmenides*: 5th Century BCE Oracle born in Elea, a Greek colony located in southern Italy. Best known for his poem "On Nature" that describes Reality as endless and indivisable.
  See: http://www.wikipedia.org/wiki/Parmenides
- *parthenia*: A virgin maiden.
- *penteconters*: Ships used in the Battle of Artemisium by the Persian navy. Heavier and less maneuverable than the Greek warships called triremes.
  See: http://www.wikipedia.org/wiki/Battle_of_Artemisium
- *Phaedriades*: The towering limestone cliffs of Mount Parnassos often referred to as the Shining Cliffs because of their stark reflected light.
  See: http://www.wikipedia.org/wiki/Phaedriades
- *phalanx*: A military formation used effectively by the ancient Greeks. Heavily armed men (usually armed with spears) masses together tightly as they approach the enemy. They protect one another with closely packed shields and move en masse.
- *Phocaea*: An ancient Ionian Greek city on the western coast of Anatolia.
- *Phocian wall*: A wall (about twelve feet high) at Thermopylae. The Greeks fought in front of this wall as the defended Hellas.

- *Phoenicians*: A people who occupied the eastern Mediterranean. Byblos was a Phoenician city.
- *Pythia*: The Oracle who proclaimed Apollo's prophecies. Named after the Python that Apollo slayed to claim his power at Delphi, wresting that power from the Earth Goddess Gaia.
  See: http://www.wikipedia.org/wiki/pythia
- *Python*: Though we think of this as a snake, it is more a dragon-like creature with four legs. The famous Python of Delphi was a very ancient companion of Gaia and supposedly killed by the god Apollo.
- *River Styx*: A river that flows into Hades. (The Greek Underworld also known as Erebos.) The boatman Kharon guides the recently dead souls down this river to the Land-of-the-Dead.
- *rizogalo*: Delicious rice pudding.
- *Rock of the Sybil*: A large boulder found in the sacred Sanctuary of the Temple of Apollo, Delphi.
- *satyr*: A creature of Greek myth: Half man/ Half goat
  See: http://www.wikipedia.org/wiki/satyr
- *satyr plays*: Ancient Greek play that tended to be tragicomedy and often somewhat bawdy.
- *scree*: Rubble of rock
- *Shades*: The name for the spirits of the dead.
- *Sirens*: Mentioned in The Odyssey by Homer, these creatures were birdlike women who lured sailors to their death by singing irresistible songs.
- *Solon*: An Athenian statesman and poet born around 638 BCE. Reputed to have written the words "Know Thyself" carved in stone at the Temple of Apollo, Delphi.

- *Spartan*: A citizen from the city of Sparta located in the Southern Peloponnesus of Greece. King Leonidas who faced the Persian army with his 300 elite guard was king of Sparta 480 BCE.
- *syrinx*: Panpipes. A shepherd's flute played by the nature god Pan. See: http://www.wikipedia.org/wiki/panpipes
- *Teleste*: An Initiate into the Mysteries
- *temenos*: The sacred Sanctuary of the temple.
- *Thanatos*: God of Death. Not to be confused with Hades, king of the Underworld.
- *The Hot Gates*: Another name for Thermopylae because of the natural hot springs that steamed from rock fissures. See: http://www.wikipedia.org/wiki/thermopylae
- *The Underworld*: Also known as Erebos. Greek souls (psyche)were carried here after death. Unlike Christian Heaven or Hell, all souls traveled to this Land-of-Shades.
- *therapon*: Attendents who often assist heros to put on their armor and help in many ways. In the Iliad by Homer, Patroklos is Achilles' therapon.
- *thumos*: A many-meaning Greek word used by Parmenides in his poem "On Nature." It's hard to assign an exact English equivalent, but it means yearning and longing and heart.
- *thyrsus*: Any ivy-twined staff carried by the maenads when they went off in the night to worship the god Dionysus.
- *Toi pant' onom' estai*: "And his name shall be all things."

- *Treasury of the Sikyonians*: Along the Sacred Way leading up to the Temple of Apollo in Delphi, there were small treasuries (built like miniature temples) that held god coins and jewels given to the gods as tribute and honor.
- *tripod*: A three-footed leather sling seat upon which the Pythia sat and inhaled the fumes from the Earth's cleft in order to commune with the god and declare his oracles.
- *triremes*: Swift war vessels sailed by the Greeks in battle against the Persians.
  See: http://www.wikipedia.org/wiki/triremes
- *Tyche*: Goddess of Fortune
- *Women & Men's Quarters*: In many parts of ancient Greece, men and women had separate rooms to sleep and gather in.
- *Yia sas*: A formal way to say hello. "Health to thou."
- *Yia sou*: An informal way to say hello. "Health to you."
  I've taken liberties here… these are used in modern Greek.
- *Zeus*: Supreme ruler of Olympian gods and mortals. God of sky and thunder, known for his punishments by lightning bolts.
  See: http://www.wikipedia.org/wiki/zeus

RECOMMENDED READING

These are reading adventures! Jump in with both feet if you're curious about the ancient mysteries, philosophies and the nature of reality.

- *The Illiad* and *The Odyssey*

  by Homer, Translations by Bernard Knox and Robert Fagles
- *The Oracle: Ancient Delphi & The Science Behind its Lost Secrets*

  by William J. Board
- *Plutarch: Moralia, volume V, Isis and Osiris.*

  The E at Delphi. The Oracles at Delphi

  (Loeb Classical Library No. 306)

  Translated by Frank Cole Babbitt
- *Herodotus: The Persian Wars*, Books 5-7

  (Loeb Classical Library No. 119)

  Translated by A.D. Godley
- *The Hero with a Thousand Faces, Power of Myth*

  Joseph Campbell (Really, anything by J. Campbell)
- *The Ancient Greek Hero in 24 Hours*

  Gregory Nagy
- *The Golden Bough*

  Sir James George Frazer
- *The Terrestrial Gospel of Nikos Kazantzakis*

  ("a powerful and poetic work…" ~Bill McKibben)

  Thanasis Maskaleris

- *Reality* (to learn more about Parmenides)

  Peter Kingsley

- *Fractals: The Patterns of Chaos* (Ever wonder about the universe?)

  John Briggs

- *The Holographic Universe: The Revolutionary Theory of the Universe*

  Michael Talbot

- *Beyond Forgiveness: Reflections on Atonement & The Oldest Story in the World*

  Phil Cousineau

- *The Secret History of Dreaming*

  Robert Moss

Great websites to research the Greeks gods and goddesses as well as anything pertaining to ancient Greece:

- www.theoi.com
- www.wikipedia.org
- www.history.com (for some interesting videos about Greek myth)

STUDY GUIDE QUESTIONS

1. What does Thaleia mean when she says to the old priest Diokles and all the men of Delphi, "You can't kill the song?" What is the song?

2. Do you think *Night of Pan* is a "real" story? Was Thaleia a real person? Did an Oracle declare the four prophecies about the Persian invasion 480 BCE? Was there ever an Oracle of Delphi who stopped the Persians?

3. Why doesn't Pan just tell Thaleia what to do? Why does he give her a choice?

4. How does *Night of Pan*, a story about an ancient time (about 2500 years ago!) relate to us today? And how can words of those in power sway people to do things they may not have dreamed of otherwise? (This may be both for the good and the bad.)

5. What does it mean when some Greeks "carry earth and water" to the Persians?

6. Do you think you'd like to be the Pythia-Oracle? Why or why not?

7. When I wrote the scene about Thaleia's initiation with Pan in a cave, I thought I made up the cave. About a year later, I discovered there actually *is* a cave on Mt. Parnassos about seven miles above Delphi called the Cave of Pan! I couldn't believe it. Have you ever written something or said something you thought you made up only to find out later that it is real? Why do you think this happens? (Hint: Have you ever heard of synchronicity?)

8. What different meanings do you think the saying carved on the Temple of Apollo—*Know Thyself*—has? (Hint: Does it refer only to an individual knowing whether she/he is out-going or shy? Or is there much, much more to it?)

9. Why were both Apollo and Dionysus worshipped at the Temple of Apollo? Were they worshipped at the same time or different times? What is the relationship between the two gods?

10. Why don't the gods help Thaleia, when she commands them to destroy Brygos and the soldiers up on the mountain? (Hint: What is *hubris?*)

11. What do you think Thaleia means, when she tells the fake Pythia, The Child-of-the-Clouds: "Then I would dig two graves… one for you… and one for me?"

12. What is the Python? Is it a snake like the massive serpents in the tropics?

13. How do you determine your role in the world if you don't have a satyr-god like Pan telling you what to do? (Hint: There is no right or wrong answer here… just *your* answer.)

Go to my website: http://www.gailstricklandauthor.com to find the answers to these questions. Don't forget to have fun coming up with your own answers! Know thyself!

DAD'S FIRST CAMERA

I know of many boys
and just as many girls
who wanted to scrape
farm clay from work-worn shoes.

I can tell you of one—
only thirteen when he lost
his Dad.

I'd seen a photo of the boy—
seven or eight at most,
dressed in aviator clothes
just like Charles Lindburgh.

The hat with earflaps,
leather jodphurs,
knee-high boots,
even goggles in case of enemy fire.

But that was before—
only thirteen when he lost
his Dad.

Those years that followed
piled together like their
hard-scrabble life.
The boy and his mom.

He made dinner for them both:
bacon fat on white bread,
so she wouldn't need to cook,
just home,
bone-tired from her seamstress job.
He joined ROTC.
Wore his uniform
Most every day,
so she wouldn't have
to buy him clothes.

Took a job in a bakery
minding the day's bread.
Four in the morning.
Work before school.

Until one sleepy dawn,
he fell asleep,
burned each and every loaf.
Only thirteen when he
lost his Dad.

There was that time…
He took his hard-earned nickel
to buy a Milky Way.

"Here, son. Buy this one."
"No, the wrapper's torn."
"Just take it, boy."
"No," he said and "No," again.

The kiosk owner
pushed the candy into
the boy's grasp.
"Just take it, boy."
His eyes pleaded,
tried to tell.

At last, the boy relented.
Took the candy and
with one small bite—
chocolate melting sweet on his tongue—
he glanced at the waxy wrapper,

hoped as always for the contest star.
the star to win a camera—
his Brownie.

His way to scrape farm clay
from work-worn shoes.

Only thirteen when he
lost his Dad.

Gail Strickland
October 2011

ACKNOWLEDGEMENTS

The Greeks have a word very dear to me: θυμοσ (thumos). It means heart and yearning. Θυμοσ is my passion to understand an ancient world peopled by bold mystics and philosophers and poets. Θυμοσ led me to write this book. This longing brought me to unexpected places and friendships. I met Virginia in a tiny village in southern Greece. She taught me how to dance and laugh and collect shells offered by the sea. And Thanasis Maskaleris, Greek scholar extraordinaire, who taught me about Dionysos and Apollo: two sides of the Mystery creating the whole. (He was also an endless supply of jokes.)

My passion for Homer and Parmenides and young Oracles who lived over two thousand years ago gathered a community around me who helped me when I was down and danced with me in the good times. There are so many I wish to thank: My mentors—gentle and wise Linda Watanabe McFerrin, fearless leader of The Left Coast Writers and Phil Cousineau whose invaluable help and sage advice never let me down. The independent bookstores who not only provided most of my source material, but conferences and readings: Book Passage (Kathryn, Tina, Sam, Susan and Elaine…what am I saying? All of you!) Rebound Books (Joel and Toni who advised and encouraged and gave me a constant supply of hard-to-find books.) and Kathleen at A Great Good Place for Books who was the first to read my manuscript, look me in the eye and say, "This book *will* be published."

How can I possibly thank all my writer-friends who helped me? Peter S. Beagle for his inspiration and kind words. Joanna Biggar for editing and unfailing friendship. This book would never have seen the light of day without patient guidance by my Willful Writing Sisters: Adrienne, Mary Brent, Kim, Catherine, Ellie and Anne. And there's my first writing group: Penny, Toni and Maggie who fed me cookies and tea and lots of advice about commas. And Debbie Goelz who keeps me laughing through it all. Thank you to my birthday club gals: Fran, Diana, Nancy and Linda and all my dad's friends (and mine) at The Meadows retirement home. A grateful thanks to Lauri who believed in my book even on those days when I didn't. Gregory Nagy doesn't know how much I learned from his talks about Greece's song culture. "You can't kill the song!"

Several conferences helped and encouraged me: The Squaw Valley Community of Writers (A workshop with Sands Hall? Priceless.) Kachemak Writers' Conference (where I met poet Anne Caston, novelist David Bradley and Lee Gutkind "godfather of creative nonfiction" who cajoled me to read for them in the green room and shared a glass of wine or two over discussions about Point of View.) Book Passage Children Writers' Conference and Walter Jon Williams at Taos Toolbox. Finally, there was AuthorSalon where the inimitable Michael Neff taught me the nuts and bolts of publishing. I learned something from them all.

So now I find myself working with yet another amazing community: the hard-working, perceptive, patient and kind people at Curiosity Quills Press. Alisa Gus (who always knows just the right questions to ask), Eugene Teplitsky, Mark, Nikki, Ricky (the talented artist who designed my cover!) Andrew and Clare. Thank you does not begin to describe my gratitude.

Every step of the way, my family read (and re-read!) versions of my manuscript. Sent me links about the Python and Parmenides and the holographic universe. For their patience and love, thank you Bram, Lara, Steve, Chris and Katie. Thank you to my brother Bob whose music cheered me when I was down and my sister Ginnie, fellow poet and lover of myth. And a huge thank you to my sister-in-law Phyllis, not only my friend but the first one to publish my writing.

And for my patient and loving husband—a line all your own. Thank you Michael. My appreciation and respect are beyond words.

As Parmenides taught me: We are never alone.

ABOUT THE AUTHOR

While studying the Classics in college, **Gail Strickland** translated much of Homer's *Iliad* and *Odyssey*, Herodotus' prophecies and *The Bacchai* by Euripides. Living on the Greek islands after college, she discovered her love of myth, the wine-dark sea and *retsina.*

The Baltimore Review and *Writer's Digest* have recognized Gail's fiction. She published stories and poems in Travelers' Tales' anthologies and the San Francisco Writer's anthology. Her poetry and photography were published in a collection called *Clutter.*

Born in Brooklyn, New York, Gail grew up in Northern California. She raised her children; was a musical director for CAT children's theater; taught music in schools; mentored young poets and novelists and introduced thousands of youngsters to piano and Greek mythology. Gail is passionate about bringing the richness of Homer's language and culture to today's youth.

Loved *Night of Pan*?

Gail Strickland on **Facebook**:

http://j.mp/GailFB

Thank You for Reading

http://www.gailstricklandauthor.com

Please visit http://curiosityquills.com/reader-survey to share your reading experience with the author of this book!

Kiya: Hope of the Pharaoh, by Katie Hamstead

To save her younger sisters from being taken, Naomi steps in to be a wife of the erratic Pharaoh.

As Naomi rises through the ranks of the wives, Queen Nefertiti seeks to destroy her. To protect herself, Naomi charms the Pharaoh, who grows to love her. But when Naomi conceives his child, Nefertiti's lust for blood is turned against her.

Obsidian Eyes, by A.W. Exley

1836, a world of light and dark, noble and guild. The two spheres intersect when seventeen-year-old Allie Donovan is placed at the aristocratic St Matthews Academy. More at ease with a blade than a needle, she finds herself ostracised by the girls and stalked by a Scottish lord intent on learning why she is among them.

Used to relying on herself, Allie must cross the guild-noble divide to keep her friend safe when she discovers he is working on a top secret military project, deep under the school.

CPSIA information can be obtained
at www.ICGtesting.com
Printed in the USA
FSOW01n2321071015
11916FS